DOCTOR WHO

AMORALITY TALE

THE HISTORY COLLECTION EDITION

AMORALITY TALE
DAVID BISHOP

BOOKS

1 2 3 4 5 6 7 8 9 10

BBC Books, an imprint of Ebury Publishing
20 Vauxhall Bridge Road, London, SW1V 2SA

BBC Books is part of the Penguin Random House group of companies, whose
addresses can be found at global.penguinrandomhouse.com

 Penguin
Random House
UK

This book is published to accompany the television series *Doctor Who* broadcast
on BBC One. *Doctor Who* is a BBC Wales production.
Executive producers: Steven Moffat and Brian Minchin

This edition published in 2015 by BBC Books, an imprint of Ebury Publishing.
First published in 2002 by BBC Worldwide Ltd.

www.eburypublishing.co.uk

A CIP catalogue record for this book is available from the British Library.

ISBN 978 1 849 90904 4

Editorial director: Albert DePetrillo
Series consultant: Justin Richards
Project editor: Steve Tribe
Cover design: Two Associates © Woodlands Books Ltd, 2015
Production: Alex Goddard

Printed and bound in the USA

Introduction

History has always been a rich tapestry of opportunities and inspiration for *Doctor Who*. The end of the very first episode saw the TARDIS travel back to Earth's distant past, and the Doctor has been hopscotching his way through human history ever since. But stories where the TARDIS materialises at a notable moment in history purely by chance have always niggled me. When I started work on *Amorality Tale*, I vowed that his intervention in history should be properly motivated and not just a coincidence. (Keep reading past this introduction and you can judge for yourself whether I succeeded.)

Amorality Tale came from two seeds of inspiration fusing together in my imagination. One of them was a place. When I moved to London in 1990, my first job was at a small magazine company in Old Street, an area on the fringes of the East End. Back then it was a decidedly down-at-heel part of the city, forlorn and far from fashionable – now it's an enclave for artists and hipsters, a dramatic transformation in a quarter of a century.

Travelling to work in Old Street gave me a thrill because it took me close to Shoreditch, a place long associated with *Doctor Who*. I used to explore the nearby streets at lunchtime, fascinated by local landmarks like St Luke's with its curious obelisk steeple. The church is now home to the London Symphony Orchestra, but in 1990 it was abandoned, almost a ruin. The look of that lonely building lingered long after the few months I worked nearby.

The second seed was a historical fact I stumbled across one day. Early in December 1952, smoke from coal fires in London merged with a heavy fog hanging over the city to form deadly smog. This greasy yellow shroud brought traffic and transportation to a halt, choking the city and its people, especially in the East End. Between 4,000 and 12,000 Londoners died in just four days. The effects were so bad, funeral directors ran out of coffins and overwhelmed mortuaries had to stack the excess bodies outside.

The magnitude of this terrible event was not immediately apparent, but became notorious. It led to the Clean Air Act of 1956, which banned domestic coal fires and made London a much healthier place to live. These days the Great Smog has largely been forgotten, but the scale of that disaster haunted me. Imagine the impact now if 12,000 Londoners died in four days. Imagine what it would be like to live through those deadly days and nights.

My mind kept replaying the image of smog-filled streets, people unable to see further than they could reach, the paralysing fear it could create. What if there was something else lurking in the smog, using it as a weapon? And what if that malevolent threat was centred around Old Street, on the edge of the East End?

So I had a time and place for my novel – now I needed a Doctor to intervene in events, and a companion to stand by him no matter what. While working in Old Street I got to interview Jon Pertwee, the actor who played the Third Doctor. (He had retired to the sunshine by then, it was a terrible telephone line, and my tape recorder failed to capture a single word of our conversation – not my finest hour as a journalist.)

The Third Doctor was my Doctor growing up, the one I saw first, so he was an obvious choice. Other authors had featured him before, but nobody had written a novel set during the Third Doctor's final days. There's an inherent sadness to Season Eleven, as if the Doctor senses what is coming – indeed, he has a near-death experience in his penultimate story. That set the tone for *Amorality Tale*, with the Doctor all too aware time is running out.

His companion for those final stories was sparky journalist Sarah Jane Smith, played to perfection by Elisabeth Sladen. Everyone who watches *Doctor Who* has a favourite companion – Sarah Jane was mine. I wouldn't be surprised if my choice of journalism as a career after high school owed at least something to Miss Smith.

Amorality Tale is unusual because the TARDIS crew goes back only two decades in time, moving from the 1970s to the 1950s. Most historical stories relocate the Doctor and friends by centuries, even millennia, but I wanted the novel to show how much London had changed in just 25 years. Sarah Jane was the perfect companion to experience the shock of the past, a feminist displaced a generation to an era when women had far fewer opportunities.

I spent a lot of time researching East End life during the early 1950s in a bid to make sure the novel would effectively recreate that time and place. Hopefully the resulting narrative wears that research lightly, adding little touches of authenticity rather than stopping the story to lecture readers on life as it used to be. (In some writing circles, that tendency is known as 'I've suffered for my art, now it's your turn' syndrome.)

One last thing: the title. I'm terrible at devising suitable names for stories and my editors often have to intervene with a better suggestion. *Amorality Tale* was a working title that stuck, inspired by sixteenth-century morality tales. They were a popular form of drama where the characters represented different virtues and vices.

I knew the supporting cast of my novel would not be full of heroes. Some of them lived and worked outside the law but would fight for the greater good when required. Others were law-abiding citizens and guardians of justice who would have to confront their own flaws and frailties when facing terrible tests of courage. My novel adopted an amoral standpoint, inviting readers to judge each character by their actions, not their rhetoric.

Everyone faces crucial moments during their lives, decisions that could alter their future irrevocably. *Amorality Tale* is about how we make those choices and how we cope with the consequences. In the end, that's all we can do…

David Bishop
August 2014

Alison, for loving me

Religion blushing veils her sacred fires,
And unawares morality expires.
Nor public flame, nor private, dares to shine;
Nor human spark is left nor glimpse divine!
Lo! thy dread empire, Chaos! is restored;
Light dies before thy uncreating word;
Thy hand, great Anarch! lets the curtain fall
And universal darkness buries us all.

Alexander Pope, 1688–1744

Morality Tale: *n.* a kind of drama (popular in the sixteenth century) in which the characters represent virtues, vices, etc.

PROLOGUE

London – December, 1946

Ernie Evans stamped his boots on the stone steps outside St Luke's Church, trying to keep his feet warm. The temperature was close to freezing and Ernie's breath hung in the air like a cloud. The short, pinch-faced man blew on his icy fingers and pulled the heavy greatcoat tighter around his chest. In the distance a bell mournfully chimed twelve times.

Ernie had been waiting for nearly an hour and his patience was wearing thin. Five more minutes and he was leaving. Didn't matter how good a deal the Yank was offering for the hooky cigarettes, it wasn't worth freezing outdoors in the middle of winter. You could catch your death of cold doing this. Ernie was just about to give up and go home when he heard the sound of approaching footsteps, coming from the west. The black marketeer slipped back into the church doorway, melting into the shadows.

A lone figure was walking along Old Street from Charterhouse. The man was tall and broad-shouldered, with a face some would consider handsome. His black hair was swept back from his forehead with Brylcreem, making it shine beneath the street lights. Metal buttons glinted on his

American army greatcoat. The end of a cigarette glowed red in his left hand. The soldier stopped outside the gates to St Luke's and took one last draw on the cigarette before crushing it underfoot. He turned and looked up at the church entrance.

'You got the money?'

'What took you so long?' Ernie demanded.

'Had to dodge the military police.' The soldier smiled wolfishly. 'Apparently there's a crackdown on American troops fraternising with your wives at night. We've been leaving behind a few too many unwanted pregnancies.'

Ernie emerged from the shadows and skulked down the steps. 'Bloody Yanks. The war's been over a year – why don't you go back home?'

'My unit's shifting back to the States next week. Soon enough for you?'

Ernie shrugged his round shoulders. 'Got my stuff?'

'Got my money?'

'You first.'

The soldier pulled a carton of cigarettes from within his coat. 'The rest is nearby in a truck. Now where's the money?'

Ernie dug a roll of bank notes from his pockets and began counting them out. 'One hundred, like we agreed.'

'Two hundred. The price is now two hundred.'

'You what?' Ernie squinted up at the American. 'That's well out of order!'

'Take it or leave it. I've got plenty of buyers if you're not interested.'

'Flaming daylight robbery, that's what it is!' Ernie grumbled, digging into another pocket for more money.

'Not at this time of night.'

Ernie pulled out a second roll of notes, much larger than the first. The soldier's eyes widened at the size of the roll – it was big enough to hold several thousand pounds. Ernie counted out two hundred pounds and offered it to the American. 'Here's your money – I hope it chokes you!'

The soldier's face hardened to a malevolent glare as he pulled a revolver from his pocket. 'Change of plan. Give me all your money and I'll let you live – probably.'

'You bloody…' Ernie began as he stared at the gun. 'You won't get away with this. I've got friends who don't take kindly to strangers with shooters invading their patch.'

'You forget, I'm being demobbed back home in a week. I'll be long gone before your friends can do a thing.' The American smiled blithely at Ernie. 'So, what's it to be? Give me all your money and walk away alive. Sounds like a good deal to me. I mean, I wouldn't have thought your pathetic life was worth half the cash you're carrying. But still, considering the alternative…'

'What's that?'

'I shoot you and take all your money anyway.'

'You won't shoot – too much noise.'

'You want to take that chance?'

Ernie swallowed hard. He knew he should have brought a weapon along tonight but hadn't counted on things turning nasty. The Yank had seemed a safe bet when Ernie met him in the pub two days ago, charming all the women and buying all the men a drink. Later the soldier had approached Ernie, saying he understood there was a market for surplus US Army items missing in transit. A deal had quickly been struck and a meeting arranged for the following night. Now Ernie was regretting the greed which had led him to this situation. He reluctantly handed over all his cash.

'Good choice. I like the English – so polite, so trusting.'

Ernie resisted the urge to attack the soldier. Don't let him goad you, the black marketeer repeated to himself, don't let him goad you. 'You've got all me money, what do you want now?'

'I want to see the look on your weasel-faced features when you realise I'm going to kill you anyway,' the soldier replied.

'What?' Ernie asked, not immediately understanding. Then realisation was swiftly followed by incredulity and anger. 'Why you—' His words were cut short by the American smashing the revolver into Ernie's face. The soldier beat his victim repeatedly about the head with the butt of the pistol. Ernie collapsed to the ground, trying to call out for help. Still the blows rained down on him, one crushing his windpipe and silencing his voice for ever.

As Ernie lay on the cold stone steps gasping for breath, the American serviceman straightened up and looked around him. Nobody was watching, nobody had seen what happened. He smiled at his victim. 'You know the best part of all this? The gun wasn't even loaded.'

Ernie was fighting to stay conscious. He knew he was badly hurt and probably dying. His legs had gone numb during the beating and his arms did not respond when he tried to protect himself from the blows. Stupid way to die, he thought. Survived a war just to get beaten to death less than a mile from home over some stolen smokes.

Ernie felt himself drifting away but a voice caught his attention. It was the American talking, but he sounded more like a frightened child now.

'Who are you? What do you want?'

Ernie was confused. It sounded like the American was having a conversation, but there was nobody else speaking.

Ernie's eyes had swollen shut but he could still feel a bright light blazing down on to him from above.

The American fell to the ground beside him, like someone kneeling in genuflection at a church service. What was going on?

'Forgive me and I will become your servant for the rest of my days!'

Ernie decided it didn't matter any more. Cold and exhaustion overwhelmed him. He relaxed, as if he was sliding slowly down into a cold sea. He remembered going to Margate as a child on a Bank Holiday outing with his mum. The scorching sun turned the beach into a hotplate as he ran down to the water's edge, burning the soles of his feet. But that was years ago and his mum had died soon after…

WEDNESDAY, DECEMBER 3, 1952

The heavy key rattled as it turned, opening the lock on the small door. The prison officer withdrew the key and pulled the door back, before stepping to one side. The prisoner was waiting with another guard, patiently watching the procedure. For some inmates, this day never came. They waited for the rest of their lives but never saw what lay outside the towering metal gates. For others, being released from prison was something to fear. Inside you could be a big fish in a small, enclosed pond of incarceration. Outside you were just another minnow in the big, wide world.

Tommy Ramsey had no such fears. He had been respected and feared inside, and life outside would be much the same. Tommy had earned his position in the community by a dedicated campaign of brutality, terror and cunning. Six months away should have made no difference to that. If it had, he would soon set things to right.

The prison officer looked at Tommy, 'Ready Mr Ramsey?'

'You bet!' Tommy replied in his rasping East End accent. He plucked a stray thread from his charcoal grey Savile Row suit before shaking hands with the two warders. Each smiled to acknowledge the twenty-pound note slid into their hands, which they both pocketed. 'You boys look after yourselves, all right?'

Tommy took one last look around the prison walls before stepping out of the doorway into freedom.

Jack Cooper was waiting outside Wandsworth Prison by the long black Bentley. He saw Tommy emerge and tried to assess the mood of his boss. Tommy seemed happy, a smile creasing his severe features. His receding brown hair was cut close to the scalp – Tommy had no time for elaborate hairstyles or the men who wore them. The immaculate double-breasted suit was straining a little to fit his barrel-shaped chest. It looked like the boss had been exercising. Prison seemed to agree with Tommy Ramsey. But then most things did, if they knew what was good for them.

By rights Tommy should have swung for murder. The evidence against him at the trial had seemed overwhelming, but the gangland boss had left nothing to chance. Two key witnesses had disappeared, another developed a bad case of amnesia after a visit from Jack and crucial evidence was mislaid while being kept in storage by the police. A few thousand pounds spread around the jury members hadn't hurt matters either.

So it had come as no surprise when Tommy was found not guilty of murder. The East End gangster had been startled when he was convicted of firearms offences but accepted his prison term magnanimously. A woman was dead and somebody had to be seen to be punished, even if the sentence hardly matched the alleged crime. Tommy went to Wandsworth for six months and Jack had been chosen to take care of the business in the meantime.

Tommy embraced Jack warmly before getting into the back seat of the Bentley. Jack climbed in after and closed the door behind him. In the driver's seat was a huge man, a black peaked cap perched incongruously on his massive head. He turned to look at the passengers.

'Mr Ramsey, good to have you back! How was your holiday?'

'Good, Brick, very good. But they need to do something about the food in there. These trousers are almost hanging off me!' Tommy replied happily. 'Take me home – the sooner I get north of the river, the happier I'll be.' Tommy nodded to Jack, who turned a handle set into the back of the front seat. A glass partition slowly rose in the middle of the car, providing the passengers with some privacy from the driver. Brick started the car, which purred into life. He carefully drove away from the prison, making for the nearest bridge over the Thames before steering the vehicle towards the East End.

In the back seat, Tommy looked down at the floor of the car. 'I was going to ask you for the latest news. But first of all, perhaps you can tell me who's this lying here, all trussed up like a turkey? Did Christmas come early this year?'

In front of Tommy lay a young man, bound hand and foot with a gag through his mouth. His clothes were dirty and torn, one shoe was missing and his greasy black hair hung down over his bruised face. An attempted moustache was just visible above his upper lip. His eyes were full of terror at his predicament. Jack kicked the unfortunate youth before explaining.

'There's a rival gang hanging around Old Street, mostly kids, no more than seventeen. They've been busting up businesses under our protection, trying to grab the patch for their own. Brick caught this one watching the house. His name's Jamie. He won't say anything else.'

Tommy's smile curled into a sneer. 'I don't like people taking liberties.' He glared down at the captive. 'Cat got your tongue, has it? Well, let me give you a message to take back to your little gang. Old Street belongs to Tommy Ramsey and nobody, but nobody, looks after it. You got that?'

The youth nodded, tears of terror brimming in his eyes. Tommy kicked the captive in the crotch for good measure.

'I said, you got that?!?'

The youth nodded vigorously this time. Tommy looked to Jack. 'I think he's going to cry. Should we send him home to his mummy?'

'Guess so. How's he getting there?'

Tommy smiled. 'Express delivery. Get that door.'

Jack opened the car door on his side and held it ajar. Beyond it the road and gutter were visible as the Bentley sped across London. Tommy used his feet to shove the youth towards the doorway. The captive was crying out in protest but his words were muffled by the gag and noise of traffic.

'Seems to have found his voice again,' Tommy noted. 'Too late, mate.'

A final shove from Tommy pushed the bound man out onto the road. Tyres screeched as cars swerved to avoid the body that had suddenly appeared, rolling along the kerbside. Jack shut the door as Brick drove on.

'Little toerag,' Tommy said bleakly as he lit a cigarette. 'What's next?'

'Some of the shopkeepers along Old Street have been slow paying their insurance money lately. They say if we can't protect them from outside gangs, why should they pay us? The ringleader seems to be a watchmender who's just set up in the shop opposite St Luke's Church.'

'So? Make an example of him. Get someone to smash the shop up. The others will come around quick enough after that,' Tommy said.

Jack smiled at his boss. 'Billy is doing it this morning.' He glanced at his watch. 'He should be there by now.'

*

William 'Billy' Valance walked along Old Street towards St Luke's Church. A thick-set, imposing figure in a brown suit, he had a bland face disguising a menacing temperament. For the past seven years Billy had been a lieutenant for Tommy Ramsey. They first met while in military prison for violent behaviour. Once the war was over, Tommy returned to his native East End, keen to get a piece of London's burgeoning black market economy. He prospered amidst the austerity of post-war rationing and offered Billy a job as one of his enforcers. Within a few months Tommy had grabbed control of all illegal activities around Old Street and Shoreditch. Within a year he was taking good money out of Spitalfields Market and extending his reach into nearby Finsbury and Bethnal Green. The Ramsey Mob was something to be feared, and Billy had rejoiced in the power and prestige he received by association with it.

But the last year had not been so happy for Billy Valance. Jack 'The Lad' Cooper had emerged from the ranks to become Tommy's right-hand man. Jack was only just twenty and had not seen service during the war. Billy disliked taking orders from anybody younger than himself – especially an upstart like Jack, with his pretty-boy looks and curly blond hair. Then Tommy was distracted by the murder trial and got sent down for six months. But the biggest shock of all came when Tommy left Jack in charge.

Billy had hoped to get the top job himself, but Tommy was adamant. Billy was a good enforcer but he didn't have the nous to lead the firm, Tommy had said. The months had crawled by ever since and Billy had watched as Jack let things slide. It was just as well Tommy was getting out today – he would sort the mess out, once and for all. If he had any sense, he'd sort Jack out at the same time. Billy believed the lad was far too lax with old enemies like Steve MacManus, who had

11

begun to encroach into Ramsey territory.

Billy stopped outside the church and looked across Old Street to the shops opposite. One stood alone, a rare detached building in the traditional terraced row. The shop façade had recently been repainted, with a new sign over the door: FIXING TIME – YOUR WATCHES AND CLOCKS MENDED. PROPRIETOR: DR J. SMITH. Billy consulted a scrap of paper to check he had the right address. Smashing up the wrong shop would not look good now that Tommy was back on the streets.

Billy crossed the road and peered in through the shop window. The watchmender's was furnished like a front parlour, with plush leather chairs, a sofa and several standard lamps. But the most striking part of the shop was the clocks – dozens of them. The walls were almost completely obscured by the timepieces hung on them, while tall grandfather clocks stood back to back on the floor. Any flat surfaces such as table tops were also laden with more clocks.

Billy pushed open the front door and stepped inside. As it closed, he heard a bell ring at the back of the shop behind a red velvet curtain. Back office, he thought to himself – probably got the workshop out there. In front of the curtain stood a glass-topped display counter filled with dozens of different watches. A cash register stood at one end of the counter, near the curtain.

'Anybody home?' Billy called out. There was no reply. He peered at the face of an ornate ormolu clock. 'Weird.'

'Really?' a plummy voice asked, startling Billy. He turned around quickly to find the watchmender standing behind him. 'I've grown to like it.'

'Where'd you come from?' Billy demanded, trying to hide his surprise.

'Are you speaking rhetorically or philosophically, old chap?'

The watchmender smiled, his eyes glinting with mischief and intelligence. His face was careworn and tired, with a prominent nose and a mass of curling grey hair framing the features. He was dressed in a green velvet smoking jacket with matching bow tie, a white ruffled shirt with further ruffles protruding from its cuffs, dark trousers and shining leather boots. A small, strange amulet hung on a thin chain around his neck.

Billy was determined not to be distracted by the watchmender, no matter how outlandishly he was dressed. 'I meant, where'd you come from a minute ago – there was nobody here when I walked into the shop.'

'Appearances can be deceptive. You shouldn't judge a situation just by the way it looks from outside.' The watchmender wandered away to examine a grandfather clock which had begun chiming the hour, even though its hands suggested the time was only ten to. 'How can I help you?'

'It's more to do with how I can help you. Word on the street is that you don't believe in having insurance.'

The watchmender opened the face of the clock to wind forward the minute hand. 'You're not another of those tiresome fellows who wants to offer me their protection, are you? I told the last one to go away. Perhaps you'd be a good man and follow his example.'

Billy was nonplussed. The watchmender couldn't be local – his accent alone put paid to that idea – but even newcomers to the area knew better than to refuse the protection of the Ramsey Mob. Yet this old man seemed determined to sign his own death warrant. Billy decided that mere threats were obviously not going to do the trick. He reached up and knocked a clock off its wall mounting. The timepiece fell to the floor where it smashed to pieces.

'Oh dear. What a shame. But accidents like this can happen,

if you know what I mean. You really should think about getting some insurance.'

The watchmender finished adjusting the grandfather clock and turned to face Billy. 'This really is quite unnecessary. If you leave me in peace, I will leave you and your fellow thugs in peace. Why don't we leave it at that?'

Billy nudged another clock off its mounting so it crashed to the floor.

'Tsk, tsk. Clumsy me.'

The watchmender sighed heavily. 'You know, I've met cavemen who were more charming than you. And more subtle.'

'Who you calling a caveman?' Billy was getting riled by this point. The old man actually seemed to be sneering at him, as if he didn't realise Billy was in charge of the situation. 'I'll show you who's a caveman,' Billy said as he lunged at the old man, both fists raised ready to strike.

But he found himself flailing at thin air as the watchmender adroitly sidestepped his charge. A moment later Billy was spinning forwards as one of his ankles was grabbed and twisted by the old man. Billy landed upside down on the edge of an armchair, the impact forcing the air from his lungs. He struggled to right himself while gasping for breath.

The watchmender grinned down at him. 'A bull in a china shop shows more panache than you, my dear fellow.'

More than anything else in the world, Billy hated to be patronised. It was guaranteed to make his already short temper explode with anger. An upper-class twit of an officer in the army had patronised Billy on the parade ground one day during the war. Billy had beaten the officer senseless, smashing several teeth down the toff's throat. It was that incident that landed Billy in military prison where he had first met Tommy. Now the watchmender was using exactly the same tone of voice.

Billy pulled himself to his feet and swung his fists wildly at the old man. The watchmender ducked and weaved, easily evading the blows. This just riled Billy further. He scooped the ormolu clock from atop a table and raised it in the air, ready to smash it down on his foe's head. But the old man pummelled Billy with a series of short chopping motions, using the sides of his hands as weapons. Billy doubled up in pain, meekly dropping the timepiece. The old man lunged forward and Billy thought he was about to be struck again. Instead his attacker grabbed the ormolu clock, just before it crashed to the floor.

'This is a valuable antique, I'll have you know!' The old man placed it carefully back onto the table top. Moments later, Billy found himself being propelled back out onto the street. He heard a parting comment from the watchmender.

'Brute force rarely triumphs over the skilled user of Venusian Aiki-Do.'

Outside St Luke's Church, Father Xavier Simmons was saying goodbye to the congregation from his mid-morning mass. They were a mixture of older women and men, but a sprinkling of younger people from the surrounding area had begun to attend his services in recent months. Word was beginning to spread about the good work being done in this parish. He looked down at the steps where Ernie Evans' bloody corpse had been found six years ago. He remembered the epiphany he experienced that night as if it were yesterday. In appearance Simmons was much the same as he had been then, though perhaps with a little less hair and a few more pounds around the waistline. But in essence he was so very different from the murderous man who looked into the face of the Saviour. He had been reborn that cold December evening...

'Father Xavier? Father?'

An insistent voice called him back to the present. The priest turned his attention to the short, round woman talking to him. Mrs Ramsey was a regular at all the services and always gave generously to the parish collection. But she could afford to, Simmons reflected ruefully, as her son controlled all illegal activity in this area of the East End.

'Father, I can't tell you how much I enjoyed your sermon today. That passage where you spoke about the need to create a new Eden here on Earth, where no one goes hungry. A place where nobody has to steal or kill – you seemed to be speaking from the heart, Father,' she said.

The priest nodded his thanks. 'I believe everything I say, Mrs Ramsey. We have to help each other if we want others to help us. I hope you'll be along tomorrow. It's going to be a big moment for the local community...'

'I wouldn't miss it for the world,' Mrs Ramsey replied. She looked at her watch. 'I've got to go now, Father, I'm expecting my Tommy home this morning.'

The old woman made her way carefully down the stone steps before heading east towards Shoreditch. Father Xavier watched her go until he was distracted by a comical scene across the road. A heavy-set man in a brown suit was pulling himself to his feet by a lamppost. The priest narrowed his eyes as he tried to recognise the sheepish-looking man – yes, it was Billy Valance, one of Ramsey's bruisers.

Father Xavier smiled as he went back inside St Luke's Church. It seemed this would not be the happiest of homecomings for Tommy Ramsey.

The newly released prisoner's good mood was souring as Jack continued his report about recent events. 'What do you mean, takings are down? How much? Why?'

Jack shifted uncomfortably in his seat. 'We just aren't clearing as much as we used to from the brothels or the gambling rooms. The Red Room is the worst, takings are down by half since you went inside. But all our vice and gambling businesses are suffering. I blame the new priest.'

Tommy was bemused by this. 'You having a laugh? What's a god-botherer got to do with anything?'

'St Luke's has had a new priest for several months now – an American called Father Simmons. He's one of these evangelical nutters, bashing the Bible and preaching eternal damnation. The amazing thing is people seem to be lapping it up. He's organised protests outside the brothels, opened a soup kitchen for needy and getting the community involved in church activities.'

'And I thought God was dead,' Tommy said.

Jack shook his head. 'Not round Old Street, he ain't.'

Tommy pondered all this for a moment. Beyond the car window central London was being replaced with his beloved East End streets. 'Heaven can wait – we got more urgent problems. First things first – send one of our men in to get close to this new gang. Jim Harris is the youngest, he'll do. Next, I want you to dig Bob Valentine out of whatever whisky-sodden sewer he's lying in and bring him round the house. No point having a bent copper on the payroll unless he's pulling his weight.'

Tommy leaned forward to tap on the glass partition, motioning for Brick to stop the car. 'After that I want a meeting of all the lads, so I can have a word.' Tommy opened his car door so Jack could step out onto the footpath.

Once he was out, Jack turned back to Tommy. 'Where are you going?'

Tommy grimaced. 'To go see our friend Max Morgan at the

Red Room. He's always been a little too light-fingered for my liking.' Tommy rapped on the glass partition. The Bentley slid smoothly away into traffic, leaving Jack behind. He smiled to himself before looking around for the nearest phone box.

A young woman pulled open the plush red curtains at the windows of the Red Room. Weak winter sunshine fell into the illegal gambling club but shied away from illuminating too much of the gaudy crimson interior. Situated above a pub, the spieler was notorious for its violence and its décor. A previous manager had painted the walls a vivid crimson – according to local legend, this was to hide the blood stains. Naturally, the club had been renamed the Red Room. The only respite from the unrelenting red was the dark oak of the tables and chairs grouped around the large, high-ceilinged room. A long bar stretched down one wall, while two doors stood opposite each other. One led to the staircase down to a private entrance at street level. The other door opened into the manager's office, a smaller room but just as crimson in colour.

Sarah Jane Smith sighed. She had been working at the Red Room for a fortnight but felt no closer to solving the mystery which had brought her to 1952. Lately the Doctor's mood had been bleaker, more introspective. He narrowly escaped death during an adventure on a planet called Peladon and Sarah had felt the brush with his own mortality was weighing heavily on the Doctor's thoughts. She decided the best way to snap him out of this lethargic mood was a challenge to his intellect. The freelance reporter found just the thing while researching an article for *Metropolitan* magazine…

Sarah was amazed to learn that between 4,000 and 12,000 Londoners died during four days in December 1952. Most of the deaths had been concentrated in the city's crowded and run-down East End slums. The thousands of fatalities were attributed to a dense smog which settled on the city at this time, caused by lingering fog combining with smoke from the coal fires Londoners were still using to warm their homes.

To Sarah, the idea that thousands of Londoners could die in just four days because of smog seemed almost unbelievable, yet it was a matter of public record. To a city still recovering from the horrors of the Blitz, the Great Fog of 1952 was like a blow upon a bruise: painful, yet more of the same.

The second part of Sarah's puzzle for the Doctor came from the picture archives of the London *Evening News*. She had been looking for photos of East End mobsters since the Second World War. Gangland bosses like the Kray twins in the 1960s courted publicity and frequently appeared in the papers. Others were more reluctant to be seen. Sarah was digging through the files when she found a photo of Tommy Ramsey folded in half. He was smiling and shaking hands with someone in front of a church.

Sarah unfolded the photo and almost dropped it on the floor, such was her surprise at what it showed. The other person in the picture was the Doctor! She turned the print over to check the date stamp on the back: December 1952. But there was no publication date shown. It seemed the photo had been purchased for the paper's inventory stock, but never saw print. Sarah had presented her two-part mystery to the Doctor while he tinkered with equipment in his laboratory at UNIT headquarters.

'This photo proves you were in the East End of London during December 1952 – the same time that thousands of people died in mysterious circumstances,' Sarah had said. 'I can't believe the two facts are unconnected.'

'Why not?' the Doctor replied. 'Coincidence is probably one of the most underrated factors in many of history's key events.'

'Well, you can't deny this is you shaking hands with a notorious East End gangster. Has this already happened?' Sarah was becoming increasingly frustrated at the Doctor's obstinacy.

He fixed a jeweller's glass into his right eye as he adjusted a miniature circuit. 'Historically, yes – you said so yourself.'

'I meant, has this already happened to you?' Sarah demanded.

'No,' he replied. 'At least, not yet.'

Sarah stood and fumed as the Doctor ignored her for the next thirty seconds. Eventually he looked up and noticed her again.

'Sorry, were you asking me something?'

'Oh, Doctor, I don't know how you can be so wilfully obtuse!' Sarah slammed the photograph down on the laboratory bench and turned away, determined not to let him see her frustration. Behind her the Doctor was looking in fascination at the picture. But he seemed more intent on something in the background of the photograph than the image of himself or the other figure in the foreground.

'What year did all this happen?'

'I've already told you,' Sarah replied through gritted teeth. 'December 1952.'

The Doctor picked up the circuitry he had been repairing and strode purposefully towards the TARDIS, which stood in the corner of the laboratory. It was only when he reached the door that he noticed Sarah was not following him. 'Well, what are you waiting for?'

'Sorry?'

'Get your things. We leave for 1952 as soon as I get this directional finder wired back into the TARDIS!'

*

They had arrived in mid-November 1952, and spent the past two weeks establishing themselves in the local community. Fortunately, Sarah had researched the period and its people before presenting her puzzle to the Doctor. Alas, specific details about what was due to happen here were few and far between. For example, she had seen a report about large numbers of policemen dying, the cause attributed to working outdoors in the polluted air. But knowing that hardly made solving the mystery behind the deaths any easier.

Still, her research had made the task of blending in a little bit easier. Sarah talked her way into a job as a barmaid at the Red Room after learning it was one of Tommy Ramsey's illegal gambling clubs. She hoped it would get her close to the gangland leader, but was dismayed to discover he was in prison and not due for release until the third of December. She spent more time fending off the unwanted attentions of the customers than she did serving drinks. Sarah never failed to be shocked at the level of male domination and chauvinism, but she kept reminding herself that women's liberation was an alien concept in this time and place.

Worse than any of the customers was the reptilian manager of the Red Room, Max Morgan. He had a leering face, greasy hair scraped over a balding pate, wandering hands and a beer-bloated paunch hanging over the front of his low-slung trousers. Morgan was quite the most repulsive individual Sarah had ever encountered. He seemed to regard her as fair game.

Sarah had just finished sweeping the floor when she heard heavy footsteps coming up the stairs. The door swung open and a mountain of a man walked in. Nearly as wide as he was tall, he smiled at Sarah as he held the door open. She was surprised to see what gentle eyes he had, hidden behind a granite slab of a face.

A second, smaller man came into the Red Room. He glared at Sarah malevolently. 'I'm Tommy Ramsey,' he said. 'Who the bloody hell are you?'

Jack Cooper stood in a red phone box, his eyes darting up and down the road to see if anyone was watching him. Satisfied that he was not being observed, he rang a number he had memorised but never dared write down. When the call was answered on the third ring, he spoke quickly and quietly.

'It's Jack Cooper. Put me through to the boss.'

Another pause, then a gruff voice came on the line. 'Report!'

'Tommy's out, I picked him up this morning. He's gone round the Red Room to sort out the manager, while I'm rounding up the lads for a meeting.'

'What about our plans?'

Jack was confident in his reply. 'Doesn't suspect a thing. It'll just be the usual ranting and raving tonight. He hasn't got a clue.'

Tommy Ramsey cast an eye over the new barmaid. She had an inquisitive heart-shaped face, framed by dark brown hair cut to collar length. She was probably in her early twenties and seemed uncomfortable in her barmaid's uniform – a revealing red blouse and daringly short black skirt over black stockings and black patent leather stiletto shoes. Tommy found her steady gaze intriguing. Most people looked away when he looked at them, but not this one. She returned his gaze with interest.

'She's Sarah, a new barmaid. Been here about two weeks.' Max Morgan emerged from his office and walked towards Tommy, extending a handshake to his boss. 'Welcome back Tommy – how was Wandsworth?'

Tommy replied with a backhanded slap to Morgan's face. 'I

don't recall saying you could call me by my first name.'

The manager pressed a shaking hand up to his stinging cheek, bright red with embarrassment. 'Sorry, Mr Ramsey. It's just you've been away and—'

Tommy pulled back his arm as if to deliver another blow and Morgan backed away while bowing in supplication. 'Sorry, sorry, I'm so sorry.'

'Stop bloody apologising.' Tommy snapped his fingers and held out an open palm to Morgan. 'Where's the money?' When the manager didn't respond immediately, Tommy took a step towards him. 'Come on!'

Morgan ran back into his office and quickly reappeared with a cash box bulging with notes and a ledger. He laid the accounts book open at the latest entry. 'It's all there in black and white, Tomm – Mr Ramsey.'

Tommy emptied the cash box while casting a cursory eye over the accounts. 'You're only pulling in half what you were six months ago.'

The manager shook his head mournfully. 'Business is bad. Everyone's suffering, thanks to that hellfire and brimstone merchant at St Luke's.'

Tommy stared at Morgan, who couldn't meet his gaze. 'But I hear you been doing a lot worse than anybody else, even taking that into account. Got any explanations?'

Morgan looked wounded at such an accusation. 'Who's been saying that? Has Jack the Lad been spreading lies about me again? I tell you something, Tommy, that boy—'

His diatribe was cut short by another savage blow to the face. Sarah winced at the severity of it. Tommy stood over Morgan, who was now nursing both sides of his face. 'It's Mr Ramsey to you. That's two warnings. You won't get a third. And don't try to blame your troubles on Jack, he's a good boy. This used to be a good little earner but you're screwing it up.

Get it sorted or get out.'

Tommy pocketed the cash and turned towards the door.

Sarah knew it was now or never. Taking a deep breath, she spoke up.

'Excuse me, Mr Ramsey?'

He stopped in his tracks. Sarah took this as a good sign.

'I don't think you realise it but Morgan is playing you for a fool. You don't want to look like a fool, Mr Ramsey, do you?'

Tommy swivelled around and walked over to Sarah, his fists clenching and unclenching. 'Nobody calls me a fool and survives to brag about it. You've got exactly one minute to explain yourself – or else that pretty face of yours won't be pretty much longer.'

'Don't listen to her, Mr Ramsey, she's just a—' Morgan tried to interject.

Tommy silenced him with a gesture while keeping his gaze locked on Sarah.

'Start talking.'

The war had been over for seven years, but parts of the East End were still just bombsites. Derelict buildings that had once been homes for families now played house to vermin and weeds. Ironmonger Row behind St Luke's had been particularly badly hit by German bombs. Only one of the original buildings was still standing, and that had been declared unsafe. But that didn't stop it being used by those without homes.

Two teenagers tended a fire in the grate of the last house on Ironmonger Row. They were brothers, both on the run from National Service. The pair had gravitated back to their native East End but couldn't go home – the military police would be waiting for them. The brothers had adopted new names to disguise their identities, calling themselves Billy and Charlie.

For the past month they had been scratching a living from thieving and illegal bare-knuckle boxing matches, until they met Callum.

He was like nobody they had known, wild and fearless.

Callum seemed to rejoice in causing mayhem and chaos. He was only of average build but his black eyes betrayed a wanton streak that terrified ordinary people. His skin was white, almost translucent, in stark contrast to his jet black hair. He had a charisma about him that made others want to follow his lead. The two brothers soon found themselves happily joining Callum in whatever crazed enterprise entered his head.

Within weeks of appearing in the area, Callum had formed his own gang. The members were young men, between sixteen and twenty, all frustrated by a society that would not acknowledge them as adults until their twenty-first birthdays. Their fathers and older brothers had gone to war before they were twenty-one, why should this new generation have to wait?

Callum harnessed that frustration, turning them into a formidable force on the streets. Billy and Charlie felt they had found their place at last, something they could belong to and be proud of. They were part of a gang and that meant power and strength. The brothers both liked that.

They were still tending the fire when Callum appeared at the door. 'Boys, our time is nearly upon us!' He held up his right hand. It was covered in blood.

Arthur 'Brick' Baldwin stood in the doorway of the Red Room, watching as Tommy confronted the new barmaid. Brick liked the look of her and hoped she knew what she was doing. Tommy had few qualms about using his fists on anybody, or about ordering his bodyguard to deliver the beating for him. Brick hated hitting anyone. His size turned any fight into a drubbing and he would rather die than hurt a woman, especially one as pretty as her.

Sarah swallowed hard before replying to Tommy. 'Morgan is skimming money from the Red Room's profits. That book he showed you is a fake. There's a second set of accounts hidden in a safe under his desk. The combination is seven right, twelve left, five right.'

Brick noted Tommy staring into the barmaid's eyes. She held Tommy's gaze steadily. The bodyguard thought she looked nervous, but sure of herself. She seemed to believe what she was saying.

The blood had drained from Morgan's face. 'You can't believe that. I would never, never…'

Tommy walked to the manager's office.

Tommy grabbed the desk in the office and flung it over in the air. Revealed beneath was a safe. He crouched down to twist the dial through its combination, then pulled open the door. A second ledger book was inside. He opened the pages and quickly confirmed the truth of Sarah's allegation. Tommy closed the book, stood up and strode back into the main room.

'Please, Tommy, I can explain…' Morgan whimpered.

'It's Mr Ramsey, especially to thieving scum like you,' Tommy replied. He motioned for Sarah to follow him out of the Red Room. She hurriedly grabbed her coat. 'Brick, make sure Morgan doesn't leave, will you?'

'Yes, Tommy.' When they had gone, Brick stepped into the doorway and folded his arms across his mighty chest. The only exit had disappeared.

Once outside, Tommy looked up and down Brunswick Place while he talked to Sarah. 'Why?'

'I want to work for you. I can help you. I understand you reward loyalty well. Morgan was ripping you off so—'

'So you grass on Morgan to gain my trust – is that it?'

'Telling the boss the truth, no matter how painful, isn't being a grass. It's being honest.' Sarah held Tommy's gaze, trying to keep her terror hidden. What she said now could mean the difference between life and death for herself and the repulsive, reptilian Max Morgan. 'I thought you would place a value on that too.'

'How do I know you didn't set Morgan up?'

'You don't. But I didn't. He put his own head in the noose.'

Tommy lit a cigarette and sucked greedily at it. 'Never did trust him – too shifty by half.'

'So, do I get a job?' Sarah asked.

Callum stood opposite the fire as he watched his gang. The light from the flames threw dark shadows around his face. About twenty youths were gathered in the condemned building, dividing the spoils of the day. The gang was becoming more brazen by the day as the expected retaliation never came. Why bother picking pockets when you could demand people emptied their pockets for you? Callum was always urging them to take more risks.

Now he looked down at them, a motley collection of misfits and fugitives. Callum sneered with contempt. 'This is pathetic! Skulking in a bombed-out building, counting out coins – hardly rich pickings!'

The elder of the two brothers, Charlie, spoke up for the rest of the group. 'We done good today, it's our best haul yet.'

Callum shook his head in disgust. 'It's pocket change! You have no ambition, you're too scared of your own shadows. There's a power vacuum on the streets of London – those who came back from the war are getting old, past it. This is our opportunity, a chance to take control. The streets are ours for the taking, if you only have the courage to snatch them away from the likes of Tommy Ramsey and his men.'

Billy stood beside his brother. 'Like Charlie said, we done good today. Why stir things up? Why cause trouble?'

Callum grinned. 'I like trouble. Anyway, we don't have any choice. See this?' He held up his bloody hand for all to see. 'Know how I got this? From one of our own – this is what Tommy Ramsey thinks of us!'

Callum stepped out of the room. Billy and Charlie looked around the others, but nobody knew what their leader was talking about. Callum came back in, dragging Jamie's bloody body. Callum dumped him in the midst of the gang.

Tommy stared deep into Sarah's eyes. If she had been a man, he would have wondered whether she was an undercover policeman, trying to infiltrate the firm. But Tommy knew the Old Bill would never send a woman to do such a dangerous job. Perhaps that scumbag MacManus was trying to plant an informant inside the Ramsey Mob? Tommy dismissed that possibility as well. There was something different about Sarah. She could not disguise her quiet terror but there was an implacability about her that Tommy admired.

'Well?' Sarah asked impatiently.

'You've got some brass neck, I'll give you that,' Tommy replied. 'You take the rest of the day off. Come to the house tomorrow – Tabernacle Street. Know where it is?'

'I'll find it,' Sarah replied. 'What about Morgan?'

'What do you care?' Tommy said.

'He's slime but he could still be useful, if he kept his hands out of the till,' Sarah suggested. 'Better to have him scared and earning than dead and buried.'

Tommy nodded his agreement. 'I'll have a word with him. Off you go.'

Sarah put on her coat against the chill winter air and began walking towards the City Road. Tommy watched her leave before going upstairs to speak with Brick.

'You take the car and follow her home. I want to know where she lives, how long she's been there and where she comes from. All right? I'll be having a word with our friend Morgan.'

Jamie's face was a mess of cuts and bruises. His wrists were bloody and raw from the ropes that had bound him. His clothes were torn to pieces, almost falling from his body. One of his legs was broken, the jagged bone visible through the cloth of his trousers. The other gang members moved to help Jamie but a word from Callum halted them.

'No! Just look at him for now. Look what the Ramsey Mob did to one of ours. Tommy was out of prison only a few minutes when he threw Jamie out of a moving car. This is what we are up against. This is why we can't be content just to bide our time and stay out of trouble. That's not an option any more. Billy, you say you don't want trouble? Too late! Trouble has already arrived. But if you're scared, well – you can always leave…'

Charlie grabbed his brother to stop him attacking Callum. Billy spat with fury at the gang's leader. 'Nobody calls me scared! Nobody!'

Callum smiled. 'That's what Tommy Ramsey is doing. He's saying you're scared – all of you! Little boys playing at grownups, pretending to be men. Is he right? Are you just little boys?'

'No!' the gang members shouted back.

'Are you just pretending?' Callum asked.

'NO!' the teenagers roared in unison.

Callum's eyes blazed with fury, the flames from the fire reflected in the blackness of his pupils. 'The Ramsey Mob struck at us today, they hurt one of ours. Tomorrow we strike back. Tomorrow, we kill one of them.' Callum looked around his followers. They were all standing now, a group united by their burning hatred for Tommy Ramsey.

'Are you with me?' Callum asked.

'YES!'

Sarah walked for nearly a mile to reach the boarding house in Great Sutton Street. She stopped outside St Luke's to adjust her stiletto shoes, which were causing blisters on the backs of her ankles. Whoever designed these instruments of torture obviously hadn't walked any distance while wearing their own creations, Sarah decided grumpily.

She looked up at the church. It was an imposing building with the stained-glass windows lit from within. An enclosed area of grass surrounded the church on all sides, with tall wrought-iron fencing at the perimeter. The building's most impressive feature was a massive steeple at its western end, stretching up into the sky. Atop it was an obelisk with a statue. Sarah had to crane her neck backwards even to look at it. She wondered how the original builders had ever managed to get the structure so high up, with only the steeple as support. The church must have dominated the local skyline when it was first constructed. Sarah imagined it would soon be overwhelmed by the skyscrapers she knew were coming to London.

She was tempted to go inside and have a look around, but remembered that Tommy had given her the night off. Best to keep walking towards the boarding house, otherwise the burly man following her in Tommy's Bentley might become suspicious. Sarah risked a glance across the road at Fixing Time, the Doctor's watchmending shop. The lights were off inside and a closed sign was hanging on the front door. It seemed everyone was having the night off. After one last tug at her uncomfortable footwear, Sarah continued walking along Old Street. The black Bentley gently rolled after her, maintaining a respectful distance as it passed St Luke's.

Inside the church Father Xavier was kneeling on the steps before the altar, his arms flung out sideways. He had been praying for more than an hour but he refused to stop until his supplications were answered.

'I try to do your will, but there is violence all around me. I try to bring your word to the people, but science is taking the place of faith. I try to make them see, but they are blinded by their own greed. What must I do?'

The priest waited but received no reply.

'Everything is getting out of control. I fear blood will be spilled, innocent blood on the streets, pain and hurting for the good people of this parish. Is that your will? Are you not just? How can such acts be allowed?'

A single tear ran down Father Xavier's face from his right eye.

'Please, my saviour, tell me what I must do…'

Tommy Ramsey was just sitting down to dinner when he heard a knock downstairs at the front door. His mother emerged from the kitchen carrying a plate laden with cottage pie, cabbage and buttered bread.

'Who could be calling at this hour? Sensible people are home having their dinner,' Mrs Ramsey said, tutting to herself. She lovingly put the plate down in front of her only child, next to a cup of steaming hot tea. 'Here you are, Thomas, cottage pie – your favourite. I made it special for your homecoming.'

Vera Ramsey was the only person who ever called Tommy

by his given name. She had married young, after being swept off her feet by a local lad called Herbert Ramsey. He was killed during the Great War, the war to end all wars they had called it. He never knew he was going to be a father. So Vera was left to raise Thomas on her own, bringing in money with sewing and knitting – she was a dab hand with a pair of knitting needles. Even now, Vera spent most of her spare time knitting a pullover or a scarf for one of Thomas's friends. She never remarried because she believed no man could ever stand comparison to her Bert, the war hero. Every night she prayed to Bert, hoping he was waiting for her in Heaven. One day she would be reunited with him. In the meantime, she had Thomas to look after and a house to keep. That was more than enough for any mother.

'Don't worry, Mum, one of the lads will get the door,' Tommy said. He tucked into the cottage pie, hungrily gulping down mouthfuls of the minced meat with its mashed potato topping. 'Lovely grub – we didn't get dinners like this in Wandsworth, I can tell you.'

His meal was interrupted by an insistent knock at the dining room door. Tommy sighed with exasperation, put his fork down and wiped his mouth with a linen napkin. 'What is it? I'm trying to eat in here!'

Jack Cooper opened the door and put his head around the corner. 'Sorry Tommy, but you've got a visitor. It's Valentine.'

Tommy swore beneath his breath, just quiet enough that his mum would not hear. She didn't approve of blasphemy or foul language, especially at home. Tommy composed his face into a smile before turning around.

'Sorry, Mum, but I've got a man downstairs who's come to talk some business. Why don't you go next door and listen to the radio?'

Mrs Ramsey did not look impressed. 'I'll put your dinner

back on the stove, then, shall I?' She picked up the plate and took it back into the kitchen. She soon returned, pausing to pick up her knitting and kiss Tommy on the forehead. 'Don't you be talking all night. I know what you boys are like when you get going. You be sure he finishes that dinner, Jack.'

'Yes Mrs Ramsey,' Jack replied meekly from the doorway.

Satisfied, she retreated into the parlour next door, closing the door gently behind her. Tommy waited until he could hear the radio warming up and the sound of his mother's knitting needles klakking together before nodding to Jack. 'All right, bring him up.'

Tommy tried to take a sip from the cup of tea while he waited but it was still too hot. Why his mum insisted on making all tea at such a temperature was beyond Tommy, but he didn't like to mention it. She put up with a lot but never complained. For that he was very grateful.

Jack reappeared in the doorway, holding it open. In shuffled a bedraggled, unhappy figure.

'Dear oh dear,' Tommy commented. 'Look what the cat's dragged in.'

Bob Valentine was a mess. His face was pallid and drawn, with black rings beneath the eyes and two days' stubble across the jowls. His hair was a tangle of knots, streaked with clumps of grey amidst the black. His clothes were wet and crumpled, a once respectable suit ruined from too many nights of disgraceful behaviour. Suspicious stains lingered in all the wrong places and the stench of body odour, urine and cheap whisky began to fill the room.

Tommy pushed his chair back from the dining table and stood up. 'One look at you has put me right off the lovely dinner me mum cooked. The state of you! I'm amazed you've still got a job with the Old Bill.'

Bob Valentine swayed on his feet, staring at the maroon

carpet on the floor. He was still a detective in rank, if not demeanour. Years ago he had been considered a rising star in the London police force. Now he was an alcohol-sodden joke, the punchline to a dozen jokes about cops gone wrong. Gambling had been his downfall. The first time he went to a dog track the young copper had won three weeks' wages in a single night. The thrill of betting, the sickening danger and the unbelievable high of winning proved far too addictive for Bob Valentine. One way or another, he'd been going to the dogs ever since.

When his gambling debts got out of control, one of the bookie's minders had approached him. His slate would be wiped clean in exchange for a little inside information. His conscience had troubled him for days, but his mouth had answered instantly. He would do it, he would trade his honesty for relief from the burden of debt and threat of a beating. Bob Valentine made a terrible discovery that day, far worse than realising he was addicted to gambling. He was a coward – and everybody knew it.

For the past five years he had been in Tommy Ramsey's pocket, a bent copper swapping police canteen gossip for favours. His self-respect was long gone, his health was failing fast thanks to drink and cigarettes, and his career was in tatters. It was only a matter of time before he lost his job or his life. It was only his fear that stopped Bob Valentine topping himself. He was terrified of death, a coward to the end.

Tommy picked up his cup of tea and threw it in the detective's face. The pain caused by the hot liquid jolted the policeman back to life. He wiped the tea from his eyes and strained to focus on Tommy's face.

'Mr Ramsey! You're out! That's good news,' he slurred. Valentine reached into his pocket and pulled out a hip flask of whisky. Tommy grabbed it from his hand and the detective burst into tears, sobbing pathetically.

'You're a mess. I've seen prettier sights at the bottom of a budgie cage.'

Valentine tried to pull himself together. 'You owe me, Tommy.'

The gangland boss raised an eyebrow. 'How'd you figure that?'

'I got those witnesses nobbled at your trial. I even got you the home addresses of the jurors. You'd have been hung if it wasn't for me.'

Tommy leaned into Valentine's face. 'How come I still got sent down for six months, eh? Answer me that!'

Valentine shrugged. 'But you still owe me for the rest,' he insisted.

'Yeah, yeah.' Tommy's eyes lit up. 'Tell you what – I'll clean your slate in return for some information. Tell me about this new gang round Old Street.'

Valentine sagged, his face ashen. 'They're bad, Tommy – vicious. I think most of them are just boys really but the leader... His name's Callum, can't be more than twenty. He seems to love hurting people, it's like he enjoys it. Sick, that's what the boys down the station are calling him. He's the key to the whole gang. Take him away and I think the rest would fold up.'

Tommy handed Valentine back the hip flask. The detective drank gratefully from it, like a baby sucking at its mother's breast. 'Anything else you can tell me?' Tommy asked.

'Only that they hang round near the public baths behind St Luke's. I think they sleep in one of the bombed-out houses nearby.' Valentine dared to look Tommy in the face. 'Did I do good, Tommy?'

'You did great.' Tommy folded a fifty-pound note into the top pocket of the detective's suit, then rammed a knee upwards into Valentine's groin. The detective collapsed in a heap on the floor. 'Just don't ever call me Tommy again. It's Mr Ramsey to you. Get up.'

Valentine was still writhing on the rug in agony. 'I said get up!' Tommy demanded. The detective slowly, painfully got back to his feet.

'Now, you hear anything else – anything – about this gang, I want to know about it first. You got that?'

Valentine nodded, the colour returning to his cheeks. Tommy gently slapped the policeman on the side of his face twice. 'Now get out of here, I got business to attend to.'

Valentine smiled and backed out of the room, almost bowing as he left the presence of Tommy Ramsey. The gangland boss shook his head sadly once Valentine had gone. 'He used to be a good little copper. Now look at him. You learn a lesson from that, Jack – gambling is a mug's game.'

Jack nodded. He was always on the receiving end of Tommy's little homilies but he paid them no mind. 'What's next?'

'Me dinner's probably ruined by now. I'll come downstairs and talk to the lads. There's a few things that need sorting out.'

Sarah arrived at the boarding house. It was run by Mrs Kelly, a friendly Irish woman with a lecherous husband. Like most of the homes in the surrounding streets, it was a humble dwelling split over several floors. Sarah had taken lodgings here soon after arriving in 1952. It was essential to establishing her new identity in this time and place that she have a home somewhere other than the TARDIS.

For a small sum Sarah had a room of her own with a single bed, a wardrobe and a chest of drawers. If she wanted to wash, there was a tin bath that could be laboriously filled with water heated on the stove. The bath was put by the coal fire in the front room and all other guests were banned from entering. That didn't seem to stop Mr Kelly from accidentally wandering into the room by mistake while she was bathing. Sarah decided to take her ablutions in the TARDIS after that incident, even if her apparent lack of cleanliness did raise eyebrows amongst the other boarders.

The toilet was an outhouse off the narrow courtyard behind the house, or a chamber pot beneath her bed at night. Sarah had been shocked to find that modern conveniences like indoor plumbing were still rare luxuries in inner city areas. What she wouldn't give for central heating and an en suite bathroom!

Sarah stepped into the house and hung her coat on one of the hooks in the doorway. Mrs Kelly came out to see her. 'Will you be wanting a bath tonight, Miss Smith?' she asked politely.

Sarah could see Mr Kelly lurking in the front room hopefully. 'No thanks, Rose. I'll just be going straight to bed. I'm bushed.'

'Oh, all right then.'

Sarah made her way up three creaking flights of stairs to her room. Once inside, she made a great show of turning on the light and closing the curtains on the window that looked out on to the street. She then undressed near the window, making sure her silhouette fell on the curtain, before turning out the light. Sarah waited another five minutes before sneaking a look through the gap in the curtains at the street below. The black Bentley was just pulling away. It seemed her performance had convinced Tommy's bodyguard that she had indeed gone to bed for the night.

Sarah slipped into a warm dress and pulled on some more sensible shoes before venturing out of her room. She slowly descended the stairs, counting steps and carefully avoiding those that creaked loudest. She paused by the front door to get her coat. Mrs Kelly was talking loudly, trying to be heard over the radio which her husband preferred for company.

'I don't know when that young lady plans to bath next. It's shocking.'

'Maybe she goes to the public baths,' Mr Kelly replied wearily.

Sarah opened the front door, stepped out and closed it carefully behind her.

Tommy Ramsey was meeting with his key men. The Ramsey Mob was more than fifty strong, but most of those were only associates. The inner circle was just seven: Tommy himself, Jack and five lieutenants – Jim Harris, Dave Butcher, Mike Gilmore, Norman Page and Billy Valance. Each lieutenant was responsible for different areas of the Ramsey Mob's empire. Harris covered race meetings for horses and dogs, Butcher managed the brothels, Gilmore was responsible for illegal gambling clubs, Page looked after robberies and theft, while Valance was in charge of the protection rackets. Each lieutenant could call on up to a dozen men at any time to support their actions.

That night seven men sat round the long table where Tommy liked to hold his business meetings. Normally Brick stood near Tommy, in case the boss had any orders which required urgent attention. But Valance was conspicuous by his absence, so Brick had taken the empty seat. The other chairs were occupied by Tommy, Jack and the other lieutenants.

'Right, we can't wait for Billy any longer – let's get down to it,' Tommy announced, calling the meeting to order. The gathering fell silent as their leader prepared his thoughts.

'It's good to be back. I don't mind the occasional holiday but six months in Wandsworth was a bit too long, even for my liking!' Everyone laughed heartily. Tommy seemed to be in a good mood and that helped them all to relax. 'Jack's given me a brief report but I'd like each of you to say what's been happening in my absence.'

The four lieutenants present outlined the events of the past six months. Takings had been sharply down in recent times, especially since the evangelical crusading of Father Xavier started to hurt the businesses. The new gang was another factor but Jim Harris was confident of infiltrating its ranks within days. 'I've seen them around and they look like a bunch of kids to me. Upstarts who need to get wrists slapped,' he said.

Tommy smiled with the others before becoming more serious. 'That may be, but I seem to recall we were still just upstarts when we all got out of the army. It didn't take us long to push the old-timers out of the area. That's not going to happen to us.' He slammed a fist down on the table. 'These are my streets and nobody is taking them away from me!'

Tommy made eye contact with each one of his men as he looked around the table. 'Jack's done a good job in my absence but I'm taking control again now. Any resistance is to be crushed – everybody got that?' Nods all round. 'Now get out there and spread the word – Tommy Ramsey is back!'

The meeting at an end, the lieutenants filed out one by one. Brick made his own report to Tommy once the others had gone.

'I followed the girl like you said. She lives in the boarding house on Great Sutton Street run by Mrs Kelly. Been there two weeks, no bother to anybody, no visitors, keeps herself to herself.'

Tommy nodded his appreciation. 'Good work Brick. Tomorrow you—'

He was interrupted by the arrival of Billy Valance, who staggered into the meeting room and collapsed onto a chair.

He looked dishevelled and disorientated.

'Where the hell have you been?' Tommy demanded. 'Meeting finished five minutes ago!'

'Sorry, Tommy,' Billy said. 'I've been wandering the streets in a daze, hardly knowing who I am or where I was.'

'You're not making much sense now. What happened?'

'I don't know,' Billy replied, forlornly shaking his head. 'It was the watchmender, I think – he used some trick. It all happened so fast, I hardly knew what hit me.'

Tommy lifted Billy's face up by the chin and stared deep into his lieutenant's bloodshot eyes. 'You telling me the truth or you having a laugh?'

'It's the truth, Tommy, I swear!'

The gang boss slapped Billy across the face – once, twice, three times. He drew his hand back for another swipe and Billy cowered before his cold fury. 'Please, Tommy, I'm sorry. It won't happen again!'

'You better be right. I've just told the others that Tommy Ramsey is in charge and you come in here saying you can't even rumple the clothing of an old man! What kind of fool do you think that makes me look, eh?'

Tommy slapped the whimpering man again for good measure.

'Now listen to me carefully. Tomorrow, you go back to the watchmender and you make an example of him.' Tommy looked to his bodyguard. 'You better take Brick – for your own protection!'

Billy nodded his understanding, his bottom lip wobbling like a blubbering infant.

'Now get out of my sight!' Tommy snarled.

A police call box stood in Whitecross Lane, just around the corner from the Fixing Time shop. A gentle humming could be heard near the tall blue structure but an Out of Order notice was pasted to its front door.

Sarah approached the TARDIS nonchalantly and knocked three times on the door. It opened after she had waited a few seconds and Sarah stepped inside. No matter how many times she entered the TARDIS, that first moment after coming through the doorway always left her disorientated. Intellectually, she knew that the time machine was bigger on the inside than it was on the outside – dimensionally transcendental was the Doctor's tongue-twisting explanation for the phenomenon. But her senses still rebelled at the sudden shift in reality. As far as Sarah's body was concerned, she should be inside a rather cramped upright cupboard. Nothing could be further from the truth.

The control room was a many-sided chamber that gleamed with light and energy. Dozens of roundels were set into the walls. In the middle of the room was a central console, with a cylindrical rotor at its heart that rose and fell when the TARDIS travelled through time and space. Around the rotor were set panels of switches, dials and buttons. The operation of the TARDIS remained a mystery to Sarah. To her it was like a Boeing 747 – she didn't need to know how it worked, she just wanted to be sure she would arrive at her destination safely. The Doctor often complained about the TARDIS's erratic sense of direction but he seemed to have tamed its liking for the scenic route of late. The time machine had been arriving at its intended destination safely, even if the destination had proven to be anything but safe for the travellers.

The Doctor looked up from the central console and smiled at Sarah as she entered. 'Here at last! I was beginning to wonder if you would make it.'

Sarah took her coat off and hung it on a hat stand in one of the room's many corners. 'Tommy Ramsey had his bodyguard follow me back to the boarding house. I took the long way here to make sure I wasn't followed.'

The Doctor returned to fiddling with a mess of wiring that had been pulled from one of the central console's panels. 'And were you?'

'No, I don't think so.'

'That's all right, then,' the Doctor replied soothingly. He plucked a burnt and blackened circuit from the wiring and held it up in front of his face. 'This is the culprit.'

He walked to a door on the far side of the control room. It led off to a bewildering array of corridors, rooms, chambers, storage spaces and even a swimming pool. Sarah had once tried to explore the labyrinthine interior of the TARDIS, but the closer she got to its heart the more confused she became. She contented herself with converting a large, friendly room into her living quarters and raiding clothes from an immense walk-in wardrobe. It had provided her period clothes for this sojourn in 1952. She decided that the trouser suits for women and artificial fabrics from her own time would attract unwanted attention in this era. The Doctor never seemed to bother trying to blend his attire with his location, yet his clothes seemed to match his manner no matter where or when he went.

'Doctor, I—' Sarah began.

'Be right with you,' he replied, his voice echoing as if it were coming from the other side of a vast cathedral. When he returned to the console room his travelling companion was visibly shaking. 'Now, what were you – my dear, what's wrong? What is it?'

Sarah told him about her encounter with Tommy. The Doctor placed a reassuring hand around her shoulders.

'I – I almost got a man killed today,' Sarah stammered. She walked away from the Doctor, hugging her arms around herself. 'Perhaps coming here was a mistake. Perhaps the photo is wrong – perhaps we aren't meant to be here, not now, not in this place.'

'I only wish that were true,' the Doctor said quietly to himself.

'Thousands of people will die in the next few days,' Sarah continued, not hearing his comment. 'How can you know our coming here doesn't cause those deaths? We could be responsible for what is about to happen!'

'We are no more responsible for what is about to happen than you are responsible for the actions of Tommy Ramsey,' the Doctor replied. 'He seems to be the key to the next few days – if only we could learn how he is involved, we could unlock the mystery…'

'You know, sometimes Doctor, I don't understand you at all. We've been here two weeks and in all that time all you've done is mend clocks and watches in that shop of yours. It's like you don't care, don't want to get involved. Thousands of people are going to die in the next few days—'

'Don't you think I know that!' he said. 'Do you think I enjoy waiting to be a witness to tragedy and death?'

'Then stop waiting! Do something to stop it!'

'I can't! Don't you understand that? I can't stop it!' the Doctor replied, his eyes blazing fiercely.

Sarah took a step back. She had never seen him like this before.

'Those people that die must die. It's history, it's already happened and there's nothing we can do to prevent it, Sarah.'

She was horrified by his fatalism. 'Then why did we come here at all?'

'To prevent a much greater tragedy, one that can still be undone.'

'I don't understand,' Sarah said. 'How can we stop one part

of history but not another? Surely that's a… a…'

'Paradox?' the Doctor replied. 'Perhaps. But that doesn't stop it being real. Let me try to explain. We came from the future, where the events of the next few days have already happened. Thousands died and I had my picture taken alongside Tommy Ramsey. But I believe something far more terrible could happen in the coming days. That's why I have to be here, to try and prevent it. The photograph proves I will be here – I just don't know what my role is to be.'

'A bit like a chess piece that can move itself,' Sarah said, beginning to understand his argument. 'Someone else is controlling the game…'

'But I can still influence the outcome. My actions could save the lives of thousands or condemn them to a terrible, unnecessary death.' He smiled at her kindly. 'Now do you understand? I do care. I am involved. But it has to be at the right time and place, or all of mankind could suffer the consequences.'

Sarah nodded, feeling a little of the burden that he must be carrying. 'You're scared. You don't want to play god with people's lives.'

'Something like that.'

She gave the Doctor a hug. 'I'm sorry about what I said before. I didn't mean it really, I was just angry and frustrated.'

'I know.' He lifted her face up and looked into her eyes. 'People will get hurt, Sarah. People will die. We can't prevent that. But we must do all that we can…'

'To do the right thing.'

'Exactly.'

Sarah picked up her coat. 'Well, I'm going to have a bath before I go back to the boarding house for some sleep. Tomorrow I have a job interview with the Ramsey Mob – want to look my best for the new boss. What will you be doing?'

The Doctor returned to examining the troublesome circuitry. 'I am expecting another visit from Ramsey's thugs. I've become quite a thorn in their sides. Goodnight, Sarah.'

'Goodnight, Doctor.'

THURSDAY, DECEMBER 4, 1952

Jim Harris blew into his cupped hands, trying to keep his fingers warm. He had been watching the Callum gang since dawn but had gathered little information of use. The youths had risen with the sun, stolen their breakfast from the window of a nearby bakery and lifted bottles of milk from an unattended cart. Hardly the work of a terrifying new force on the East End streets. Now they had returned to their condemned headquarters in Ironmonger Row.

Harris resented being given this job. By rights it should have gone to one of the Ramsey Mob's underlings, who were ever eager to catch the eye of the boss. But Tommy had insisted that a lieutenant study this new threat and Harris had drawn the short straw, thanks to his youthful features. How Tommy expected him to infiltrate this bunch of scruffy teenagers was a mystery! Harris prided himself on his appearance, wearing the sharpest suits and finely woven silk shirts. Callum and his gang looked like they hadn't seen hot water for weeks.

Normally Harris would have been collecting information from his many contacts in the racing industry by now. Horses would be coming back from their early morning rides, some with old injuries flaring up, others fully fit again. That sort of intelligence was crucial in setting the right odds for local gamblers wanting a flutter. Harris prided himself on running the most profitable book in the East End. It helped having the full weight of the Ramsey Mob at your disposal when it came to collecting bets from reluctant payers. It also helped having a handful of the major trainers for both horses and greyhounds in your pocket, making sure races came in with the right result.

Like the other lieutenants in the Ramsey Mob, Harris had met Tommy during the war. Harris was the unofficial turf accountant for their unit, but the odds he offered were rarely to do with horses. He found soldiers were willing to bet on almost anything, even their own chances of surviving the next battle. One soldier always bet against himself coming back alive. He claimed his bad luck at gambling would protect him when the bullets started to fly. It worked for five months. When his luck finally turned, Harris had shared the winnings around the unit so everyone could raise a glass to the dead man.

After the war, Harris had contemplated getting a straight job at a legitimate bookies, but he couldn't stick the hours. Nine to five was never his game. He liked the excitement of the dog track, the thrill of a fine filly emptying the pockets of his punters. When Tommy took control of the streets around Shoreditch, Harris had been one of the first invited to join the Ramsey Mob. It was among the proudest days of his life. So being asked to snoop on a bunch of unwashed teenagers with attitude problems was not high on Harris's list of desired jobs for a chilly December morning.

Harris was contemplating sloping off for a cooked breakfast when he noticed someone was missing from the gang. A quick headcount confirmed his suspicions – one of them had slipped away in the last few minutes. But which one? Harris was still scanning the faces of the gang when he heard the voice.

'Nice threads. Shame about the spying git wearing 'em.'

Harris swivelled to find Callum close behind him. 'What the—?!'

'You're not very observant for someone who's been watching us all morning. What's your name?'

Harris stared into the black, pitiless eyes of his interrogator. 'Harris. Jim Harris. You're in trouble, you and your gang.'

Callum grinned. 'How do you figure that?'

'Tommy Ramsey knows all about you. He'll crush you lot like bugs.'

'Is that right? Him and what army?' Callum's hand flashed forward and Harris caught a glimpse of something silver, shining brightly, along with the swish of fabric being sliced apart. He looked down and was shocked to see a burgeoning red stain across his stomach.

Callum shook his head ruefully. 'That's a nasty cut. You should get that seen to. Don't want to get an infection.' His hand flashed forwards again. This time the sound was more like pork being trimmed from the bone. Harris sat backwards on the ground, no longer able to catch his breath. Something damp and warm was running down the insides of his legs.

Callum leaned over and glared into Harris's eyes. 'I've got a message for your boss. If you're lucky, you might live long enough for him to get you to a hospital. But I doubt it. Here's the message.'

Callum whispered a few words into the left ear of the fallen lieutenant before walking away. He wiped the blood from his hands onto a brick wall. When he got back to the rest of the gang, Callum called Charlie and Billy over.

'There's a spy from the Ramsey Mob across the road, badly wounded. He'll probably try to stagger back to his boss. You two watch him. Let me know if anything interesting happens.'

The two brothers nodded in unison and made for the stricken gangster.

A small crowd had gathered outside a humble shop on Old Street, just east of St Luke's Church. Most were parishioners from the church's congregation, but some people from outside the local area were present. Mrs Ramsey was at the front of the crowd, glaring at the man standing behind a red ribbon with Father Simmons. The guest of honour was Derek Carver, Chief Superintendent for much of the East End. A robust, ruddy-faced man, he filled his immaculate uniform to bursting.

The police chief had been invited by Father Simmons to officially open the first Bread of Life retail outlet. But the priest had been distracted from beginning the ceremony by a local newspaper reporter eager to get his story before a fast approaching midday deadline.

'You see, this helps the community in two ways,' Father Simmons explained. 'The factory where we make the bread is run by local people who would not otherwise be able to get work. A lot of them have been laid off from the docks or by factories which are shifting out of the area. So Bread of Life gives these people a pay packet, even if it is only a small one so far. But more important than that, it gives them back their self-respect. Give a man a job and you give him a sense of purpose, a reason to get up in the morning.'

The reporter was rushing to scrawl down the quotes as shorthand in his notebook. 'And the other way? You said it helps the community...'

'Oh yes! Well, of course, it provides cheap food for those who can't afford very much. Bread is part of the staple diet of people in this part of London but many struggle to afford even such a basic foodstuff. So this shop helps them to buy bread cheaply, made locally. That's why we call it the Bread of Life.'

The priest was on a roll now, talking faster than the journalist could keep up with his meagre shorthand skills. 'It's about giving pride back to the East End, really. This area was worst hit by the Blitz and it's still waiting for many of the bombed-out buildings to be cleared.'

Father Simmons was interrupted by a gentle nudge from Carver. 'Excuse me, but the – err – opening ceremony?'

The priest blushed with embarrassment. 'I'm terribly sorry, Chief Superintendent! Once I start talking about this project I get completely carried away. You must forgive me for holding you up!'

The police chief waved away the apology. 'There's nothing to forgive. I like to see a man who is passionate about doing good. We need more people like you to help get the East End back on its feet!'

Father Simmons nodded eagerly. 'I'm glad you said that. I have a proposal which I would like you to consider…'

'After the ceremony, perhaps?'

The priest blushed again. 'I'm terribly sorry, I'm doing it again. Let's get started, shall we?' Father Simmons clapped his hands together, getting the attention and the silence of the chattering crowd. 'Welcome, one and all to this very special occasion for the people of Old Street and the surrounding area. As some of you may know, we have already begun selling the Bread of Life in parts of the East End, but this is our very first shop. If everything goes to plan, we hope to be opening similar shops across London in the coming weeks and months – all with their own factories offering work to local people!'

The crowd applauded spontaneously. Chief Superintendent Carver was quite swept along by the priest's fervour. Simmons was a powerful and charismatic speaker, able to reach out to his audience as if speaking to each person individually. It was a rare gift, something Carver wished he possessed himself. But the policeman knew his rough voice and gruff words were never likely to move anybody to applause, let alone religious belief.

'I now invite Chief Superintendent Carver to officially open this shop!' Father Simmons handed a pair of scissors to the police chief before stepping aside. Carver gripped the red ribbon tied across the shop front in one hand and prepared to cut. He paused to allow the newspaper photographer to get a good angle, then sliced through the ribbon. It fell neatly aside and everyone surged toward the shop. Inside, workers from the factory were handing out slices of bread, laden with rich, creamy butter.

'I am the Bread of Life. He who eats of me shall live for ever,' Father Simmons called out to the crowd as they entered the shop. 'Everybody's first loaf is free! Make sure you share this bounty with your family!'

Mrs Ramsey had been elbowed aside in the rush to get inside the shop. She cleared her throat loudly several times to get the attention of those around her. Once the others recognised her diminutive figure, they stepped hastily aside. In moments a path had cleared for her to reach the counter. Father Simmons thought it best resembled the Red Sea parting for Moses, but in this case the red came from the threat of bloody vengeance Tommy Ramsey would dispense if his mother was denied anything she wanted.

Jim Harris felt a hollowness in his chest, as if his very being was slowly oozing from the vicious wounds to his body. He couldn't die like this, lying in some alleyway, beaten by a smirking youth. He had a message to deliver and he had never let Tommy down before. He wasn't going to start now, even as his life was dripping away between his fingers.

Somehow Harris pushed himself up against a brick wall, both hands clutching at his wounds. He steadied his shaking legs then began to stagger towards Old Street. If he could make it to a main road, he could wave down a car and get taken to hospital. There was still time, if only he could make it to a main road. He took one hand away from his stomach and felt something shift inside, something not meant to move like that. It was all he could do to stop from throwing up. Choking down the bile, he staggered on, one bloody hand propping him up by leaning on the wall.

Brothers Billy and Charlie followed Harris at a discreet distance.

Chief Superintendent Carver finished his third slice of bread with unexpected enthusiasm. He looked around for more but was disappointed to discover the shop had run out of supplies after only an hour. Father Simmons saw the look on Carver's face and smiled.

'Chief Superintendent! You look unhappy – I hope our bread isn't to blame,' the priest said.

'Quite the reverse. I was hoping to take some away with me – very tasty. Very tasty,' Carver replied, licking his lips. His eyebrows rose in gratitude as Father Simmons presented him with a wrapped loaf.

'I wouldn't want you to go away empty-handed,' the priest said. 'In fact, I have a proposition for you. How much do the East End police canteens pay for their bread?'

'I don't honestly know.'

'I'm guessing that Bread of Life can undercut whatever price you do pay. And, as you testify, our bread is the equal of any other loaf.'

Carver nodded enthusiastically. 'Better, I would say.'

'Well then, that's settled. I'll put your stations down as our first major business customers.'

The chief superintendent held up his hands in mock protest. 'I only came down to open a shop, Father!'

The priest looked crestfallen. 'I'm sorry, Chief Superintendent – I hope I haven't offended you.'

'Not at all, I'm just not used to your American hard sell.'

Father Simmons nodded. 'Well, I wasn't always a man of the cloth. I used to be quite the wheeler dealer before I saw the light – not always on the right side of the law, either. But those days are long behind me. Now I only want to spread the good word and do my Saviour's bidding.'

'Well, let's just say I'm very impressed by what you've managed to achieve here. I only wish we had more men like you,' Carver replied.

'And the bread supply contract?'

'You don't give up, do you?' the chief superintendent said with a smile. 'All right, if you can match or better the price the canteens are currently paying, then the contract is yours on a trial basis.'

Father Simmons grabbed Carver's right hand and began to shake it enthusiastically. 'Thank you, thank you – you won't regret this!'

Tabernacle Street was one of Shoreditch's side roads, close to the junction of Old Street and the City Road. Terraced housing lined both sides of the street. Few cars were parked on the road, except for a black Bentley outside number 15. All along the road women dressed in aprons were scrubbing the front steps of their humble homes. It was a local daily ritual, handed down by generations of East End wives and mothers to their daughters. A young woman approached the women, walking hesitantly down the footpath. One of the scrubbers stopped and looked up.

Mary Mills had lived in the same house on Tabernacle Street all her twenty-nine years. She had been born in her parents' bedroom upstairs, the last of five daughters. Her mother had died soon after due to complications, a fact Mary's father had used as an excuse to beat his daughters every Saturday night after he staggered home from the King's Arms. Each daughter left the house as soon as they could, marrying the first man to offer a chance of escape. The old man finally died of liver failure when Mary was sixteen. She inherited the crumbling house, red hair and freckles from her father – but nothing else.

Life ever since had been a struggle. Mary got pregnant after a moment of passion with a sailor during the Blitz. She was glad her parents were dead when it happened, as the shame would have killed them. But Mary refused to apologise for her behaviour and kept working at both of her cleaning jobs until the day before the baby was born. She named the child Jean after her mother. After that Mary took in laundry to meet the bills. Two more fleeting romances led to two more girls – Rita and Bette (Mary had always been fond of going to the pictures, when finances would allow). The family trait of only having daughters was as strong in Mary as it had been in her mother.

The three girls were all school age now and Mary found the days empty without one of them tugging at her apron strings. The house was badly in need of repairs but there were so many problems and so little money it hardly seemed worth making a start. The outdoor toilet had overflowed again this morning. Mary would be thirty soon but on days like this she felt closer to fifty.

'Excuse me,' the young woman asked Mary. 'I'm looking for Tommy Ramsey's house. This is Tabernacle Street, isn't it?'

The sound of scrubbing stopped as one by one the women

looked at this strange outsider. Who could possibly want to visit Tommy Ramsey of their own volition? Only the criminal or the insane. Yet this young woman seemed like neither. Mary looked up at the visitor. She was well dressed with a pleasant, inquiring face. Her voice sounded posh to Mary, but anybody not born within earshot of Bow Bells sounded posh to Mary.

'It's Tabernacle Street all right. What do you want with Tommy Ramsey?' Mary asked, giving voice to the question every other woman on the street was eager to ask.

'I've got an appointment to see him, about a job,' the visitor explained. 'Which house is his?'

Mary just pointed across the road to number 15. The new arrival smiled a thank you and crossed the road, aware of at least a dozen pairs of eyes watching her every movement. She knocked on the door and waited. It creaked open and she couldn't help but be startled by the appearance of Brick. He filled the hallway like an enormous piece of inherited furniture in too small a home.

'My name's Sarah Jane Smith – we met yesterday at the Red Room. I'm here to see Mr Ramsey.' Sarah made sure her voice was loud enough to carry to the women still ignoring their scrubbing.

Brick looked up and down the road before stepping aside to let Sarah squeeze past him into the hallway. 'You better come inside – he's waiting.'

Once the door had slammed shut, the street was filled with the sound of furious scrubbing and gossip. Mary Mills just smiled, keeping herself to herself. Many on this road lived in terror of the Ramsey Mob and few of the women would have dared knock on the front door of number 15. But the visitor looked almost entirely unconcerned at entering the most feared home in the East End. Good for you, girl, thought Mary as she resumed scrubbing.

On the other side of the road, Brick and Billy Valance emerged from number 15. They climbed into the Bentley and Brick drove away, carefully observing the local speed limit.

The Doctor was late opening his watchmender's shop that morning. He had been up all night running experiments in the TARDIS. He had considered not opening at all, but knew that another visit from one of Ramsey's thugs was likely. Better to be present for it and take advantage of the visit, than take the day off and have to deal with the consequences afterwards.

He was just checking the results of his latest experiment when a black car stopped outside the shop. Two men got out, although the driver had great difficulty in extracting himself from behind the steering wheel because of his massive frame. The Doctor busied himself in the shop, taking notes on the different times showing on several of the clocks. A grandfather clock made of oak and brass was displaying the correct time – 11 o'clock. Beside it was a carriage clock of silver and gold, which showed the time as 11.30am. Beyond that was a cheap wall-mounted timepiece that seemed to think the time was midday. The Doctor removed a small device attached to the side of the wall-mounted clock. He was deactivating the device's power source when the two men walked into the shop.

'Fascinating,' the Doctor announced to the room without looking around. 'This cannibalised circuit was able to create an acceleration effect in a localised area, as I surmised. But the chronometric warp leaks beyond its pre-set boundaries. Perhaps if I reverse the polarity of the neutron flow…'

Valance cleared his throat to get the watchmender's attention. The Doctor turned around and smiled at him. 'Back again so soon? I think you must be my first regular customer!' The Doctor slipped the circuit into his jacket pocket. 'How can I help you today?'

Valance scowled. 'I don't know what trick you pulled on me yesterday but it won't happen again. I brought company,' he said, nodding to Brick. The man mountain flipped over a sign in the shop window, so it now read CLOSED when seen from outside.

'So I see. Who's your friend?'

'None of your business. Will you be taking out insurance with us or do we have to get nasty?'

The Doctor sighed. 'You really are a most tiresome chap, aren't you?'

'Yes or no?' Valance demanded.

'No.'

Valance nodded to Brick, who leaned against the front door, blocking anyone from leaving or entering. Valance moved to the counter at the rear of the shop, preventing any escape by that exit. The Doctor was trapped.

'Another cup of tea, Miss Smith?' Mrs Ramsey stood over Sarah, teapot at the ready in one hand. In the other she brandished a china plate laden with slices of homemade cake. 'Or perhaps another slice of cake?'

'No thank you, Mrs Ramsey – I'm trying to watch my figure,' Sarah replied. She had already had four cups of tea and three slices of cake. She couldn't face more food or drink.

'Why? You look like you need feeding up, if you don't mind my saying say. It's not healthy to be so thin. You'll waste away to nothing.'

Sarah had been waiting in the upstairs parlour for twenty minutes, with Mrs Ramsey keeping her company. Thomas was busy elsewhere, according to the gangster's mother. Sarah guessed Mrs Ramsey was probably about sixty-five years old. She barrelled around the house in a floral print dress, slippers and apron, making tea and cakes for the burly men who were constantly coming and going. They deferred meekly to her requests, as if terrified of their own shadows. The boss's mother was not to be crossed.

Sarah settled back in a plush armchair and looked around the parlour. A thick rug covered most of the floorboards. A heavy wooden radio stood on a vast oak sideboard, opposite the fireplace. The remains of last night's fire were still in the grate. The walls were covered with family photographs, all framed in solid silver or gold. Pride of place went to a sepia-tinted portrait of a man in uniform who had an uncanny resemblance to Tommy. Mrs Ramsey caught Sarah looking at the photograph above the mantelpiece.

'I know what you're thinking, Miss Smith – he looks exactly like my Thomas. That picture was taken nearly forty years ago, when my Bert went off to fight in the Great War.' Mrs Ramsey sat down in another armchair opposite Sarah, looking up at the photo. 'The war to end all wars, they called it. But my Bert never came back and then my Thomas had to fight in the next war. I was so worried I would lose both of them. I don't think I could have taken that.'

'It was tragic the way two world wars decimated succeeding generations,' Sarah said. 'Patriotic communities suffered more than most.'

Mrs Ramsey pulled a rolled handkerchief from inside her sleeve and dabbed at her tearful eyes. 'Mr Churchill, he came along our street during the Blitz. One of the proudest days of my life, that was.'

Sarah sat quietly, letting the old woman alone with her memories. Heavy footsteps could be heard approaching the parlour door. Mrs Ramsey stirred from her reverie.

'That'll be my Thomas. I'll just put the kettle on – you'll be wanting another cup of tea, Miss Smith.'

Sarah felt nervous enough about meeting Tommy again. She crossed her legs and tried not to think about running water.

Valance pulled a blackened metal cosh from his pocket and pointed it at the Doctor. 'You should have gotten some protection while you had the chance. Tommy Ramsey says we have to make an example of you.'

The Doctor regarded him coolly. 'Really, how interesting. I think I would like to meet this Tommy Ramsey. How do I make an appointment?'

Valance sneered. 'The only person you'll be meeting is your maker!'

'You really do have the most dreary line in threats and menaces, don't you? I'm surprised he keeps such an unimaginative person on the payroll.'

Valance snapped. 'That's it!' He lunged at the Doctor, cosh drawn back ready to strike. His target dropped into a defensive stance, then pivoted on one foot to evade the vicious blow. Valance stumbled but did not fall. He spun round and nearly succeeded in smashing the bludgeon against the Doctor's head. 'You are history!'

'My dear chap, nothing could be further from the truth,' the Doctor replied, parrying the blow expertly. He used Valance's momentum to send the thug flying headfirst into the grandfather clock the Doctor had been examining earlier. Valance collapsed to the floor in an untidy heap, unconscious.

The Doctor glanced over at the bear of a man blocking the front door. 'I don't suppose we can settle this like civilised men, can we?'

Brick shook his head regretfully. He moved away from the door into the centre of the shop, his massive hands extended menacingly forward. The Doctor retreated, careful to keep some furniture between himself and the advancing foe. Even Venusian Aiki-Do might not save him this time…

'No, Mum, I'm fine – I don't need another cup of tea!' Tommy shut the door on his mother before returning to his seat in the upstairs parlour. He sat down and regarded the young woman opposite him. She looked quite different in these surroundings, removed from the lurid interior and cheap barmaid's uniform of the Red Room. To Tommy Sarah now seemed prim and proper. She showed little fear of being in his presence. He liked that.

'So, you want to work for me. Why?'

Sarah smiled. It was a long time since she'd been to a job interview. Normally she was the one asking the awkward questions. But if she wanted to get closer to the Ramsey Mob, she needed to impress this murderous man.

'A place like the Red Room has potential – besides skimming half the profits for himself, Morgan is an incompetent manager. He lets opportunities slip through his fingers.'

'Such as?'

'He wouldn't let punters spend more than they were carrying. Gamblers always believe they can win back their losses but few ever do. I believe in giving people enough rope – a man in debt is a man in your pocket.'

Tommy nodded his appreciation. 'What else?'

'Like you, I believe in loyalty. What's good for the firm is good for everyone in it. But loyalty has to be rewarded – handsomely. Call it a profit-share scheme to motivate your staff.'

Tommy smirked. 'You're just a girl – nobody in the Ramsey Mob will listen to a girl! You're only good for one thing.'

'Really? I notice that your men all take orders from your mother.' Sarah got up to leave. 'Forget it, Mr Ramsey. I had enough trouble keeping that thief Morgan at arm's length – I don't need you chasing my skirt.' She opened the parlour door. 'Please thank your mother for the cake and tea.'

Tommy stormed to the door and slammed it shut. He leaned over Sarah, who refused to shrink from his powerful presence. 'Nobody speaks to Tommy Ramsey like that! Nobody!'

Sarah stared into his eyes, her voice level and unafraid as she spoke. 'Your mother doesn't seem to be scared of you. Neither am I.'

Tommy drew back a fist, ready to smash it into Sarah's face. But she did not flinch, continuing to stare into his eyes. Tommy stood for a moment, poised to strike. But his anger passed and his furious face relaxed into a smile.

'You've got a lot of bottle! Few people dare stand up to me,' he said, turning his fist into a gesture for them to sit down again. Sarah returned to her chair and Tommy sat opposite her once more. 'All right, you're in. I want you here beside me for the next few days. Call it probation, if you like.'

Sarah smiled. 'Of course. I'd expect nothing else. And my things?'

'I'll have Brick collect them from Mrs Kelly's boarding house. He's just off running an errand for me.'

'You know where I live...'

'Of course. You hardly think I'd employ someone who appears out of nowhere, do you? If you were a man, I'd think you were a cop or something!'

Sarah laughed at Tommy's joke, trying to keep her terror hidden.

Jim Harris staggered out on to Old Street. Twice he had fallen on the short distance from Ironmonger Row. Getting back to his feet had taken supreme efforts of will. He knew that if he should fall again, he would not be able to get up unaided. Harris looked up and saw the steeple of St Luke's Church towering overhead. He staggered to the steps and fell face forward onto them, unable to move any further.

Nearby Charlie and Billy were debating what to do. It seemed clear the fallen man would not be able to make his own way back to the Ramsey Mob's headquarters. Billy ran back to fetch Callum.

The Doctor and Brick were warily circling each other in the shop, each looking for an opening. The big man was proving surprisingly nimble. As they moved around the room, the Doctor tried to engage his opponent in conversation.

'My name's Smith, Doctor John Smith – but you can just call me the Doctor. What's your name?'

'Brick.'

'A curious pseudonym. How did you come by it?'

'Tommy took one look at me and said I looked like a brick sh—'

'I understand entirely,' the Doctor interjected. 'What's your real name?'

'Baldwin. Arthur Baldwin.'

'A pleasure to meet you, Arthur – a shame it had to be like this.'

Brick nodded morosely. 'I'm sorry about what I have to do to you. I just want you to know that I don't enjoy it.'

The Doctor smiled. 'Then why do it?'

'Because I'm good at it and this is the only work I can get. So, like I said – I'm sorry. I'll try to make this as painless as possible.'

'You have to catch me first.'

'That's just a matter of time. People assume that just

because I'm big, I'm also slow, stupid. Discovering their mistake can be a painful experience.' Brick lunged heavily in one direction, which the Doctor easily evaded. But the big man's first movement was just a feint. He dodged in the opposite direction and caught hold of his quarry's jacket. Before the Doctor could get free, Brick was crushing him in a mighty bear-hug.

'Just relax. The pain will soon pass,' Brick said, his voice soft and soothing in the Doctor's ear. 'I've seen it many times. People struggle to stay alive but when the end comes, they almost welcome it.'

The Doctor didn't reply, saving the remaining air in his lungs to keep back the blackness hammering at the edge of his thoughts. He squirmed around in Brick's crushing embrace, managing to slide a hand into the pocket of his jacket. He pulled out a fob watch and flicked open the casing to reveal the dazzling face inside. Straining with all his remaining strength, he held the watch up for Brick to see.

'I'll give you this watch if you let me go,' the Doctor gasped.

'I'm sorry Doctor, but I can't – I can't…'

Brick's words faded away as his grip slackened. The Doctor extracted himself from the giant man's arms, wincing at the constriction of movement in his chest. It felt like the muscles around his ribs were stretched and bruised. He was fortunate the ribs had not caved in from the intense pressure. Leaning on a table for support, the Doctor looked up at Brick's face. The massive figure was now impassive, his features a blank.

'Thank you, old man. I'm very grateful to say you are highly susceptible to hypnotic suggestion,' the Doctor said, ruefully rubbing his chest.

'You're welcome,' Brick replied in a lifeless monotone.

The Doctor smiled. 'I can't resist saying this. Take me to

your leader!'

Father Simmons was happily strolling back to St Luke's from the Bread of Life store when he saw a crowd gathering outside the front steps. He started running when he noticed the trail of blood leading to the crowd. Somebody was hurt and they had come to him for help. If only he hadn't stayed on at the shop, making sure everything went smoothly on the first day of business.

The priest pushed his way through the handful of bystanders. Someone had turned the injured man over and folded a jacket under his head for comfort, but otherwise his wounds went unattended. There were two vivid red slashes across the man's chest. His hands were feebly trying to hold his internal organs in place. His face was white, as if drained of blood. The evidence of where it had gone was staining his shirt and trousers.

Father Simmons demanded one of the crowd surrender their jacket. The priest tore the jacket apart at its seams to remove the lining. A single, savage glare from Father Simmons silenced the protests of the jacket's owner. The priest pressed the lining against the wounds as an impromptu dressing before looking up at the bystanders.

'Has someone called an ambulance?' he asked.

'I did. It should be here any minute,' an elderly woman replied.

'Bless you,' Father Simmons murmured. If the injured man got to hospital in time, there was still a faint chance he might survive. But the priest froze when he saw one of the other faces in the crowd grinning down at him. Without even thinking, Father Simmons made the sign of the cross.

Tommy was just sitting down to lunch with his mother and

Sarah when the doorbell rang. Tommy slammed his fork down on the tablecloth in disgust.

'Can't I have a single meal in peace? This place is worse than the nick!' he protested. Tommy didn't bother tucking into his generous serving of steak and kidney pudding. Whoever was at the door was bound to stymie his chances of finishing the first mouthful. He could hear raised voices downstairs and then several pairs of feet coming up the stairs.

Jack burst into the room, just ahead of two other people. 'I'm sorry Tommy, I told them you was having your dinner but...' He turned and looked helplessly as Brick stomped into the room, followed by the Doctor. Sarah was almost as surprised as the gangster to see the new arrival.

'Who the bleedin' hell are you?' Tommy demanded.

The ambulance drove away from St Luke's Church, the sound of its bell fading into the air. With the injured man removed, the crowd soon dispersed. But one man remained as Father Simmons was left, looking down at his bloody hands.

'Look familiar, does it?' Callum asked.

'I don't know what you mean,' the priest protested. 'Were you responsible for that poor man's terrible injuries? He could die, you know!'

'I'm just surprised he lasted this long. I got a bit overenthusiastic, you might say.'

'Callum – that's your name, isn't it? Callum, you've got to stop the violence between your boys and Tommy Ramsey's men. It's been building up for weeks. You've got to stop things escalating any further!'

Callum smiled. 'Why should I?'

'You're only drawing attention to yourself.'

'I want attention! I want everyone to know my name! I want to be famous and if I have to kill every one of Tommy

Ramsey's men, I'll do it.'

Father Simmons shook his head sadly. 'I don't doubt you believe that. But think about the effect of what you are doing. You will ruin everything I have worked for in this community. I'm trying to build a better world, starting here.'

'Then let it be ruined,' Callum sneered. 'I don't have to listen to you or anyone else.' He grabbed the priest's wrists and held them up. 'There's just as much blood on your hands as there is on mine, Father.'

'You don't understand. I've changed. I'm not the same man who used to hurt and rob and steal for his own gain, for his own pleasure.' The priest pressed his hands together as if in prayer, pleading with Callum. 'I've changed, I've seen the light of our Saviour. I believe you can change too!'

'Believe what you want – I know the truth!' Callum walked away, laughing to himself. Father Simmons sank onto the stone steps, where a dying man had lain only minutes before. The same steps where a dying man had lain six years ago…

'You'll have to excuse Arthur for bringing me here, but I hypnotised him. This should bring him round.' The new arrival in the Ramsey household snapped his fingers and Brick blinked once, twice and then looked quite bewildered.

'Where am I?'

'Home!' Tommy replied.

'How did I get here?'

'Hypnosis,' the Doctor replied. 'Dreadfully sorry, but I wanted to meet Mr Ramsey and it seemed the quickest way of gaining an audience.'

Mrs Ramsey intervened to spare Brick from the forthcoming fury signalled by Tommy's face rapidly changing to a disturbing shade of puce. 'Arthur, why don't you come in the kitchen and I'll fix you a nice cup of tea?'

'Ta, Mrs Ramsey, that'd be lovely. Don't know what's come over me.'

While she was ushering Brick out of the room, the Doctor introduced himself to Sarah. 'I don't believe we've been introduced. I'm Doctor John Smith, but everyone just calls me the Doctor. I fix problems with time – clocks and watches. My shop is just opposite St Luke's Church.'

Sarah shook his hand. 'Sarah Jane Smith. I work for Mr Ramsey.'

'Really? That must be – interesting.' The Doctor smiled warmly, winking at his companion on the sly.

'You two know each other?' Tommy demanded suspiciously.

'My dear chap, just because we share the same name, it doesn't mean we are related. Smith is the most common surname in England.'

Tommy grunted before beckoning to his second-in-command.

'Jack, I want you to go see what's happened to Billy.' Tommy whispered some additional instructions into Jack's ear before sending him away. Once he had gone, Tommy cast a careful eye over the man who had outwitted two of the Ramsey Mob's most dangerous enforcers.

To Tommy, the Doctor looked like some variety show magician. His shirt was ruffled at collar and cuffs, the green velvet smoking jacket, the careworn face and mighty nose indicated a lifetime spent jobbing around the theatres and clubs of Britain. The talent for hypnotism helped cement the impression. Yet the Doctor was obviously no buffoon, despite his extravagant gestures and supercilious accent. Tommy always looked deep into the eyes of everyone he met, to best assess the depths of their character. It was a gift which enabled him to know his friends and his enemies better than they knew themselves.

In Sarah's eyes Tommy had seen someone who was curious and caring, yet willing to be ruthless when the need arose. The Doctor's eyes were rich and strange, as if they had seen more than most. There was a sadness about them too, born of deaths and disappointments and too many goodbyes. Tommy was impressed but not afraid – the Doctor was a significant opponent. If he could be turned to Tommy's will, he would be a powerful ally.

'You've been causing my men some strife, Doctor. By rights I should have you beaten near death and dump your body outside that pathetic little watchmender's shop so everyone can see. What's stopping me?'

'Curiosity,' the Doctor replied, stroking his chin thoughtfully. 'You can't quite decide what to make of me. You'd like to know more before you act.'

'Let's suppose you're right. What do you plan on doing next?'

'Try to talk some sense into you!'

Tommy laughed. 'This should be good! Have a seat and tell me more.' The gangland boss pushed his rapidly congealing plate of food to one side and gestured for the Doctor to join him and Sarah at the table.

'I will never pay a penny for your so-called insurance. There are far greater threats facing the people of this city than the Ramsey Mob.'

'What do you mean—' Sarah began, but a glare from Tommy snapped her mouth shut. She resolved to keep silent. Having only just begun to win over Tommy's trust, she had to be careful not to throw it away again.

'I mean,' the Doctor continued, 'that Mr Ramsey and his men should be preparing their defences – not lining their pockets.'

'Talk to me, not to her,' Tommy grunted. He pulled a packet of cigarettes from his suit pocket and lit one. 'What threats? If you're talking about Callum and his gang of boys, they ain't worrying me. I seen their kind come and go.'

'Perhaps,' the Doctor replied. 'But don't say I didn't warn you.'

'Warn me? All you've done is talk in riddles. You got something to say then spit it out. Otherwise keep it shut,' Tommy said.

'For an intelligent man, you sell yourself short, Mr Ramsey. You could have been a community leader with your personality, doing good. Instead you rob from the community, taking their cash and their dignity in a dozen different ways. You and your kind are the East End's own worst enemy.'

Tommy was shaking his head. 'That's where you're wrong. I protect these people – these are my people. When a husband gets laid off, I'm the one who makes sure the kiddies get fed.' Tommy pushed his chair back and stood up, punctuating his words with jabs of his finger.

'When the fascists tried to drive the Jews out of the East End, it was me and my men who stood shoulder to shoulder against the black-shirted scum. When a factory closes down, I'm the one who makes sure the workers can find new jobs. I look after the people of Shoreditch and St Luke's and Old Street. I protect them – nobody else! Not the Old Bill, me – Tommy Ramsey!'

The Doctor looked unimpressed. 'And what is the price of this protection? You're just a minor thug of no historical importance. In twenty years' time you'll be forgotten, superseded, superfluous. There's no place for you in the modern world.'

'Is that right?'

'Yes, I'm afraid it is.'

Tommy glared down at the Doctor, sucking one last breath of smoke from his cigarette before stubbing it out on his dinner plate. 'Well, let me tell you something. There's no place for you on Old Street – you're not welcome round here. While we've been busy having our little discussion, my men have torched your shop.' Tommy consulted his watch. 'The flames should just about have finished their job. Now get out of my sight, Doctor, and don't come back again!'

The visitor stood up slowly, preparing to leave. But he had one final comment to offer before departing. 'You haven't seen the last of me.'

Tommy just waved him away. 'Yeah, yeah. Don't slam the front door on the way out, will you – it upsets me mum.'

Jack Cooper had broken in through the back entrance of the troublesome watchmender's shop, armed with a can of petrol and an American Zippo lighter. Once inside, Jack carefully poured the contents of his can around the fixtures and fittings. Satisfied with his handiwork, he retreated to the back entrance and pulled out his lighter.

Jack had taken the lighter from the pocket of a drunken US serviceman who was sleeping with Jack's mother. Jack was only ten in 1942, but he already knew his mother was no better than the whores who sold themselves on the docks. Other boys had taunted and teased him about it relentlessly. That night, Jack decided to do something about it. He stole the lighter and used it to set fire to his own home, while his mother and the soldier were still asleep inside. They might have escaped the smoke and flames if the boy hadn't pushed a wedge under the bedroom door, trapping them inside.

As he watched the flames engulf his home, Jack left childhood behind. He vowed never to be ashamed again. He would take what he wanted and damn the consequences. The boy became a man. Too young to fight in the war, he fought on the streets instead. Among the other runaways living like wild dogs on the streets of London, Jack became a legend. His baby-faced good looks and curly blond hair gave him the appearance of a little angel but his savage behaviour and fondness for starting fires were all devil.

What Jack couldn't steal he would burn using his precious lighter, the one possession he kept from his first life. But for Tommy Ramsey, Jack would probably be dead by now, or standing trial for murder like Derek Bentley and Christopher Craig. Tommy caught Jack on his sixteenth birthday, trying to torch a warehouse in Moorgate. The building was part of the rapidly expanding Ramsey empire and Tommy didn't take too kindly to attacks on his property. But he recognised a fearless ferocity inside Jack that would be useful, if directed properly. Tommy took the lad under his wing and schooled Jack in more subtle ways of achieving success.

Now Jack was Tommy's second-in-command, a rising star in the Ramsey Mob. There remained only one more obstacle to Jack's ascension to power – Tommy himself. The last six months had given Jack a taste for more power and reverting to the role of Tommy's errand boy was no substitute. Still, at least it gave him the chance to indulge his first love: firestarting.

Jack touched his lighter to the puddle of petrol on the floor. Flames spread hungrily through the shop, consuming the floor and licking at the furniture. Jack stood transfixed, watching it dance and flicker. At last he tore himself away and retreated through the back door. He walked around the block past a police call box and then stood on Old Street to watch the fire engulf the interior of Fixing Time.

'Still playing with matches, Jack?'

Steve 'Madman' MacManus was standing beside Jack, smoking a cigar. He was sharply dressed in a camel-hair greatcoat with gleaming brown leather shoes and leant on a silver-topped cane. A fanatical Tottenham Hotspurs supporter, MacManus controlled large sections of North London. He walked with a slight limp ever since an incident involving a rival gangland boss, a machine gun and a butcher's knife. Nobody knew the details but the rival's body parts had never been recovered.

Jack nodded at the new arrival. 'Nothing beats a roaring fire, boss.'

'Tsk, tsk!' MacManus waggled a finger playfully at Jack. 'You don't want the locals hearing you call me that. I don't think Tommy would be best pleased to discover his right-hand man is defecting to another firm.'

'He'll know soon enough. I can't wait to see the look on his face.'

'All in good time, my lad, all in good time.' MacManus studied the fire, the flames illuminating his thin, hawkish features. 'No fire engines rushing to the rescue?'

'Fire brigade don't know about it unless somebody tells them. People round here know better if they see me standing outside. I'll call the brigade in a few minutes myself – don't want the fire spreading, do we?'

MacManus nodded. 'So, what's been happening?'

Jack reported on the day's events before pressing MacManus to act soon. 'I don't think I can take much more of Tommy's self-serving superiority.'

'Patience, Jack, patience – you're too impetuous. Give Mr Ramsey enough rope and he'll hang himself for us. Then you can take over his patch.'

Jack nodded his reluctant agreement. 'What about this new gang – are they a welcome home present from you?'

For once, worry furrowed MacManus's brow. 'No, I don't know where they've come from. This Callum sounds like he could give you a run for your money. But anything that adds to Tommy's woes and confusion is welcome.'

'What will happen to Callum and his gang after…?' Jack ventured.

'After we deal with Tommy?' MacManus took another generous drag on his expensive cigar. 'Everyone is expendable, Jack. You would do well to remember that. Everyone is expendable.'

At 15 Tabernacle Street, Mrs Ramsey was showing Sarah to her new bedroom, at the top of the house. It was small and cosy, with just a single bed, a wardrobe and a lamp on a bedside table. 'I think you'll be comfortable here, dear,' Mrs Ramsey said hopefully. 'The linen and eiderdown are fresh on today and I've put a nightie under the pillow for you.'

Sarah sat down on the bed and sank into the soft mattress. 'It's wonderful, Mrs Ramsey. I'm sure I'll sleep like a log.'

'Call me Vera, dear. If you're going to be staying here a while, we might as well be on first-name terms.'

Sarah smiled. 'All right, Vera – and thank you.'

'Don't thank me! It's good to have another woman in the house. It's been just me with Tommy and his boys since my sister Ruth died in the Blitz. Arthur is collecting your things from the boarding house, so I'll put them outside your door in the morning. Goodnight, dear.' She closed the door as she left.

'Goodnight, Vera,' Sarah replied. She slid a hand under the pillow and pulled out the nightie. It was pink flannelette with lace around the neck, just like Aunt Lavinia used to wear when Sarah stayed with her on summer holidays as a girl.

Sarah took off her clothes and slipped into the nightie. It reached from her neck down to her wrists and ankles. She opened the wardrobe and found a full-length mirror inside one of the doors. The reflected image dismayed her. 'I keep wearing this, I'm going to start looking like Aunt Lavinia!'

'Who could be calling at this hour?' Mrs Kelly pulled her robe tightly around herself before opening the front door of the boarding house. Outside stood a giant of man, smiling apologetically.

'I've come to collect Miss Smith's things from her room. She's found other accommodation.'

'Oh!' the landlady said. 'But she's paid up for another fortnight!'

Brick pulled a wad of notes from his suit pocket. 'Mr Ramsey said to give you another fortnight's board, for the inconvenience.'

'Be my guest.' Mrs Kelly took the notes from Brick and stepped aside to allow him in. She counted the cash while he lumbered upstairs to gather Sarah's possessions. Mr Kelly appeared from the front room where he had been dozing in front of the fire.

'Who was that?' he asked.

'A man from Tommy Ramsey, come to collect Miss Smith's things.'

Mr Kelly made the sign of the cross without even realising it. He had enjoyed sneaking a glimpse at their boarder. But if Miss Smith was a girlfriend of Tommy Ramsey and she ever told him what had happened…

'What's wrong?' Mrs Kelly asked her husband. 'You've gone quite pale.'

'I'm not feeling very well,' he replied, bolting for the outhouse.

At the Ramsey household, a black ceramic telephone was ringing. Tommy stubbed out a cigarette before picking up the heavy receiver. 'Do you know what time it is?'

'I'm sorry to disturb you so late, Mr Ramsey – it's Valentine.' The caller's voice quivered with fear.

'What do you want, Detective?' Tommy replied, his voice laced with sarcasm. He smiled at his mother as she came back into the front parlour. Mrs Ramsey returned to her armchair and picked up her knitting.

'I'm at the hospital. There's been a murder and they called me in. A man was stabbed twice near St Luke's Church. He was still alive when he got here but died just after I arrived.'

'Yeah, so?' Tommy was getting impatient with the alcoholic copper. He had little time for people who could not keep control of their vices. Every man has his weakness, but he shouldn't let that weakness ruin his life.

'It was Harris. The dead man was Jim Harris. I thought you should know,' Valentine said. 'I recognised him as soon as I walked in.'

There was a long silence as Tommy absorbed this news.

'Mr Ramsey? You still there?'

'Yes,' Tommy replied, trying to keep all emotion from his voice. He didn't want his mother to know what had happened. Harris had always been one of her favourites among the lads, after Brick, of course. 'Did he say anything before he… went?'

'He had a message for you. I think that was the only thing kept him alive so long. "The Ramsey Mob are history. A new firm is taking over. Tomorrow, midday, outside St Luke's." That was the whole message.'

'Anything else? Did he say who did it?' Tommy demanded.

'Callum. He said it was Callum,' Valentine replied. 'Tommy, I'm sorry—'

'Don't be. You did good. Just make sure the Old Bill don't poke its nose in anywhere near the church at noon tomorrow.' Tommy put the phone down, his fists shaking with suppressed rage. Where the hell was Jack? Tommy's mind raced as he considered his next move.

'Anything wrong, Thomas?' Mrs Ramsey asked, not looking up from her knitting.

'I've got to go out. I might not be back tonight.'

'Well, if you must, but I think a good night's rest never hurt anyone.'

'Tell that to Jim Harris,' Tommy muttered under his breath. He left the parlour and went upstairs to Sarah's bedroom in a hurry. Tommy opened the door and walked straight in, startling Sarah. She was standing by the window, looking out over the rooftops of London.

'I've got to go out. I want you to stay here tomorrow and—' Tommy began, but was cut short by a shriek from Sarah.

'Who the hell do you think you are, bursting in here! I know this is your house, but I don't think that gives you any right to—'

Tommy held up his hands in protest. 'I'm sorry! I'm sorry!' he shouted, before lowering his voice. 'I didn't mean to burst in, I should have knocked.' He stopped speaking, distracted by the silhouette of Sarah's figure created by the moonlight falling through the window behind her.

She folded her arms across her chest. 'Well, what did you want?'

'One of my men has been murdered by a rival gang. Their leader has challenged me to fight him. I need you to stay here and look after Mum for me.' He explained before Sarah could protest again. 'I know, you didn't come here to look after me mum, but people are going to die tomorrow. I don't want you or her anywhere near the fighting – OK?' Sarah nodded her agreement grumpily.

'All right then, I'll see you tomorrow.' Tommy was about to leave but couldn't resist a parting remark. 'Nice nightie, by the way.'

Sarah looked down and realised what effect the moonlight was having on the fabric of her nightie. She blushed a deep crimson from embarrassment.

Tommy emerged from the front door of the house just as Jack and Brick arrived back at Tabernacle Street in the Bentley. Brick had seen Jack walking home while returning from the boarding house and given him a lift. Tommy wasn't happy with either of them. 'Where the hell have you been? It doesn't take that long to torch a shop!'

'Sorry Tommy, I must have lost track of time,' Jack replied weakly.

'Too busy looking at the fire more like!' Tommy muttered. He considered Jack's love of arson a useful but dangerous obsession. 'Harris is dead – Callum murdered him in the street. He left a message for me. A meeting at midday tomorrow outside St Luke's Church.'

'Sounds serious,' Jack said.

'That little scrote thinks he can take me out. He's got another think coming. Tommy Ramsey doesn't lay down and die for anybody!' Tommy was furious but his anger was a cold fury, all the more terrifying for its icy control. 'Jack, I want you to man the phones. Get the word out – this could be a diversion and I don't want to take any chances.'

'Right!'

'Brick, you're with me in the Bentley. I'm gathering the lads. If we're facing a bloodbath tomorrow, I'm going mob-handed. Nobody kills one of my men and gets away with it. Nobody!'

Friday, December 5, 1952

Dawn brought the city slowly back to life. PC Andy Hodge was walking the beat around Old Street, nodding his good mornings to the early risers – shopkeepers opening up, a milkman finishing his deliveries, the postman beginning his round. Hodge had walked this part of the East End for two months, since finishing his initial training. He wasn't a native of the area, but he liked to think the locals were starting to accept him as part of the community. They had even stopped mocking him for the wispy moustache the ruddy-cheeked constable had been trying to grow ever since he arrived.

Hodge was still puzzled by a conversation with his desk sergeant at the station earlier that morning. 'You're relatively new here son, ain't that right?'

'Yes sir.'

'So you probably haven't seen what happens in a gang war.'

'No sir. I know we can expect trouble now that Tommy Ramsey is out of Wandsworth and back on the streets. The lads on last night were saying a watchmender's shop that burnt down looked like arson, but the neighbours didn't see anything,' Hodge had said. 'People seem to turn a blind eye when it comes to the activities of the Ramsey Mob.'

Sergeant Diggle had looked very uncomfortable at that last

statement. 'Word has come down from upstairs. According to Bob Valentine there's going to be a street fight today between Ramsey's men and that new gang of teenagers.'

'Where? When?'

'Midday, outside St Luke's Church.'

'How many men will we have there to stop the fight?'

'Nobody.'

Hodge had not understood. 'Sorry, sir – nobody?'

The sergeant smiled wanly. 'Upstairs believe this is a local dispute and we should leave the gangs to sort each other out. I mean, what does it matter if one criminal hurts another criminal? Just one criminal less for us to worry about, right? So you're to make sure you stay away from St Luke's at midday.'

'But what if an innocent bystander gets hurt?' Hodge protested.

'Trust me, there won't be any bystanders.'

'But we can't just surrender the streets to gang violence. That's wrong!'

The sergeant started to get angry. 'You're not here to decide what's right and what's wrong, Constable! You're here to follow orders!'

'I thought I was here to enforce the law,' Hodge protested.

'You are – just make sure you do it somewhere else at midday, all right?' Diggle despaired of the over-eager constable. 'I don't know. You youngsters, come in here full of your lofty ideals – the sooner you get a taste of the harsh realities of life, the better for all of us!'

An hour later and Hodge was still reliving the conversation in his head. Was he naïve? A do-gooder with no grasp of the real world? Standing back and letting two gangs kill each other on the street went against everything he believed in, everything he had been taught in training.

A pretty young woman standing on a doorstep said hello to the constable as he passed. He looked back at the property and realised where he was standing – outside the home of Tommy Ramsey at 15 Tabernacle Street.

'Morning, miss,' Hodge said before continuing on his way.

He had made his mind up. Orders or no orders, he was going to be outside the church at noon. You had to stand up for what you believed in, Hodge told himself. Otherwise, what was the point in anything?

Sarah Jane Smith watched the police constable stroll away. He had a kind face but it was creased by some inner worry. What could he have to fret about, she wondered while taking another sip from her cup of tea.

Across the street the front door of the opposite house opened and the woman who had given Sarah directions stepped out, also nursing a cup of tea. 'Hello again!'

'Hello,' Sarah replied. 'Thanks for the directions.'

'That's all right, love. You were looking a bit lost,' Mary said. She looked up and down the road, but none of the other women had come out yet to start the morning scrubbing ritual. 'Do you want to come inside?'

Sarah smiled. 'OK.' It was nice to be made welcome. She crossed the road and followed Mary inside, shutting the door behind her. They went into the front room and sat at a table in front of the fireplace. The room was tiny.

Mary looked Sarah up and down. 'I've got to say, you don't look like Tommy Ramsey's normal type.'

'Oh? What do I look like?'

'Bit posh for Tommy. He likes showgirls from the West End. He's only brought one home in all the time I've lived opposite and Vera threw her out onto the street in a moment. Called her something unmentionable, too.'

Sarah laughed. 'I can't imagine Vera swearing! She's far too nice.'

'You can't be Tommy Ramsey's mum and not know a thing or two,' Mary replied. 'So what's your story? The women on this street are all dying to know but none of them dare ask. They're all too scared of Tommy.'

'But you're not.'

'I'm the black sheep of Tabernacle Street, didn't you know? Single mum, no husband, three bastards at me feet.' Mary said all this with matter-of-fact simplicity. Sarah was taken aback by the woman's candour.

'That must have been hard for you. It's tough enough raising children on your own in my time, but back in the—' Sarah realised what she was saying and hastily changed her words. 'I mean, that's tough enough for anyone.'

Mary took a photograph of her daughters from the mantelpiece and handed it to Sarah. 'These are me daughters. That's Jean, she's the oldest. Then there's Rita who's seven and Bette, who'll be six next week. They're all off to school already.'

'I know, I saw them go this morning. They're lovely.'

'Thanks.' Mary drained her cup. 'Would you like some more tea?'

Sarah politely shook her head. 'No, I'd better get back. I promised Mr Ramsey I'd look after his mother today.'

'More like she's watching over you. Got eyes like a hawk, has Vera.' Mary saw Sarah out to the door. 'Well, come back over again. It's nice to have someone else to talk to. My daughters are growing up now. I miss having some company.'

'You could get a boyfriend,' Sarah suggested.

'No more men!' Mary exclaimed. 'Every time one of them comes near me I end up with another baby. One thing I've learned growing up – women have to look out for themselves. We can't depend on men any more.'

'Well, see you later.' Sarah went back across the road and into the Ramsey home.

Only when she closed the front door did Mary realise Sarah had avoided answering any of her questions.

Callum roused his gang with a selection of kicks to their slumbering bodies. 'Get up! All of you! The Ramsey Mob should have got my message by now.'

Billy was rudely awakened by a boot to his belly. He sat up sharply, pulling a cosh from his suit pocket. 'What is it? Somebody want some trouble?'

Callum grinned down at the snarling teenager. 'Tommy Ramsey does – and we're just the gang to give it to him. Now get up! We need to prepare.'

Billy shook his brother awake before standing up. He tried to brush the wrinkles out of his crumpled suit, feeling a churning excitement in his stomach. The prospect of a brawl always put him on edge. When it came to defending your territory, most gangs favoured unarmed fighting. People got hurt, some even died but the Old Bill didn't get involved unless weapons were used.

Despite that, you never knew when somebody would pull out a blade or a gun. There were still plenty of service revolvers available under the counter, mementos brought back from the war. Nobody liked to arrive for a fight armed with lead pipes and pickaxe handles, only to discover the other side was waving shooters. Billy looked at his watch.

It was nearly eleven already – not much time to get tooled up now. He asked Callum if they needed firepower.

'Against Tommy Ramsey? No. He's a fool who believes in honour amongst thieves. He'll turn up mob-handed, but keep his shooter in that Bentley of his, in case things turn nasty.' Callum licked his lips hungrily. 'I can't wait to get behind the wheel of that car. I plan to keep it as a souvenir.'

Tommy was standing on the bar in the Red Room, addressing his men. He had spent the night driving around the East End, gathering his troops for the coming battle. Nearly forty members of the Ramsey Mob were standing in the gambling club, all armed to the teeth with knives, pickaxe handles and coshes. They were all dressed in their Sunday best suits, with clean white shirts and silk ties. Looking good was important to Tommy. Nobody respected scruffs.

'Callum's in for a nasty surprise come midday,' Tommy said. 'How many spotty-faced jokers has he got in his pack, Jack?'

Jack Cooper stepped forward from the gathering. 'Twenty at the most. Most of them are still in nappies, Tommy!' This brought laughter from the men.

Tommy smiled at the joke before holding up a hand for silence. 'That's true, very true – but that don't mean we shouldn't take them seriously. Remember what they did to Jim Harris. He's lying on a slab now, thanks to Callum and his gang of upstarts.'

The men nodded, the smiles gone from their faces now. Tommy nodded his approval at the change in mood.

'They've been taking liberties. Now it's time they were put in their place. These are our streets. These are our people. And nothing and nobody is taking them away from us.'

Tommy reached out his hands, palms held open towards his men. 'Who's with me?'

'We are!' the men shouted in unison.

'I can't hear you! Who's with me?'

'WE ARE!'

'You better believe it!' Tommy curled his right hand up into a fist. 'I said it before and I'll say it again – Callum's in for a nasty surprise.' Tommy punched the fist into his other hand, the flesh slapping together. 'Let's go give it to him!'

The Doctor was picking through the smouldering embers of his watchmender's shop. The fire brigade had arrived eventually, but too late to save any of the contents. The structure of the brick building remained intact and could probably be salvaged. But the shop itself was a mess of blackened furniture and charred timepieces. Several of the clock faces had warped in the intense heat generated by the fire.

The Doctor ran his fingers along the scorched, soggy floor and then sniffed at his digits. An accelerant had been used – probably petrol. He stood up and brushed the soot from his hands. Not very subtle, but effective enough. The ornate ormolu clock he had rescued from the Ramsey thug had suffered in the blaze, its face melted like some surreal sculpture. The Doctor shook his head sadly. So much for valuable antiques! He left the shop, climbing out the gaping space where the front window had been. It must have shattered from the incredible heat inside. Fragments of glass were scattered across the pavement.

The Doctor looked up at the shop's sign above the door. The name Fixing Time had been crudely painted over with a single word: Fixed. Ramsey's men had certainly done their job well. The rest of the businesses along Old Street would not be late with their insurance premiums in the near future. This little rebellion had been well and truly crushed.

'A fire does so much damage,' an American accent announced. The Doctor turned to see a priest standing where Steve MacManus had been the previous night. 'It's not just the flames. There's the smoke too, and then the water. Sometimes I think the fire brigade does more harm than good.'

'The damage had already been done by the time the brigade arrived,' the Doctor said.

'I'm sorry, I haven't introduced myself. I'm Father Xavier Simmons. I take service at St Luke's, across the road.' He gestured at the church with its towering steeple before shaking hands with the Doctor. 'And you are…?'

'Smith, Doctor John Smith. But everybody just calls me the Doctor.'

'A doctor of what?' Simmons enquired politely.

'Science mostly. I'm fascinated with time. Hence the shop.' The Doctor looked at the priest curiously. 'You sound like you're a long way from home.'

'The accent. Yeah, I'm from the States. I was stationed near here during the war. Afterwards, I stayed on. I was just about to be demobbed back home when I had what I guess you would call a life-changing experience.'

'You saw the light?'

Father Simmons smiled. 'Exactly! My new life started just across the road, on the steps of St Luke's. I realised I had wasted my life, chasing worldly goods and not caring who got hurt along the way. I decided to devote myself to doing the Saviour's work. I guess you could say that I was born again that night.'

'Fascinating.' The Doctor looked up at the church's steeple. 'So you've been at St Luke's ever since?'

'Oh no. I had to go through several years of training. My vocation may have come in a flash but it takes a little longer to learn the ways of the Saviour. I've been in this parish since Fall. I mean Autumn!' The priest shook his head. 'I'm not sure I'll ever remember all your quaint English expressions.'

'Not everything about England is quaint,' the Doctor

replied, looking at the burnt-out remnants of his shop. 'Tommy Ramsey's men did this because I refused to pay their insurance premiums.'

'A protection racket!' Father Simmons shook his head sadly. 'I grew up in Chicago – I lived beside people like Tommy Ramsey. So much violence. If only people could live together in peace, as one under the benevolent eye of the Saviour. The world would be a happier place, Doctor.'

'Do you think that's realistic? Human nature fights against conformity. The herd instinct is strong but all the greatest advances in human history have been led by individuals, people inspired to push beyond the boundaries of their knowledge and experience.'

The priest pointed at the smouldering shop front. 'You think this is a worthwhile price to pay for progress? I cannot agree with your ideas, Doctor. I believe we are all but children before our creator. We should follow the Saviour's will. I am sworn to do everything I can to make that happen.'

The Doctor was distracted by two groups of men forming on the roadside outside St Luke's. 'So you consider yourself a missionary?'

'It's my mission to spread the word of the Saviour, so I suppose so. I'm a missionary for peace and harmony and this city is my station.' Father Simmons' eyes were ablaze with fervour. 'I opened a bread factory to give people jobs, put money in their pockets and pride back in their hearts. Now we've started selling that bread back to people cheaply, giving them the stuff of life itself. I even managed to negotiate a contract to supply all the local police stations with our bread. That sort of project is the key to my mission's success.'

'Well, it seems your mission is about to go very, very wrong.' The Doctor pointed at the gatherings in front of the church. 'Those men don't look like they've come to St Luke's for a prayer meeting.'

Father Simmons looked with horror at the two gangs. 'No! Not now!'

The Doctor grabbed the priest by the arm and pulled him inside the blackened shop. Nobody would be safe on the street in the coming minutes.

Callum and his gang stood in a triangle formation on the western side of the church steps. Callum was leading from the front, flanked on either side by Billy and Charlie. The two brothers were both carrying lead pipes and black leather coshes like the rest of the gang, but Callum was unarmed.

'I don't need any of your weapons to take out Tommy Ramsey,' he had said as the gang walked to the church. 'I'll tear him apart with my bare hands.'

The Ramsey Mob were gathered on the eastern side of the steps. None of the men brandished any weapons. Jack stood at the front, looking at his watch. Behind him Tommy's four lieutenants were getting agitated.

'Where the hell is he?' Valance whispered.

'Tommy'll be here – he just wants to make a big entrance,' replied Norman Page.

'Let's get this over with,' Mike Gilmore hissed. 'I'm dying for a slash!'

'You do this every time, Mikey,' Dave Butcher said with a smirk. 'Why didn't you go at the Red Room, when you had the chance?'

'Didn't need to go then, did I?'

'Every time we have a stand-up with some other gang, you have to take a slash. Your dry cleaning must cost a fortune.'

'Get it free, perks of the job,' Gilmore replied.

'Oh yeah, course.' The throaty exhaust of the Bentley could be heard approaching from the east. 'Here he comes. Not before time, either.'

'Shut it,' Jack commanded. The lieutenants fell silent.

The Bentley glided to a halt outside Fixing Time. Tommy got out and nodded to Brick, who drove away. Tommy joined his gang as the noise from the Bentley faded into the distance. He was carrying a long, curved scabbard, the golden, gleaming handle of a sword protruding from it. Tommy nodded to his men before turning to face Callum.

An unnerving quiet filled the street. It seemed everybody knew about the conflict and was keeping well away from the church. All the nearby shops had closed early for extended lunch breaks. Cars were taking scenic routes to skirt the expected violence. Net curtains were pulled in all the windows overlooking the street. The footpaths were empty. It could have been dawn on a Sunday morning but for the pale winter sun overhead and the sound of clocks chiming twelve in the distance.

'High noon,' the Doctor whispered. Beside him Father Simmons was shaking his head in anguish, rocking back and forth on his heels.

'I can't let this happen – not again. There's been enough bloodshed on the steps of St Luke's. I can't let this happen…'

On the street Callum and Tommy walked towards each other. They stopped a few feet apart, their eyes locked together, their gaze not shifting. At last, Tommy broke the silence.

'So you're the infamous Callum. Not much to look at, are you?'

'I could say the same of you,' Callum sneered. 'The way people talked while you were in prison, I was expecting some giant to turn up.'

'The giant's me driver. He's gone back home in case you tried any funny business. He'll pick me up soon, once I've removed you from the picture.'

Callum shook his head. 'You don't get it, do you? Your time is past, old man.' He gestured at the surrounding area. 'Soon this place will be swarming with my kind. You're looking at the future.'

'I don't think so, sonny. Your gang of boys is only just out of short trousers. You might scare a few shopkeepers, but you're no match for the Ramsey Mob.' Tommy clicked his fingers.

As one his men reached into their suits and each pulled out a pistol, taking careful aim at the youths standing opposite. Callum's men looked less than pleased at this development. Billy and Charlie exchanged a worried glance but stood their ground.

Callum raised an eyebrow. 'Brought your pea-shooters, have you? They must make you feel like big men.'

'I'm losing patience with your cheek. Either you and your boys take off, or my men will take you out – here and now,' Tommy snarled. 'And that's a promise.'

'But where's your gun, Tommy? Or were you planning to bore me to death with your razor-sharp wit?'

'No,' Tommy replied, drawing his sword from the scabbard. 'I let me paperknife here do all the talking.'

'STOP!' Father Simmons shouted at the two men as he ran out of the Doctor's shop. 'You mustn't do this!'

Callum and Tommy both glanced at the priest as he approached.

'Friend of yours?' Callum asked.

'Hardly. I thought it was your big brother, come to save you,' Tommy sneered.

'You mustn't do this!' Father Simmons stepped between the two men, placing a hand on both their chests to keep them apart. 'Violence is wrong, don't you understand that? It doesn't solve anything.'

'That's where you're wrong, Father,' Callum said. 'Violence is the way of this world. You of all people should know that.'

Tommy looked perplexed. 'What are you on about?'

'Xavier Simmons killed a man on the steps of St Luke's Church six years ago. That's when he saw the light. Isn't that right, Father?' Callum asked.

'I was a different man then. I begged for the Saviour's forgiveness. I'm paying for my sins by doing the Saviour's work,' the priest insisted. 'Please, my son – don't make the same mistake I did!'

Callum pushed the priest's hand aside. 'I'm not your son, Father. I make my own decisions – keep out of this!'

Tommy looked round at Jack, who just shrugged his shoulders at this turn of events. Father Simmons reached out to Callum, pleading with him.

'Don't do this, I'm begging you. All my work—'

'It's all about you, isn't it. What about me? I've waited long enough!'

'Please, you don't understand—'

Callum punched the priest in the face, knocking Simmons to the ground. 'Keep out of this. It's between me and the monkey here,' he said, pointing at Tommy. The gangland boss was infuriated by the comment.

'Who you calling monkey?' Tommy demanded, slashing downwards at Callum with his sword. The razor-sharp blade sliced cleanly through Callum's left arm. The severed limb fell to the ground, one finger still pointing towards Tommy and his men.

Callum glanced down at it and started laughing.

The priest began to scream.

Callum continued laughing, but as he did his body floated up off the ground. It hovered at head height, slowly revolving in the air. As Callum turned, his appearance began to change. His body seemed to mutate, the skin starting to glow with an unearthly radiance.

The Doctor watched this transformation from the doorway of his shop. Callum's glowering appearance had been replaced by a creature of light and darkness, terrifying to behold. His humanoid features were blurred but distinctly alien, glowing tendrils in place of hair, a hundred tiny eyes where two had been. There was no mouth, but when the creature spoke its voice vibrated in the minds of all those around.

'No need for disguise any more – I can finally purge myself of your form. Just as I intend to purge this place of you, humans. Your time is over. Soon the Xhinn shall control this world, just as we control so many others!'

The thing that had been Callum pulsed with intense radiance, forcing the astonished onlookers to shield their eyes. When they looked back, a new limb had replaced the one severed by Tommy. The alien creature raised this new arm and pointed it at Tommy. Blue light formed at its end, growing ever brighter like some savage flame.

On the ground Father Simmons had been cowering before the Xhinn. Now he reacted while the others stood gaping. The priest threw himself at Tommy, just before a bolt of blue light spat from the alien's arm. The two men tumbled to the ground, just evading the energy discharge.

It flashed into Tommy's men, searing a round hole through the stomach of Gilmore. He collapsed to the ground, hands twitching in shock. The fist-sized hole did not bleed, the energy having cauterised the wound as it passed through his body. Blue light continued to dance around Gilmore's body. The fluorescence winked in the air, then was gone – the body disappearing with it. But the air was still filled with the smell of roasted pork. Several of the Ramsey Mob began to vomit involuntarily. They had all seen death before, but none had seen a man simultaneously gutted and cooked alive.

The rest of the men opened fire, shooting repeatedly at the alien. Their bullets flew towards it but seemed to melt away as they neared the floating figure. It replied with more of the unstoppable blasts of blue light, indiscriminately scything down both Tommy's men and what had been Callum's gang.

Billy and Charlie stood their ground at first, but bolted when the alien cut down the teenager standing behind them. Better off staying alive to fight another day than be fried alive by that thing. The rest of the gang followed their lead and tried to escape. Several of the stragglers were cut down by the Xhinn.

PC Hodge was running late. He had planned to be outside St Luke's Church by midday, hoping to stop the simmering gang war turning to violence. But a dispute between two female neighbours had delayed him by several minutes. Apparently one of the women had dared to say the other's children were dirty. By the time Hodge arrived, the two women were rolling around on the footpath, pulling each other's hair and shouting obscenities that made the young constable blush. He managed to pull them apart but it had taken nearly half an hour to get the warring women to shake hands.

He began running towards St Luke's when he heard a nearby clock chime twelve. Minutes later he saw a cluster of ashen-faced youths running towards him. Hodge called for them to stop but they did not even slacken their pace. He managed to grab hold of one of the lads as they passed him, running away from Old Street.

'What's going on? What's happening?' the constable demanded.

'You wouldn't believe me even if I told you,' the youth

replied. He shoved Hodge to the ground and then ran after his friends. The policeman considered chasing the youth but decided he was better finding the cause of this hysteria. Hodge resumed running towards Old Street, quickening his pace when he heard a sickening sound. Just before he came within sight of St Luke's, the constable recognised the noise – it was men screaming.

Then he saw what was making them scream.

'Run! Run while you still can!' the Doctor yelled. Tommy and Father Simmons were still lying on the ground. They stared up at the inhuman creature. It had forgotten them for the moment, but that could soon change.

Glancing around, Tommy saw the severed limb from what had been Callum, still twitching its fingers. Tommy grabbed the arm and his sword. He had to get his men to safety. Crouching low, he ran away from the creature.

'Move! Move! Everybody, back to the house! Now!'

Tommy's words seemed to galvanise Jack and many of the men into action. They turned and ran for their lives. But others stayed, reloading their pistols and firing repeatedly at the alien. The Xhinn slowly floated towards them, passing over the prostrate figure of Father Simmons, who was praying with his eyes closed.

The Doctor saw his chance and ran forward into the mêlée. He grabbed the priest by the arm and began dragging Simmons towards the steps of St Luke's. After agonising moments the priest got to his feet and followed the Doctor into the safety of the church. He collapsed into a pew, sobbing.

'I tried to stop them. I begged them not to fight,' he cried in anguish.

The Doctor was watching the horrific slaughter on the street outside through a crack in the doorway. 'They wouldn't listen, and now they're paying the price.'

Father Simmons wiped the tears from his face. 'What was that – that thing out there? It called itself the Gin…'

'Xhinn. It's called the Xhinn,' the Doctor replied, correcting the priest's pronunciation. 'I've heard of them but never encountered one before. I had hoped I never would.'

'Who is it? What is it?'

'The Xhinn is a much feared species that colonises other worlds. They strip a planet of all its natural resources and either subjugate or exterminate the native species. All to fuel the colonisation and plunder of more worlds. A never-ending cycle of pillaging and destruction.'

Hodge stood outside Fixing Time, rooted to the spot. A floating monster was destroying the Ramsey Mob, firing bolts of blue light from its arms. The light would shoot through the men, then engulf them. Finally, while they still lay screaming for mercy, the men simply winked out of existence.

Hodge could not understand what was happening, could hardly believe the evidence of his own senses. It was like some nightmare made real. As a boy he had enjoyed novels by writers like H.G. Wells, fantastic tales of Martian invaders who attacked places like Leatherhead. He had even looked for Leatherhead in his atlas of the world, where so many countries were shown as pink – part of the mighty British Empire. It was his father who pointed out that Leatherhead was near London.

'That just proves those books you read are rubbish. As if creatures from another planet would attack London! What nonsense!' his father said.

Now Hodge was confronted with just that situation and all he could think about were his father's words. Brandishing his truncheon, the constable took a deep breath and stepped towards the creature.

'Stop in the name of the law!' he shouted.

The floating apparition slowly revolved to face him. It had no mouth, but Hodge could hear a voice inside his head.

'Or else what? You'll arrest me?' The voice began laughing. Hodge took off his helmet and put his hands over his ears, trying to block the noise.

The creature glared at him with a hundred tiny eyes. 'Run!' it commanded. 'Run!'

Hodge realised the apparition was pointing at him. The glowing limb was burning ever brighter – it was going to fire one of its death rays at him! The policeman turned and fled into Whitecross Street. To his immense relief there was a police call box standing just around the corner. He pulled a key from his pocket and tried to push it into the lock. But there was something wrong with the mechanism. His key wouldn't fit.

Hodge was aware of a crackling noise behind him and the hairs on the back of his neck stood up. The creature must be right behind him! He hammered at the door but it would not be forced. Finally, he noticed the sign across the door: Out of Order. The constable slowly turned around.

The apparition was within inches of his face. Hodge could feel his cheeks beginning to glow, as if he'd been lying in the sun too long. The voice sounded in his head again.

'Run!'

Hodge dropped his policeman's helmet and ran away from Old Street as far as he could. Every moment he expected to feel the searing heat of one of those blue bolts blasting through his body. His mind was filled with the sound of alien laughter.

'Run for your life! Ha ha ha ha ha ha ha!'

Father Simmons was baffled. 'Where do the Xhinn come

from?'

'Nobody knows. According to legend, they were created from fire millions of years before mankind. They rebelled against their maker and were cast into this universe for their pride,' the Doctor explained. He turned away from the sickening scenes outside and sat wearily beside the priest.

'Like fallen angels,' Simmons said, struggling to understand.

'If you like.'

'Then they can still be saved!' the priest gasped, rising from his seat. He started walking towards the doors. 'They can be made to love the Saviour again and be returned to his mercy!'

The Doctor grabbed Simmons and forced him to sit back down. 'If you go outside now you'll be murdered like all those others. Don't throw your life away like that!' The Doctor began to pace in front of the pew, rubbing his index finger thoughtfully across his bottom lip.

'We can't take on the Xhinn singlehandedly, without weapons or a plan. From all I've heard the Xhinn are a methodical species who see themselves as fulfilling some divine quest. What just happened seems wrong, far too precipitous. It could be a single Xhinn, or a rogue element – I don't know. I just don't know…'

He made up his mind. 'If Earth is the Xhinn's next target for colonisation, there may still be time to stop them. I need to get back to the TARDIS.' The Doctor looked at Father Simmons, who was shaking his head in bewilderment. 'Will you be all right here?'

'I don't know. I don't know anything any more…'

'Well, you just stay here, there's a good chap,' the Doctor said soothingly.

He opened the church doors and peered outside. Old Street was empty again. There was no sign of the Xhinn or anybody else. The Doctor closed the doors behind him and then ran across the road into Whitecross Street, where the TARDIS was stood. A discarded policeman's helmet was lying beside the door. The Doctor hoped its owner had escaped unharmed.

Billy and Charlie were the first ones to make it back to Ironmonger Row. The brothers could hardly believe what they had witnessed.

'It had to be some sort of trick,' Charlie decided. 'Callum was trying to fool Tommy Ramsey – and it worked.'

'That was no trick. I don't know what it was but Callum ain't human. He's some kind of monster,' Billy insisted. 'Gives me the creeps just thinking about it. We was here with him all that time…'

Two more of the gang returned to the condemned house. They were pale and shaking, unable to speak. The brothers tried to convince them to stay but the youths just collected their things and ran off.

'Go on then, run home to your mums!' Billy shouted after them.

Charlie was deep in thought, still trying to get his head round what had taken place. 'Nobody's ever gonna believe this happened, you know. We can never tell anybody about this – they'll think we're off our nuts.'

'I know somebody who'll believe us – Tommy Ramsey,' Billy said. 'He saw it all too. I reckon we throw our lot in with him.'

'Why?'

'This ain't over, Charlie. It's just beginning. We thought Callum was starting a gang war and that was right. We just picked the wrong side.' Billy realised his brother wasn't listening. Charlie seemed to be transfixed, staring over Billy's left shoulder. 'What is it now?'

Billy turned round to find the Xhinn floating in the air a

few feet away from him, arms raised to blast them to oblivion. 'Blimey!'

Callum's cruel voice echoed in the brothers' heads. 'So you two are all that's left of my little gang. No matter. The Xhinn will soon have no need of your species. I give you a choice – serve us, and you will be given unimaginable power when the Xhinn conquer this world.'

Billy swallowed hard before replying. 'Or?'

The Xhinn's arms began to pulse, readying for the killer blow. 'Or I kill you, here and now. Even your puny intellect should understand that.'

Charlie stood up and joined Billy, facing the floating alien. Around them the shattered building was ablaze with brilliant blue light, sending rats and cockroaches scuttling for shelter in the shadows. But the brothers stood firm.

'Well,' Billy began, 'I guess we'll just have to—'

Before he could finish the Xhinn lowered its arms, as if distracted. The alien's head cocked to one side. 'I hear you.'

Billy was taken aback. 'What you mean, you hear me? I ain't even—'

'Yes, I abandoned human form. But the—'

Charlie tapped his brother on the shoulder. 'He ain't talking to us. He's talking to somebody else.'

'His boss, you mean?' Billy replied.

'As you command.' The Xhinn began to fade away. Just before it disappeared, the alien glared at the brothers. 'I will return for you.' Then the creature was gone.

Charlie looked at his brother and laughed.

'What's so bleedin' funny?' Billy demanded.

'You look like you've caught the sun, that's all!'

Billy put a hand to his face. It felt dry and stretched, as if all the moisture had been baked out of it. 'Never mind that. Let's get out of here. I ain't sticking around until that, that – that thing – comes back!' He started running, his brother close behind.

'Where do we go?' Charlie asked.

'Only one bloke round here has got the firepower to stop these scumbags. It's time we joined the Ramsey Mob!'

Sarah was on the roof at Tabernacle Street with Brick when the first man got back from the rout at St Luke's. The bodyguard was showing her his most precious possession.

'So you've kept pigeons all your life?' she asked politely.

Brick nodded. 'Me granddad got me started. He used to race pigeons. He took me down the Sclater Street Sunday bird market in Bethnal Green when I turned five and bought me my first pigeon. Tommy lets me keep them up here, out the way.' The burly enforcer was tenderly cupping one of the birds in his hands, cooing softly to it.

Sarah smiled. 'You're so gentle with the pigeons and yet…'

'I act the heavy for Tommy.' Brick sighed. 'Generally I can just turn up and most people will pay up or shut up, whatever Tommy wants. When you're my size, not many will take you on in a fight.'

'I suppose not.' Sarah pointed at the pigeon in the big man's hands. 'Can I hold him?'

'He's a her actually. I call her Annie, after me mum. She died in the war.' Brick carefully transferred the pigeon into Sarah's hands. 'She likes it if you stroke her neck feathers.'

Sarah followed his advice and was rewarded with a gentle cooing sound. Brick smiled proudly. 'She likes you.'

Sarah looked around from her vantage point. If she wanted, Sarah could have walked the length of Tabernacle Street without ever touching the ground, just by clambering along the rooftops of the terraced houses. From up here she could see for more than a mile in all directions. Blue lights seemed to be flashing near the steeple of St Luke's Church but the cause was unclear.

'I wonder how the meeting with Callum's gang is going,' she said.

Brick looked at his watch. 'I better go and collect Tommy. He—' The big man was interrupted by a shout from downstairs from Mrs Ramsey.

'Arthur! Miss Smith! Come quick – something's happened.'

Brick took the pigeon back from Sarah and slipped the bird into its cage. Then he led her back downstairs, clambering down a precarious ladder, through the skylight and onto the upstairs landing.

By the time they reached the front parlour, Tommy had returned. He was clutching a man's severed arm and a long, wickedly sharp sword. Only twenty of his men had made it back from the confrontation at the church, and several of them were wounded. Mrs Ramsey busied herself tending to the injured while Tommy called a meeting of his senior men around the dining room table. While Jack was busy gathering the surviving lieutenants, Sarah cornered Tommy in the hallway and demanded to know what had happened.

'You wouldn't believe me if I told you,' he said wearily.

Sarah was having none of it. She fixed him with a steely gaze. 'I've seen stranger sights than you can possibly imagine. Try me.'

'All right, but don't say I didn't warn you.' Tommy gave her a broad outline of events, culminating in the transformation of Callum into a deadly monster that shot blue murder from its limbs. The gangland boss didn't get the astonishment and disbelief he expected.

'That's a new one on me, but anything's possible. What are you going to do next?' Sarah asked.

'I'm meeting with the men to decide. Until I know how

many men got away alive, I won't know whether we can take on these things by ourselves or not. We may need help from outside.' Tommy fastened the buttons on his jacket and brushed down his hair. 'How do I look?'

Sarah straightened his tie. 'Better. More in control.'

Tommy nodded. He opened the door of the dining room and stepped inside. Just before closing it, he made a final comment to Sarah. 'Make everyone a cup of tea, will you? Thanks.'

He shut the door on Sarah, leaving her fuming in the hall.

Hodge ran into the police station, breathless and wild-eyed. It took the desk sergeant ten minutes just to calm the constable down enough that Hodge could speak. Even when he did, his explanation didn't make any sense.

'Monster – killing men. Screaming, terrible screaming. There was blue light coming from its hands. The Ramsey Mob were being torn apart. Don't know what happened to Callum. His gang were scattering when I arrived. It was terrible, terrible…'

Hodge collapsed, his eyes rolling back into his head. Sergeant Diggle wasn't sure what to make of it all. The new constable had been a good lad, quiet but diligent, fair and thorough. The force needed more men like Hodge. But this story! Monsters on the streets of London, flashing blue lights and murder at midday. All sounded like a bad dream, or the ravings of a madman.

Diggle shook Hodge's shoulders, reviving the constable. 'Now, lad – you sure you didn't dream all this? Monsters that float in the air? Death rays shooting out of their hands? On Old Street?'

The young policeman was adamant. 'I didn't dream it, sir. I know what I saw! If you don't believe me, come and see for yourself!' He got up to leave but the desk sergeant grabbed his arm.

'You've obviously had a shock, whatever it was you saw. I want you to go down the canteen. Get yourself a cup of tea and a sandwich. I'll go have a look at all this, err, business. Where did you say it happened?'

'Outside St Luke's Church, just after midday.'

'I told you to stay away from there, sonny.' Sergeant Diggle picked up the keys to a patrol car and walked out of the station. 'These youngsters, think they know it all. It was different when I started out…'

Elsewhere, three Xhinn hovered in a chamber of unending darkness. They moved through the air in a complex pattern of pirouettes and spirals, tracing out paths invisible to the human eye.

For millennia, the Xhinn had travelled the universe. Their craft were like shadows, fleeting and hidden, unnoticed in the vacuum of space. Only by the desolation left behind could the progress of a Xhinn mission be charted. Even the name of the Xhinn was a mystery, spoken in a whisper, born of terror. Few who stood against the Xhinn survived. Fewer still succeeded.

The triumvirate slowed in its movements, sharing a thought as one.

'He returns.'

The Xhinn that had been Callum shimmered into existence, afloat in the centre of the three. He looked around himself, unsure about the summoning.

'Why have you brought me here? Are you not pleased with me?'

'No.'

'But I did as you asked. I walked among the native species, taking its form. I explored their primitive ways, exposing

DOCTOR WHO

them to our ideals.'

'You acted unwisely.'

'Precipitously.'

'Without consultation.'

'Action without consultation is unauthorised.'

'Unwelcome.'

'Unwanted.'

The triumvirate spat the words at him, like daggers into his mind. Their thoughts overlapped and oscillated around each other, in a graceful savagery.

'You revealed us.'

'Too soon.'

'Too hasty.'

'Now we must act.'

'Before we are ready.'

'Before it is time.'

'But these creatures – they are no threat to us! We are the Xhinn! We have colonised thousands of worlds, subjugated species after species. What can we fear from these primitives?'

'That is not for you to decide.'

'Not for you to know.'

'Not for you.'

'You were a mistake.'

'Too young.'

'Too much.'

'Why do you hide away here? Why wait? We can take this world for our own. We are the Xhinn! We are all powerful!'

'You forget yourself.'

'Unfortunate.'

'Unwise.'

The triumvirate began to pulse, changing from creatures of light to beings of darkness. As one, the three Xhinn reached out towards the creature that had been Callum.

'No! No! You can't do this to me! You need me! I know the ways of these primitives! I can still be useful! Wait! Wait!'

Then he was no more, subsumed into the triumvirate. They pulsed with the extra energy, then resumed their delicate patterns of hovering.

'A mistake.'

'Deleted.'

'Our plans.'

'Advanced.'

'Success.'

'Inevitable.'

The triumvirate nodded in agreement.

In the TARDIS, the Doctor had been busy lashing together a handheld device from circuits and wiring plundered from the central console. He was running a test on the prototype when the ambient light began to dim in the control room.

Some kind of energy drain. What could be causing that, he wondered. Several of the indicator needles on display dials in the central console were flickering wildly between zero and off the scale. The Doctor ran from panel to panel, trying to absorb all that was happening. According to the TARDIS instruments, someone had just operated a matter transmission system. It could only be the Xhinn!

Suddenly the room was ablaze with light for a second, before slowly returning to its normal level. The Doctor stood, scratching his head. A massive energy surge, which was then slowly reabsorbed, he decided.

He examined the handheld device. The Xhinn vessel must be nearby. He began to adjust the circuits. If he could re-route the wiring, he might be able to turn it into a homing device. But the apparatus did not respond. The display winked once, then died away. The Doctor looked at it despairingly. The energy surge must have overloaded the circuits.

Outside the TARDIS, a police patrol car was parked in Whitecross Street, near the intersection with Old Street. Sergeant Diggle clambered out from the vehicle, his ample belly struggling to free itself from behind the steering wheel. His wife was always complaining about having to adjust his uniform to allow space for his ever widening waistline. Was it Diggle's fault that he had a weakness for jellied eels and mash?

The police sergeant checked his wrist watch. It was nearly two o'clock. The sun would not be setting for another two hours, but already he could feel the night drawing in. Diggle hated these long winter nights. If he didn't get outside during his lunch break, he never saw the sun at all. It was dark when he arrived at the station and dark again by the time he left for home. Like living in a tunnel, he thought bleakly. Oh well, better go see what young Hodge was fussing about. Then he could get back to the station before the shift ended.

The sergeant strolled around the corner into Old Street. Nothing seemed out of the ordinary, and yet – there was something strange here, Diggle decided. But he couldn't put his finger on it. At last, realisation struck home. Where was everybody? The street was deserted. No cars or lorries moving in any direction, and no pedestrians on the street.

A glint of metal caught his eye. Diggle walked over to the gutter where a knife had been dropped. A drop of blood was visible on the blade. The sergeant dipped his finger into the redness. It was still tacky, like discarded paint. Probably two or three hours since this blood was spilled, which would partially confirm Hodge's wild story. There had been an altercation outside St Luke's Church and somebody was hurt, probably stabbed. But Diggle could find no evidence of floating monsters or mass murder.

He looked up and down the street. Just in the few minutes he had been here the far reaches of the long, straight road had disappeared, swallowed up by a gathering fog. Looked like the city was in for a real pea-souper, Diggle thought. He fancied a nice bowl of pea soup right now, perhaps with some tinned ham chopped into cubes and dropped into the swirling liquid.

The police sergeant knew there was little point in asking local residents if they had witnessed anything. For a start, people knew better than to discuss Ramsey Mob business with the police. Secondly, they would probably think him mad if he started asking them about blue death rays. They'd probably be right, too. But Diggle did know one place he could be sure of getting a straight answer. He walked up the stone steps and opened the door into St Luke's Church.

Father Simmons was lying face down on the steps of the altar, his arms extended out sideways in a crucifix position. He prayed fervently, his eyes clenched shut, his lips mouthing the words of his mental supplication.

'My Saviour, why have you forsaken me? I have done your bidding, I have worked to extend your ministry, to bring your ways to the people of this parish. Is this not enough? Why do you send these fallen angels to test me? Saviour, give me a sign that I may better do your will…'

Sergeant Diggle cleared his throat to get the priest's attention. Simmons rose to a kneeling position, made the sign of the cross and then stood up. He genuflected to the altar before turning to face the policeman.

'Yes, my son?'

Diggle smiled nervously. He had never been a religious man, preferring to put his faith in things he could see, touch and taste. He pointed at a pew. 'Can we sit down? I have to ask you a few questions.'

'Of course.' The priest took a seat next to the police sergeant. 'Now, how can I help you?'

'We've received reports about a disturbance outside this church at noon today. Have you seen anything?'

Father Simmons grabbed the policeman by the arm. 'Yes! I had been wondering whether I should report it. I was praying to the Saviour, asking for guidance when you came in. Your appearance is obviously a sign!'

'Well, I wouldn't go that far,' Diggle replied. He carefully removed his arm from the priest's grip, while taking a notebook and pencil from his breast pocket. Diggle licked the end of his pencil and got ready to take notes. 'If you could just tell me what you saw…'

'It was an angel – a fallen angel,' Simmons said.

Diggle began writing. 'An angel…' He stopped. 'Sorry?'

'Yes, it was a fallen angel. The Doctor said so.'

'The Doctor. Who is he?'

'He has the watchmender's shop across the road. Or, at least, he did before that fire yesterday. You should investigate that – most suspicious, it seemed to me.'

Diggle refused to be distracted. 'Father, you were talking about an angel.'

The priest described what had happened outside, with particular emphasis on the vengeful angel which came down to Earth and smote the unrepentant criminals. But it had spared his life, obviously recognising Simmons as a faithful servant of the Saviour.

Sergeant Diggle listened through all of this, not bothering to take notes. If Hodge's story had seemed like the rantings of a broken mind, the priest was giving the lad a good run for his money. Diggle nodded politely as Simmons tried to impress upon him the need for vigilance in the days ahead. There could be more angels and only the pure of heart would survive their fiery judgement, full of divine wrath and fury.

'Right,' Diggle replied, snapping his notebook shut and returning it to his pocket, along with the unused pencil. 'I'll be sure to tell the rest of the lads at the station about that.' He stood up and shook the priest's hand. 'Thank you for your time, Father. I'll let you get back to your, er, prayers.'

'No need,' Simmons said, his face at peace. 'You arrived in response to my pleas. Now I have given you this message, I need not fear the future. All will be well, as long as we believe.'

The police sergeant just nodded politely and left. Once outside, he shook his head in bewilderment. 'If that nutter's got a direct line to God, then I'm the next Chief Constable!' Diggle made his way back to the patrol car. In the short time he had been inside the church, the fog had drawn in even closer. It would soon become difficult to drive if visibility continued to shrink. The police sergeant determined to get back to the station in good time.

Something had definitely happened on Old Street but exactly what was another matter. The only two witnesses had given such wildly varying accounts as to cancel each other out. Diggle decided to forget the whole thing. Unless somebody else came forward with a sensible statement, this incident was not going to be officially recorded.

Tommy watched his lieutenants arguing. Jack suggested caution in the face of this fresh enemy. They didn't know what this creature was capable of, but it had eradicated nearly two dozen men. Best to stay back, let others fight this monster. Once the conflict was over, the Ramsey Mob could step in and pick from the spoils.

Billy Valance was terrified. He had escaped one of the death blasts by mere inches and just wanted to get out of London. Who knew how many of these creatures were in the city, pretending to be something they were not? How could anyone be trusted any more?

Dave Butcher favoured an all-out attack, guns blazing. If they hit it with enough firepower, the thing had to go down, didn't it? Stood to reason. He wanted to make an alliance with the other gangland bosses, get their support.

If they were going to fight this creature, they were going to need all the men and machine guns they could get.

Norman Page thought the whole thing had been a trick, a mirage like he used to see in the desert during the war. They were all having some sort of mass hysteria, where they thought they saw this creature. But it couldn't have been real, could it? Just nonsense. It was all a trick, probably by a rival gang. Yeah, that was it, a trick.

Brick said nothing, keeping his own counsel and tending to the coal fire warming the room. He hadn't seen what happened and found the other men's descriptions of events hard to grasp. But they all seemed to believe themselves, except the sceptical Page. Something strange had taken place. Whatever Tommy decided to do, Brick would go along with it. He always did.

Tommy listened to them all while staring at the severed limb on the dining table. It had stopped twitching but he still found the pointed finger disturbing. Stranger still, the arm had never bled. After being sliced from Callum's body, the severed end just seemed to seal itself – like it was waiting for something. Or somebody, Tommy thought with a shudder.

Just as he was about to speak, a sour-faced Sarah entered carrying a tray laden with cups of tea. She went round the table, slamming the tea down in front of each man. She left Tommy's until last, then stood to one side, waiting for his reaction. 'Ta very much,' he said, smiling at her.

'Don't thank me, thank your mother – she made the tea,'

Sarah replied. Tommy expected her to leave but she stood her ground, obviously determined to stay. So be it. He stood up to address the men.

'I listened to what you've all had to say. Everybody's had something useful to offer – except Page, of course, but he always talks out his arse.'

The other men all laughed at that. Page was infamous in the Ramsey Mob for his contrary opinions and unfeasible notions. But he also ran the best robbery crew in London and was one of Tommy's best earners. That gave him merit and the respect of the other lieutenants.

'I agree that we probably can't beat this thing on our own. For that, we're going to need help from outside. So I'm going to summon some of the other gang leaders from the East End to a Council of War. Jack, when we're done here, I want you on the blower, calling round. It'll be better coming from you. Meeting's at midday, here.'

Jack nodded his agreement. Tommy walked slowly round the table, giving each man their task for the next few hours. 'Billy, I want the word spread on the street. Anybody who knows anything is to come to us first. Don't matter how trivial, I want to know about anything out the ordinary people have noticed. There'll be a generous reward for information.'

'How generous?' Valance asked.

'Never you mind!' Tommy snarled. 'Dave, I want you to send the girls on holiday – we're closing down the cat houses till this is over. We need every man we've got, we can't afford to be caught short.'

'Done. Where should I send the girls?'

'Use your initiative. Do I have to think of everything meself? Last but not least, Norman – shooters. We need to be well and truly tooled up. We got no idea what this monster is going to throw at us, so better safe than sorry. Lay your hands on every weapon you can.'

'Got it, boss.'

Sarah could stay silent no longer. 'What about the police? Why don't you tell the police what's happened? They could call out the army…' Her voice trailed away as she realised everyone was staring at her. 'What?'

Tommy gave voice to what all the others were thinking. 'For a start, we look after our own. We don't need the Old Bill sniffing around here. Second, do you really think they'd believe us? We ain't got any proof. All the bodies disappeared after that thing blasted them. The plods would just lock me in a nut hatch if I came forward with a yarn like that.'

'What about the arm?' Sarah asked, pointing at the severed limb. 'That's proof. You could give it to the police.'

Sergeant Diggle parked the patrol car outside the police station. It had taken him nearly an hour to drive less than a mile back from Whitecross Street. The fog was closing in with alarming ferocity. Twice the policeman had needed to swerve onto the footpath to avoid a collision with vehicles that had strayed across the centre line. It was a great relief when he caught sight of the shining blue lamps outside the station.

Once inside he went straight to the canteen and demanded a mug of hot, sweet tea. He returned to the front desk and added a generous nip of whisky from a hip flask hidden in a drawer. Purely for medicinal purposes, he told himself – to ward off the biting cold outside.

He was swirling the last dregs of his tea around in the bottom of the cup when Hodge appeared at the desk. 'Well, how are you feeling now, son?' Diggle asked.

The constable smiled at him. 'Much better, sir. You were right, I must have bumped my head before. It's funny, what I said happened earlier – it hardly seems real now. Did you find anything outside the church?' Hodge asked.

Diggle shook his head. 'I did talk to the parish priest. He told me some fantastic story about a fallen angel purging the world of its sins. I'd rather he purged us of that flamin' fog outside, it's a menace!'

The constable's face darkened at the mention of a fallen angel, but Hodge quickly resumed smiling. 'I know what you mean, sir. We've had three car crashes reported in the last hour. I'm not looking forward to patrolling tomorrow if it's still like this.'

Tommy snatched the severed limb up from the table. 'All this shows is that I cut somebody's arm off. I give this to the police and it might get me another stretch in Wandsworth, but it don't prove anything that's happened, does it?'

Sarah was not giving up that easily. 'But you could—'

Before she could finish her sentence, the severed limb began twitching again. The fingers flexed and strained. Tommy looked at it in amazement. 'What the hell?'

The severed arm twisted in Tommy's grasp and then launched itself at his throat. The fingers clenched the gangster's neck in a choke hold, trying to throttle him. Tommy pulled at the disembodied limb while gasping for breath.

'Get – it – off – me!'

Brick ran to Tommy and pulled at the arm. With a supreme effort he pulled it off his boss and threw the limb into the blazing fireplace. The arm scuttled around in the flames, ready to launch itself again. But then the fire caught hold of the sleeve still encasing the limb, which burst into flames. The dining room was filled with a screaming noise as the flesh burned. Within moments it had seared away to nothing, leaving just the last scraps of cloth.

Tommy stood staring at the fireplace, one hand rubbing his

neck. Angry red finger marks were already beginning to form beneath the skin. 'Thanks, Brick. I owe you one,' the gangster said, his voice reduced to a rasp. He looked at the others. 'Fat lot of use you all were.'

Jack and the lieutenants sank back into their chairs. 'I wouldn't have believed it if I hadn't seen it,' Butcher muttered.

'Exactly,' Tommy agreed. He approached Sarah and placed a hand on her shoulder. 'That's why we can't go to the police. They'd never believe it.' Tommy clapped his hands, snapping everybody back to reality. 'Enough of this sitting about. You've got your jobs – get to them!'

The four lieutenants filed out of the dining room, followed by Brick. Jack stayed behind to talk with Tommy.

'We need to think about security for the house. No knowing if that monster is a one-off. There could be others,' the younger man said.

'Good point. I want two men near the front door of the house at all times. Nobody comes or goes without my say-so, I don't care who they are.'

Sarah had been pondering Tommy's description of how Callum had transformed. 'From what you told me, these creatures can imitate people – change shape. How will you know if somebody is actually who they say they are?'

'I been worrying about that too,' Tommy replied. 'It didn't like the fire, did it? We'll use that as a test. Jack, you still got your lighter?'

'Of course!' He pulled it from his pocket and gave the lighter to Tommy. The gangster snapped back the lid, lighting the Zippo.

'Now, put your hand out.'

'But, Tommy—' Jack protested.

'Put your hand out,' Tommy growled. 'Otherwise, I'll have to assume you're not being completely honest with me.'

Jack put out his hand and held it over the lighter's flame, his face creasing at the pain as his skin burnt. After a few seconds Tommy took the lighter away. Jack rubbed his scorched palm, a hurt look on his face. 'I thought you trusted me!'

'After what I've seen today, I don't trust nobody anymore.' Tommy looked at Sarah. 'You next.'

'You can't think I—'

'You've been in the area less than a month, you've wormed your way into my home and you're the last person I'd suspect.' Tommy loomed over her, his expression bleak and pitiless. 'Now put your hand over the flame!'

Sarah reached out her hand tentatively. Tommy grabbed the wrist and held her open palm over the flame. Jack looked on appreciatively, enjoying the spectacle of her pain. Sarah cried out but refused to pull away. She wouldn't give Jack the satisfaction.

After what seemed an age, Tommy was satisfied. Without comment he put his own hand over the flame and kept it there longer than either of them. He showed no pain in his expression or in his eyes – only steely resolve. In the end Sarah could stand it no longer. She pulled the lighter away from Tommy. He smiled at her.

'Thanks. So, no monsters in this room. Jack, test the lighter on Brick. If he passes, get him to test the others. Nobody's going to give him any grief.'

Jack left the room, his eyes dancing at the prospect of using the lighter on another person's flesh. Tommy watched him go. 'I worry about that boy, sometimes – he's a little too fond of fires for my liking.'

'Hmm,' Sarah agreed, nursing her burnt hand.

'You were right – that arm I sliced off Callum might have helped convince the Old Bill. But I couldn't admit that in front of the lads,' Tommy said.

'Couldn't admit a woman was right and you were wrong.'

'Something like that,' he said, looking at the fireplace. 'Doesn't matter now. Our only piece of evidence has gone up in smoke.'

Outside, the smoke from the chimney of 15 Tabernacle Street rose up into the twilight sky. Across London residents were lighting coal fires to ward off the chill winter evening. Factories belched out smoke and fumes, joining the pollution from the domestic fires. The worst concentration was in the East End, where many streets were little more than slums.

As night fell, the temperature began to drop rapidly. A dense layer of fog settled over the city, enveloping streets and lamp lights. By four o'clock, the smoke began mixing with the fog to form a thick, yellow smog. Visibility was soon down to a few feet.

Billy and Charlie only found the Ramsey family home because of the two men standing guard outside the front door. The brothers would probably have stumbled past otherwise, squinting to see the house numbers in the gloaming. 'Is this Tommy Ramsey's place?' Billy asked.

'What's it to you, sonny?' Both men standing guard were wearing scarves around their faces to keep out the acrid smog.

'Nobody calls me sonny, I'm—' Billy began to rage but Charlie kept him in check. Starting a fight would not help their cause.

'We want to join the Ramsey Mob. We want to help you,' Charlie said.

'Weren't you two of the scrotes we were going to fight outside St Luke's today? Why the hell should we trust you?'

Billy was getting impatient. 'Maybe you didn't notice, but that thing was killing our gang at the same time it was killing

116

your men. Now, can we come inside or not?'

The two guards whispered between themselves before letting the brothers in. Billy and Charlie were escorted into a small, windowless back room and told to wait. A few minutes later, the massive figure of Brick appeared in the doorway.

'Bloody hell,' Billy whispered. 'Talk about out of the frying pan…!'

Brick loomed over them, holding Jack's flaming Zippo lighter. 'Put your hand over the flame.'

'What?'

'If you want to join the Ramsey Mob, you have to put your hand over the flame,' Brick explained.

'Like an initiation test,' Charlie speculated. He held his palm over the flame, gritting his teeth against the pain. After a few seconds Brick pushed him away. Billy followed his brother's lead and subjected himself to the test. Satisfied, Brick closed the Zippo.

'You can sleep in here for the night. Tommy'll talk to you in the morning.' Brick stepped out into the hallway. 'I'll bring you some food later.' He closed the door and then locked it. Billy hammered against the heavy wood but could not move it. He glared at his brother.

'Well, this was another of your great ideas!'

Upstairs, Tommy and Sarah were having dinner. Mrs Ramsey had already eaten and gone to bed early, leaving them together. Sarah picked at her food. Spam fritters were hardly the height of haute cuisine and Mrs Ramsey liked to boil all vegetables until they resembled an unhappy mush of different colours. Tommy shovelled his food with gusto, then helped finish off the remains of Sarah's helping.

'One thing I learned in the army – never turn your nose up at a meal. You never know when you'll get the chance of another,' he said between mouthfuls. 'Don't you like vegetables or something?'

'I just prefer them to be a little less well done. Boiling them just drains away all the natural goodness, especially if you pour the water away after.'

'You don't like me mum's cooking, you can always sling your hook.'

'No, it's not that,' Sarah replied. 'I'm just not very hungry.'

Tommy pushed his plate to one side. 'What did you mean earlier when you said you'd seen stranger things? That creature today – it wasn't human. I don't know what it was, but it wasn't human.'

Sarah had been dreading this question. Should she tell Tommy the truth? How would he respond to her announcing that she came from more than twenty years in the future to help save the people of London – and perhaps the world? That she came with the Doctor, a man who had made himself into a significant irritant for the gangland boss? That she knew thousands of people would be dying in the next few days? Sarah wasn't sure he was ready for the whole truth just yet.

'I've travelled a lot, been to many strange places. I've seen things I didn't believe were humanly possible,' Sarah said.

'I know what you mean,' Tommy replied. 'During the war I was stationed in Egypt. They had markets there with freak shows – creatures that shouldn't be alive. Horrible, they were, horrible. But that was nothing to what happened today. I'll never forget that for the rest of me days.'

He dug a packet of Players out of his pocket and offered her a cigarette, which Sarah declined. 'Smoking gives you lung cancer, you know.'

'Gotta die of something, don't we?' Tommy said, gratefully inhaling the cigarette's fumes. 'Anyway, helps settle the nerves.'

'Do you get nerves? I'd have thought—'

'You thought a big-time boss like me wouldn't get nerves, is that it?' Tommy said, getting up to stoke the fire. 'Everybody gets scared, no shame in that. The only men who ain't nervous going into battle are already dead or bound for the graveyard, know what I mean?' He flicked his cigarette ash into the fireplace, staring at the glowing coals. 'But that thing today…'

'You don't know how to stop it,' Sarah said. She thought of the Doctor. Right now, he was probably facing the same dilemma. He would be trying to find a way of defeating the monster. She wished there was some way of helping him, but knew the best thing she could do was stick close to Ramsey. He was crucial to what lay ahead. If only she knew how.

'No. All we can do is prepare for the worst and hope it don't happen.' Tommy looked at her. 'Do you think this is what that watchmender, the Doctor, was talking about yesterday – about there being greater threats to London?'

'Maybe,' Sarah replied. 'Maybe he could help you.'

'I don't see how an old watchmender can be much use. I meant what I said to him yesterday. I'm the best protector the people of these streets have got. The Old Bill can't stop a kid stealing apples off a market stall – how can they stop that thing?'

Sarah stood up and went to Tommy, resting a hand on his shoulder. 'You're not alone, you have to believe that. Have faith in yourself. When things are at their worst, help can come from the most unexpected places.'

The gangster looked at her. 'Sarah, I—'

'Tommy, you should take a look outside!' Jack burst into the room. He stopped in his tracks, taking in the closeness of his boss and Sarah by the fireside. 'Sorry, Tommy, I didn't realise you two were—'

'Ain't you heard of knocking?' Tommy demanded furiously.

'Now what's so important you can't remember the manners I taught you?'

Jack blushed with embarrassment. 'Outside, there's a fog like you've never seen before. It's so bad I had to bring the guards in from the street – they could hardly breathe out there.'

Tommy strode to a window and pulled back the curtains. Beyond the window was just a haze of yellow and grey, a lamp light just a few feet away only just visible through the smog cloud. 'Just another London Particular,' he said dismissively.

'But it came down so fast! It's not natural,' Jack insisted.

Tommy was having none of it. 'That monster's got you all scared of your own shadows! It's just a bit of fog. Now get back on the phone and keep calling round the other bosses. I want them all here tomorrow – fog or no fog.'

Jack nodded, retreating backwards out the door. Sarah looked out the window. It had started, she realised. Soon people would be dying, gasping for breath, unable to clear mucus from their lungs, airways clogged with soot. The killer smog had arrived. Unlike Tommy, she believed it had to be connected to what happened earlier. This was just too much of a coincidence. In the morning she would sneak out to the TARDIS and compare notes with the Doctor. A solution had to be found before things got any worse.

'I'm going to bed,' Sarah announced. 'See you in the morning.'

Tommy watched her go. The fire threw dark shadows across his face.

Jack watched Sarah ascend the stairs to her bedroom. He didn't trust the new arrival, especially as she seemed to be wielding undue influence over Tommy. Jack resolved to tell her a few home truths once he had finished his phone call.

'Can I speak to Mr MacManus? It's Jack Cooper calling.'

The familiar North London accent soon replied. 'Do you know what time it is? I'm trying to eat here!'

'I'm calling on behalf of Tommy Ramsey, Mr MacManus,' Jack said, making his voice as formal as possible should anyone be eavesdropping on the conversation. 'He's called a Council of War. All the bosses are gathering here at Tabernacle Street tomorrow, midday.'

'What's this all about, Jack?'

'I can't tell you that, Mr MacManus. But Tommy promises to make it worth your while if you attend. He's already had assurances from the other bosses that they will be here.'

'All right, have it your way. Midday tomorrow. But I won't be coming alone. Steve MacManus doesn't walk into a trap unarmed.'

'Noted. We'll see you tomorrow.' Jack hung up, his spare hand toying with the lighter he had reclaimed from Brick. He looked down at the flame lovingly. Time for that little chat with Miss Know It All...

Sarah had just changed into her nightie when there was a knock at the door. She pulled the curtains shut before responding.

'Who is it?'

'Jack. I've got a message from Tommy.'

'All right,' Sarah said reluctantly. She pulled her coat on over the nightie and opened the door. Jack stepped inside and leered at her. 'What is it?'

'I think there's something you ought to know about your knight in shining armour – Tommy Ramsey is no saint,' he replied.

'I have no illusions about that.'

Jack stepped closer to Sarah, lowering his voice to a whisper.

'But did you know why he spent six months in Wandsworth?'

She shook her head.

'It's because of what happened to his last girlfriend. Let's just say she had a nasty accident and the police thought Tommy was responsible.' Jack grinned at Sarah's discomfort.

'But murder is still a hanging offence in 1952,' Sarah said.

'Oh, they couldn't prove murder. She died in a fire, you see.'

'You did it!'

Jack clamped a hand over her mouth, his other hand grabbing her through the fabric of her nightie. 'Just remember this – if anything happens to Tommy, then I'll be taking over. Everything that's his will be mine. And that includes you!'

Sarah thrust her right knee upwards, catching Jack squarely in the groin. He crumpled with a howl of pain, hands clutching at his wounded pride.

'Sorry to disappoint you Jack, but I'm nobody's possession – not even Tommy's. Now get out before I scream rape,' Sarah said, fighting to keep her voice calm and even.

'I'll get you—' Jack gasped, staggering from the tiny bedroom. He found Tommy standing outside.

'You'll get what?' the gangster demanded.

Sarah came to the door and smiled sweetly. 'Jack was just offering to get me a cup of tea, but I declined. Thanks all the same. Good night!' She shut the bedroom door and pushed her bed in front of it. Nobody would be paying her any unexpected visits tonight.

Tommy burst out laughing. 'She's more than a match for you, Jack. I'd pick on someone your own size.' He leaned into the face of his second-in-command, his good humour replaced with savage ferocity. 'Just remember this. Anything happens to her and you'll pay for it – in blood!'

In the TARDIS, a red light began to flash on the central

console. The Doctor noticed it and set aside his repairs on the handheld tracking device to investigate. There had been a dramatic drop in the air quality outside.

He switched on the TARDIS's scanner to show an external view of conditions outside. The screen was filled with a swirling mist through which no light could penetrate. Visibility was next to nothing.

The Doctor analysed the results of several further monitoring systems on the central console. A large centre of high pressure had settled over London and the Thames Valley, forming an inversion. It trapped a layer of cool air near ground level, which was causing the fog. That was mixing with the local pollution to create smog.

He switched off the scanner. There was nothing to see outside, thanks to the dense cloud enshrouding the city. He could not believe this was a natural phenomenon, it was too much of a coincidence. The build-up must have been triggered deliberately, almost certainly by the Xhinn. The Doctor realised that if his tracking device could find the aliens, he would probably also find the source of the smog.

He patted the central console affectionately. 'Don't worry, old girl – we'll find a way to solve this, you'll see!'

The smog was causing chaos across London. Train services in and out of the capital were cancelled because drivers could no longer see the signals at the side of the tracks. Traffic ground to a halt as cars collided in the mist, unable to see each other or the lights changing. Many motorists simply abandoned their vehicles at the side of the road and tried to walk home.

Ambulances continued working but one of the crew had to walk in front, carrying a lit flare to provide guidance for the driver. Healthy, able-bodied people were collapsing in the street suffering from asthma and bronchial complaints.

Hospitals were soon overflowing with patients. Policemen stood on street corners, waving flaming torches to alert travellers to danger. Bus services ceased as drivers could not see more than a few feet ahead.

London Airport closed as incoming flights were diverted to Hurn or Blackbushe in Hampshire. The Underground was still running but queues for tickets at some stations stretched around the block with thousands trying to get home from work. Nobody could get in or out of the city. London was close to a standstill, cut off from the rest of the country. But the worst was yet to come...

SATURDAY, DECEMBER 6, 1952

Dawn brought no relief for the smog-choked streets and citizens of London. The winter sun rose above the horizon, but not high enough to burn away the dense cloud of fog and smoke that cloaked the city. The temperature stayed close to freezing, so families kept coal fires burning to warm their homes. But this just contributed to the problem. London was poisoning itself, hour by hour.

Shops stayed closed as staff stayed home, unable to travel in the smog. The weather was getting worse, not better. An eerie silence gripped the city as the stagnant mist absorbed any noise. Public transport was suspended. Few vehicles ventured onto the roads, except ambulances and hearses. The grim task of collecting the dead and dying had begun…

It was eight o'clock when Billy and Charlie were woken by the sound of a key turning. The brothers had spent an awkward night in the cramped back room. Billy sat in the only chair, while Charlie stretched out on the floor. They slept fitfully and were grateful for morning's arrival.

Brick unlocked the door and opened it, letting Tommy step inside. He glared down at the two teenagers. 'They don't look like much, do they, Brick?'

'No, Tommy.'

'You two have got sixty seconds to tell me why I shouldn't just throw you back out onto the street,' Tommy announced, looking at the second hand on his wrist watch. 'Starting now.'

Billy clambered to his feet, brushing his dark hair in place and trying to smooth the creases from his suit. 'We made a mistake. We thought Callum was the future. We found out different.'

Tommy just raised an eyebrow. 'Forty-five seconds.'

'We want to join your firm, Mr Ramsey. We ain't scared of nobody and we'll back you to the hilt,' Charlie said, joining his brother's efforts. 'We're loyal to the death.'

Tommy smiled at Brick. 'Hear that, Brick? They ain't scared of nobody. Didn't stop them running away yesterday, I noticed.' He consulted his watch again. 'Thirty seconds.'

Billy was getting desperate. 'How many men did you lose yesterday, Mr Ramsey? A dozen? Twenty? You're going to need all the help you can get to beat that thing Callum turned into.'

'True, but you're just boys. I need men. Fifteen seconds.'

'We're local boys, born and raised in Bethnal Green. We look after our own, Mr Ramsey, and so do you. Let us help – please,' Charlie pleaded.

'Time's up!' Tommy dug his cigarettes out of his suit pocket and offered them to the brothers. They nervously declined. Tommy lit one for himself and sucked hungrily on it. 'All right, you're in. But one step out of line and you're history. Be loyal to me and you'll get your reward. Cross me, and all you'll get is an unmarked grave. Understand?'

The brothers nodded gratefully.

'Good. Now get yourself cleaned up and then go to the kitchen. Me mum will cook you some breakfast. You two need feeding up!' Tommy whispered something into Brick's ear before heading for the front door.

*

Sarah was woken by the silence. All her life she had been a city dweller, moving in time with the metropolis. London in 1952 had been a massive culture shock. Traffic levels were as nothing to that of her own time. People dressed differently, had different attitudes. Ethnic minorities were hardly seen. Women wore dresses past the knee. Hairnets and cross-over aprons were like a uniform for wives and mothers. Sarah found herself missing television. She pined for a good cup of coffee. The sexism and racism were startling to Sarah. This world seemed so familiar, yet it was almost as alien to her as Peladon or Exxilon.

Despite all that, London was still a noisy place. The East End streets pulsated with the chatter of women gossiping, men arguing and children playing. But that morning, she could hear none of the usual din outside. She almost wondered if she had gone deaf overnight, until she heard Mrs Ramsey's footfalls on the landing.

'Would you like a nice cup of tea, love?'

Sarah sighed. The world might be coming to an end, but there was always time for another cup of tea in the Ramsey household. 'That would be lovely, Vera – I'll be down in a few minutes.'

'All right dear. Mind you don't let it go cold.'

Sarah got up and changed from her nightie into a floral dress and woollen cardigan. The clothes had appeared on her bed the previous day, carefully laid out by Mrs Ramsey. They had belonged to Vera's sister Ruth and were a good fit.

Sarah pushed her bed away from the bedroom door and stepped out onto the landing. Brick was standing outside, looking embarrassed. 'I've got a message for you from Tommy. He says it's best to stay indoors today. The smog is getting worse. He needs you to meet the other bosses when they start arriving. The meeting is set for midday.'

'Thank you, Arthur – I'll be here for the meeting. But I have to go out this morning to run an errand.'

'But Tommy says—'

'Mr Ramsey can say what he wants,' Sarah replied brusquely, 'but I'm not a slave at his command. And you can tell him I said that!'

In the Xhinn vessel, the triumvirate was monitoring the build-up of smog over London. A three-dimensional hologram of the city and its weather system rotated slowly in the air, keeping time with the movements of the three aliens.

'It has begun.'

'Weaponry?'

'The dominant native species' own effluvia.'

'Target?'

'Absolute environment control.'

'Progress?'

'Achievement imminent.'

'Threats.'

'Minimal but not inconsequential.'

This brought the triumvirate a moment of pause.

'Explain.'

'Another alien presence.'

'Identity?'

'Unknown.'

'Significance?'

'Unknown.'

'Response?'

'Activate the drones.'

'Activated.'

'Let these primitives be their own undoing.'

Sarah entered the kitchen to find two teenage boys shovelling massive fried breakfasts into their mouths. They ate like they hadn't enjoyed a home cooked meal for weeks. Mrs Ramsey was watching them proudly.

'Does my heart good to see people enjoying their food.' Vera noticed Sarah was wearing Ruth's old clothes. Tears brimmed in her eyes at the sight. She pointed at the kitchen table. 'Your cuppa's there, love.'

'Thank you, Vera.' Sarah sat down opposite the two new arrivals, who paused briefly to acknowledge her presence before returning to their meals. 'Where is everybody?'

Mrs Ramsey shook her head sadly. 'Tommy says some of the boys didn't come back last night. It's like they just disappeared into that fog. He's gone out looking for them in the car.' The front doorbell rang. 'That'll be them now, I expect. I'll go let them in.'

But when Mrs Ramsey returned, she was accompanied by a woman. It was Mary Mills from across the street. She was carrying a tiny box painted with the Union Jack symbol. A hole for coins had been crudely sliced in the lid.

'It's young Mary, she's come for the collection.'

'Hello again!' Mary said, recognising Sarah. 'Can you believe this smog? I've never seen it so bad before, have you, Mrs Ramsey?'

'Never, and I've lived in this street nearly forty years.' She pulled her handbag down from a hook on the back of the kitchen door and extracted a handful of coins. 'Will that do you for this week, dear? If Tommy were here I could give you more. You could always wait…'

Mary looked nervous at mention of the gang boss's name. 'No, that's all right, Mrs Ramsey. That'll do fine.'

Sarah could not help but ask, her journalist's curiosity getting the better of her. 'What are you collecting for?'

Mary and Mrs Ramsey looked at Sarah as if she had grown

129

an extra head overnight. 'For the street party, of course,' Mary replied, as if to a child.

'Street party?'

'For the Coronation next summer.' Mary and Mrs Ramsey exchanged a look of bemusement at this display of ignorance.

'Oh, of course!' Sarah said, embarrassed. 'Queen Elizabeth's coronation. Stupid of me to forget!' She desperately racked her brain for a way of changing the subject away from her blunder. 'How about this fog, eh?'

Mrs Ramsey nodded vigorously. 'It's shocking. I was scrubbing the front doorstep this morning and I only saw three other women scrubbing their steps. Disgraceful, that's what it is – disgraceful!'

'I've got to get back,' Mary said. 'My Bette's in bed with a terrible cough, the poor mite. She was up all night coughing. Now I think my Rita's coming down with it too. It's the smog, I swear it's coming in through the windows!'

Sarah grabbed the opportunity to get out of the house. 'I'll walk you back across the road.'

'Oh, there's no need for that—'

'No, I insist,' Sarah said firmly, taking Mary by the arm and escorting her out of the kitchen. 'I could do with getting out myself,' she whispered conspiratorially to Mary. 'If I drink any more of Vera's tea I'll drown!'

The two women giggled as they stepped out onto Tabernacle Street. Sarah grabbed a coat and scarf as they left number 15. Once outside, she made her excuses. 'I'd best be off, I've got to visit a friend nearby. He's only a few minutes away, but it'll probably take me all morning in this weather.'

Mary waved a finger at Sarah, giving her a mock scolding. 'I hope you're not keeping a fella on the side. There'll be hell to pay if Tommy finds out.'

Sarah smiled. 'I can deal with Tommy. You just look after

your girls.'

A wave of worry passed over Mary's face. 'I'll see you later.' She disappeared across the street, swallowed up by the smog before reaching her own doorstep. Sarah wrapped the scarf around her face several times and set off for Whitecross Street.

At Bethnal Green Police Station, Chief Superintendent Carver was addressing officers drawn from across the East End. The policemen were all gathered in the canteen, where steaming enamel mugs of tea and hot buttered toast were being served.

'Men, we have a difficult task ahead of us today. The smog will make that job even harder. You may get some resistance. People round here can be a surly lot at the best of times, but that's no excuse for not treating them with courtesy and respect. We are doing this for their own good.'

Hodge held up a hand nervously. 'I'm not sure I understand. What is this special task?'

'Hasn't it been explained to you constable?' Carver asked. He looked to Sergeant Diggle despairingly.

'Sorry, sir. Several of the men only just arrived in time for the meeting. I didn't get a chance to brief them,' the desk sergeant explained.

'Hmm, well, that's understandable,' Carver admitted. He looked at the young constable. 'Hodge, isn't it?'

'Yes sir!' The policeman smiled, happy for the recognition. He must have made a good impression for the chief superintendent to know his name.

'It's been decided to evacuate those parts of London worst hit by the smog. We've been getting reports of rapid rises in mortality rates across the capital since the smog settled in last evening. Unless we get people to safety, the effects could be catastrophic.'

Hodge still had a question. 'But I listened to the news on

the wireless this morning. They said nothing about any evacuation.'

Sergeant Diggle answered that. 'Panic, lad – the authorities want to avoid a panic. If the evacuation was announced, everyone would rush to get out of the city simultaneously. Can you imagine the effect of several million people all trying to get out of London at once?'

'Utter chaos,' Carver chimed in, nodding sagely. 'So we'll be taking people out street by street, house by house. They go to a holding centre first, before being evacuated from the city entirely. Our goal is to empty London before the smog reaches fatal levels.'

'Surely the army is better suited to evacuating people?' Hodge asked.

'Perhaps,' Carver acknowledged, 'but we're already here and the local citizens know our faces. The smog has delayed attempts to call the army in for help.'

He paused to see if any more questions were forthcoming. Satisfied at last, Hodge was tucking into a plateful of hot buttered toast.

'All right then,' Carver said with a smile. 'Everybody has their orders. Let's make this operation as quick and efficient as possible. The vans are waiting outside. Good luck!'

Tommy wearily opened the front door of 15 Tabernacle Street. He had spent three hours out in the smog, visiting the homes of his missing men. Billy Valance had disappeared during the night – Tommy suspected the cowardly lieutenant of doing a runner – but Dave Butcher was also missing. Several of the Ramsey Mob's best henchmen had also disappeared. Nobody could explain their absence or suggest where they might have gone. Tommy tried the Red Room but it was empty and abandoned.

At least he had managed to find Norman Page, the last of his lieutenants. Norman had dug up a cache of weapons hidden away after the war and was arming all the men he could muster. They would be standing ready to respond to a phone call from Tommy.

The gangster stepped inside and slammed the front door behind him. He coughed and spat repeatedly, trying to clear the acrid stench of smog from his lungs. He felt dirty, as if he was covered in soot and sweat. The cloud seemed to wrap itself around you, like some deadly embrace.

Tommy strode into the kitchen, his throat dry and wretched. 'Mum, tell me you've still got a cup of tea in the pot,' he pleaded.

Mrs Ramsey beamed happily. 'I've always got a cuppa ready for you, Thomas, you should know that by now.'

The mention of Tommy's given name brought a snigger from the two brothers, who were still sat at the kitchen table. The gangland boss glared at them, silencing any mirth in a moment. 'What are you two still doing here?'

'We're waiting for orders,' Charlie replied, avoiding Tommy's gaze.

'Well, go and guard the front door. I'm expecting most of the major faces from the East End here by midday. I don't want any unpleasant surprises.'

The two brothers vacated the kitchen, leaving Tommy to put his feet up.

'Still bad outside, is it Thomas?'

'Mum, I never seen anything like it. Ain't normal!' He listened for the sound of other voices in the house. He could hear Jack upstairs on the phone and floorboards creaking heavily overhead indicated Brick was still in. Probably fretting about his pigeons, Tommy thought.

'Where's Sarah?'

'Oh, she went across the road with that Mary Mills nearly an hour ago. I'd of thought she'd be back by now,' Mrs Ramsey replied.

Tommy consulted his wrist watch. 'She better not miss the meeting.'

Sarah almost missed the TARDIS, so bad was the smog becoming. She only found it by groping her way around the corner from Old Street into Whitecross Street. Visibility was down to a few feet and still contracting. Eventually she bumped into the tall blue box and thumped three times on its side.

'Doctor, it's me!' she hissed.

After a long, agonising wait, the door finally opened and she slipped inside. Sarah unwrapped herself from the combination of scarf and coat, dropping the soot-soaked clothes onto the floor.

'I swear that smog's getting worse all the time. It took me forever to get here, you know,' she said. As usual, the Doctor was absorbed in checking the many dials and displays on the central console. 'I said that smog's getting worse all the—'

'Yes, I heard you the first time, Sarah,' the Doctor replied. He looked up at her and smiled. 'Have you changed your make-up?'

'No, why do you ask?'

'Try that mirror.' The Doctor pointed at a small mirror perched precariously atop an open trunk piled high with wiring, metal and oddities. Sarah followed his advice and was shocked to see a horizontal band of black and grey soot across her face, where she had peered through a gap in the scarf to see her way forwards.

'I look ridiculous!' she cried out, pulling a handkerchief from a pocket and wiping the sticky soot from her features.

'Urgh! This stuff is horrible!'

'Just imagine what it's doing to your lungs, and to the lungs of everybody else in London. Chest and bronchial infections will be up by a factor of ten. Anyone already suffering from asthma or other breathing difficulties will be dead if they can't escape the city soon.' The Doctor pointed to a display on the central console. 'Take a look at this.'

Sarah joined him by the display. It registered external air quality in the area immediately surrounding the TARDIS. The needle usually stayed in the large white space to the left of the display. Now the needle was just in the amber section in the middle. As Sarah watched, it shifted another fraction to the right, moving ever closer to the final, red sector.

'I know I'm going to regret asking this, but what does the red part indicate?' Sarah inquired tentatively.

'That London's air quality would be fatal to any human being who breathed it for more than a few hours.' The Doctor's face was graver than Sarah had ever seen it before. 'The smog cloud is getting worse by the hour, becoming increasingly toxic.'

'How long before that needle goes into the red zone?'

'Two days at the most, perhaps less.'

'Perhaps?'

'Probably.'

Sarah had not given up hope yet. 'What if the weather changes? Then the smog cloud would slowly break up, wouldn't it?'

The Doctor rubbed a hand against the back of his neck, stretching his muscles. 'I've been monitoring the build-up since last night, Sarah – this is not what I would describe as a natural phenomenon.'

'How would you describe it?' she asked fearfully.

'As a first strike weapon.'

'Like an atomic bomb.'

'Something like that.'

Sarah was aghast. 'Doctor, how can you be so calm about this? You're passing a death sentence on thousands, even millions of people!'

His eyes looked into hers mournfully. 'You think I don't know that? I would give anything to have stopped this ever happening – but it's already begun. Now we must do all we can to prevent a greater tragedy.'

She nodded, knowing what he said was true. But that didn't make the reality of it any easier to take. 'You said this wasn't a natural phenomenon.'

The Doctor nodded.

'So who or what is causing the smog? Does it have anything to do with the creature Tommy and his men fought outside the church yesterday?'

'You know about that?'

'Only what I've been told.' She caught some hesitancy in his voice. 'You were there! What happened?'

The Doctor related his version of events, explaining what little he knew about the Xhinn. But Sarah sensed he was still holding something back.

'What aren't you telling me?' she demanded.

'The Xhinn are a very methodical species. Before they colonise a planet, they send scouting missions in first to collect and analyse data about the world – its resources, its dominant species and what threat they might pose. These missions can take years in Earth time.'

'So you think this Callum creature was probably just an advance scout, sent ahead of a full colonisation team?'

The Doctor shook his head. 'The Xhinn never travel alone. According to legend, they use a triumvirate gestalt entity to guide any mission.'

'Speak English Doctor!'

He searched for an appropriate metaphor. 'Have you ever seen clover?'

'Three leaves, one plant – yes, so?'

'A triumvirate gestalt entity is like that – three Xhinn, working together as one mind for more efficient decision making.'

'Three heads are better than one, that sort of thing?' Sarah suggested.

'That sort of thing.'

'So, the triumvirate could be one Xhinn short of an entity?'

The Doctor shook his head. 'Doubtful. I suspect Callum was an external scout, sent out from the Xhinn vessel. He got ahead of himself and revealed his true identity yesterday outside the church. This smog – it's a cover-up.'

'For what?'

'I think Callum's revelation has forced the Xhinn to advance their plans by years, maybe even decades ahead of schedule. The smog is designed to lay waste to London, preventing word of their arrival being spread.'

Sarah was aghast. 'They're going to murder millions just to cover their tracks? But that's outrageous.'

'It's nothing to the Xhinn. They're playing for much higher stakes than the lives of every man, woman and child in London. They want all of Earth and its resources to feed their endless quest for more worlds, more territories.'

Sarah tried to absorb all of this information. 'So, if Callum hadn't picked a fight with Tommy, none of this might have happened?'

'We might have been able to stop the Xhinn some other way, yes.'

'We got here two weeks before the crucial moment and still thousands of people are going to die.' Sarah felt tears rolling down her cheeks.

'I know, Sarah, I know. We want to save everyone – but we can't.' He took her face in his hands and lifted it up. His thumbs delicately wiped away the tears from her cheeks. 'Remember what I said before? We're here to prevent a greater tragedy. We both have a role to play.'

She nodded, sniffing back her tears. 'So, what's our next step?'

'You need to go back to Tommy Ramsey's house. I'm convinced his part in this crisis is not yet over. But be careful, Sarah – remember what happened with Callum. Not everybody is who or what they seem to be.'

'That's all right – we developed a test for finding the Xhinn. They don't like flames or fire.' Sarah explained about the severed arm.

'The Xhinn don't just use their external scouts to carry out their plans. They employ unwitting collaborators to do their bidding, people who do not realise they will be betraying their own species,' the Doctor warned. 'Trust no one.'

Sarah nodded. 'What will you be doing?'

'Trying to avert any more deaths. I'm going to tell the Xhinn to leave Earth alone or suffer the consequences.'

'How will you find them?'

'Finding them will be the easy part.' The Doctor pointed to his handheld tracking device. 'The smog is being controlled by Xhinn technology. This device should enable me to track the source of that control. Convincing the Xhinn they should leave now will be the hard part.'

'But how can you stop them?'

The Doctor tapped the side of his nose. 'That's my little secret – better you don't know. Let's just say I haven't been wasting my time here in the TARDIS.'

Sarah fetched a new coat and scarf from her bedroom.

Before leaving she said goodbye to the Doctor. 'Please be careful. I don't want to be trapped in 1952 – these shoes are killing me!'

He smiled and watched her go. 'Goodbye, Sarah,' he said to himself, the smile fading from his features. 'Good luck.'

Frank Kelly had never been a hard worker. He spent the war avoiding active duty with a series of mysterious illnesses. These helped earn him a medical discharge and small pension once the fighting was over. Most of that went on beer and betting. When he wasn't supporting his local bookmaker, Frank liked to eye up the barmaid in the neighbouring pub.

He had only married Rose because she was pregnant and named him as the guilty party. Her father turned up with a shotgun and a marriage licence. Two days later Frank was on honeymoon in Eastbourne, his feet having hardly touched the ground. Two months later Rose had a miscarriage. She wanted to try for another baby but he was having none of it. He had been blind drunk the night she first surrendered to his charms. Once he sobered up, Frank decided the slightly overweight, pleasant-faced Rose wasn't to his taste. But he couldn't escape the marriage. Rose was a fervent Catholic and would not countenance divorce. So they stayed together, hating each other more as each day passed.

Rose put all her energies into the little boarding house, trying to make it a home away from home for the guests. Mostly they were travelling salesmen, or families evicted after missing rent payments. The Kellys were luckier than most. They actually owned their house, a rarity in this part of London. Rose's father had given it to them as a wedding present. She was turning the business into a going concern. They certainly couldn't have survived on the military pension or the pittance Frank earned helping at the local market.

When the weather was bad like this, Frank stayed in the front room, always in the chair nearest the fire. Rose bustled around cooking meals for the boarders or washing the bed linen. She was arranging sheets to dry in front of the fire when a Black Maria police van pulled up outside the house in Great Sutton Street.

'Who could that be?' Rose wondered. She was about to peer out the curtains when a heavy banging rattled the front door. The little woman glared at her indolent husband. 'What have you been up to, Frank Kelly? If that's the Old Bill, I'll have your guts for garters!'

He protested his innocence. 'I ain't been out of this house in three days and you know it, woman!' He always called her woman, never Rose. Any trace of affection between them had worn away years ago. He shifted in his seat before settling down again to gaze into the fire.

'Well, you could at least get off your fat bum and answer the door! It'll be more than you've done round this place for months!' Rose put her hands on her hips, exasperated at Frank's laziness. But he just ignored her, as always.

The front door took another battering from the impatient visitor. Rose looked to the ceiling for guidance. 'Lord, save us all from lazy, good-for-nothing, bone idle men!' She stomped to the front door and opened it. 'Yes, what do you—'

Sergeant Diggle was standing outside, his truncheon raised to start knocking again. 'Good morning, madam. Could you tell me how many people there are in the house?'

'Just me and Frank – me husband,' Rose replied. 'Normally we'd expect to have boarders but this weather is terrible for driving off any casual trade. Is something wrong?' She feared the worst, as always. Frank had a habit of acquiring misplaced goods from dubious salesmen in pub bars. Any police search of the boarding house would probably find enough evidence to lock both of them away for many, many months.

'We're evacuating everyone from the local area, due to the inclement weather,' the policeman explained. 'The authorities believe this smog could pose a health risk to residents, especially in the East End. We've been asked to move people to a holding area. From there you'll be taken outside the city.'

'Like the kiddies during the war?'

'Something like that, yes, madam.'

Rose smiled excitedly. She had never been out of London, never been further than the West End. A free trip to the countryside sounded like just the tonic she needed. But a worry was hampering her happiness.

'What can we take with us? I don't want anyone breaking in and stealing all our valuables.'

Sergeant Diggle smiled. 'Don't worry, madam. Everybody is being evacuated over the next few days, so that shouldn't be a problem. As a safeguard, we shall have a constable on every street corner to stop any looters or criminals from taking advantage of this situation.'

Rose turned to shout along the hallway. 'You hear that, Frank? We're being evacuated to the countryside! The police think the smog's not safe.'

She was rewarded with a grunt of disinterest. Rose rolled her eyes at the policeman. 'How long have we got to pack?'

'Actually, madam, the van is ready to leave now. We need to get everyone out of this street in the next few minutes.' He pointed at a Black Maria parked in front of the boarding house. Through the mist Rose could see several of her neighbours being helped up on the back of the vehicle.

'But I need to take some things – a nightdress, my jewellery,' she protested, one hand reaching for her neck. Frank had only ever given Rose one gift in all their time together, a pearl necklace he claimed to have found on the street.

She wore it whenever she was expecting guests, or on the rare occasions she got out of the house. She couldn't leave without the necklace.

'You'll be provided with food and clothing at the holding area. If you lock up the house securely, your valuables will still be here when you get back.'

Frank had finally pulled himself out of the armchair and joined his wife at the front door. 'Valuables? What's all this about valuables?'

Rose looked at her husband with worried eyes. 'We have to go now. The policemen want us to leave everything behind.'

'That can't be right, can it?' Frank looked at the sergeant with suspicion. He had a natural distrust of the police anyway but this seemed too sudden. Since when did the authorities care what happened to the residents of Great Sutton Street? All the local people had felt was neglect and contempt.

'Yes, sir. You have to leave now,' Sergeant Diggle insisted.

'What if I don't want to leave? This is my home! I own this house, you know – I don't just rent it like most round here,' Frank insisted, neglecting to mention the property was registered in his wife's name.

'It will still be here when you get back.'

'Well, when's that?'

'Probably only a few days, once the fog's cleared away.' The sergeant gestured towards the van. All the other residents had been loaded into the back of it now. Everyone was waiting for the Kellys.

Rose made up her mind. 'All right, we're coming.' She got her coat down from its hook in the hallway and pulled it around herself. Frank got the front door key from under the mat and locked the boarding house. They clambered into the back of the vehicle, Rose pushed up by Sergeant Diggle. He slammed the door shut after her and locked it tightly. The policeman slapped the back of the van twice with his hand.

'All right, this one's full – move it out!'

Rose peered out the vehicle as it pulled away from her home. How long before I come back, she wondered before her mind moved on to more exciting thoughts. 'Where do you think we're being evacuated to?' she asked Frank.

Her husband almost smiled. 'Somewhere sunny and warm, I hope!'

That brought a laugh from everyone.

A white Rolls Royce pulled up outside 15 Tabernacle Street. The driver got out and strode briskly around the vehicle to open the rear passenger's door. Out stepped Steve MacManus, his camel-hair coat pulled tightly around himself. He was wearing a brown felt hat and a matching camel-hair scarf wrapped around his face. Two men in black greatcoats also emerged from the back of the car, their identical faces dull and impassive.

MacManus knocked sharply on the front door of number 15. Tommy Ramsey opened the door and welcomed his rival into the house. MacManus looked back at his driver. 'Barry, you better stay in the car. Don't want one of the local toerags taking a fancy to it now, do we?'

The driver nodded his agreement and returned to his seat, grateful to close the door and escape the smog. The trip into the East End had been long and painful. The combination of soot and mist plastered the windscreen like paint, resisting all attempts to keep the glass clear. Thank goodness for the car's heating system which helped keep them all warm on the difficult journey.

MacManus stepped inside, followed by his two lieutenants. 'This is James and John, my offsiders. They help keep the peace.'

Tommy gave a grudging agreement. 'They can wait in the front room with the other bodyguards. The meeting is just between the top men from each firm. The fewer people talking, the quicker we get this done.'

MacManus nodded, shrugging off his coat, hat and scarf. Tommy hung them up in the hallway. 'Who else is here?'

'Fingers Blake from the docks and Stratford Simon. I was expecting more but this weather…' Tommy shrugged helplessly.

'I know, it was a nightmare getting here. Got any brandy? That smog was getting into my bones on the journey.' Tommy led MacManus upstairs to the front room, where the others were waiting. Fingers Blake was a thin, red-haired man with freckles and nervous hands. Stratford Simon was an overweight, hairless lump with bloodshot eyes and a surly mouth. Mrs Ramsey appeared and offered the new arrivals a cup of tea.

'I'm getting them something stronger,' Tommy said, nearly blushing.

'Still living with your mum, eh?' MacManus hissed once she had gone, trying to goad his rival into doing something stupid.

Tommy just smiled. 'Least I got one. Heard they found yours in a dustcart.'

Fingers Blake stepped between the two men, pushing them apart. 'All right, all right, you two. We've exchanged enough unpleasantries for one day. I thought we were here to talk some business. Shall we get started?'

Tommy and MacManus agreed, still glaring at each other. Tommy signalled to Jack, who was standing up by the door.

'Jack, will you show our distinguished guests to the dining room? We'll be having the meeting in there. Everybody else can wait here together.' He looked round the room at the half dozen burly bodyguards gathered. 'Quietly.'

As the gang bosses filed out, Tommy whispered into Jack's ear. 'Where's Sarah? She's supposed to be here!'

'What do you care?' Jack asked, genuinely surprised.

Tommy grabbed his second-in-command by the collar. 'I'll deal with you later, my lad. Just make sure nothing happens in here, all right?'

Jack nodded vigorously. 'I'll let you know when Sarah returns.'

'You do that.'

Sarah was still some distance from Tabernacle Street, trying to grope her way back to the Ramsey house. The smog was thickening, just as the Doctor had predicted. By now she could hardly see her hand if she stretched her arm out in the front. The air was sickly yellow, speckled with black and grey. Someone had turned London's street lights on, but these were hardly visible in the pall. Sarah was grateful for having memorised her route on the way to the TARDIS, otherwise she might never have found her way back again.

Ahead she could just make out shapes moving in the murky air and voices talking. She strained to hear what was being said, but the smog seemed to swallow up noise just as it swallowed up light.

'Excuse me, miss.' The voice startled Sarah. A tall, young policeman was standing beside her. She had been so intent on what was happening in front of her that she hadn't noticed his approach.

'Oh my goodness! You gave me quite a surprise, Constable!' she said. Sarah recognised the face of the policeman. 'I've seen you somewhere before. Weren't you patrolling in Tabernacle Street yesterday morning?'

'If you'd just come along with me.' PC Hodge took a firm

grip on her right arm and tried to guide her forwards.

'It's just I'm trying to get back to Tabernacle Street and I'm not sure this is the right way.' Sarah laughed out loud. 'That's funny. You must have people asking you for directions all the time. I wouldn't normally need to, but this smog is making things very difficult.'

'Yes, miss. If you'd just come along with me,' the constable replied blandly. Sarah realised he wasn't even looking at her.

'Did you hear what I said? I'm looking for Tabernacle Street.' She stood still now, forcing the policeman to a halt. 'I think I should be turning left here.'

'We're evacuating everyone from the local streets, due to the inclement weather,' Hodge explained. 'The authorities believe this smog could pose a health risk to residents, especially in the East End. We've been asked to move people to a holding area. From there you'll be taken outside the city.' He tugged at her arm again. 'So, if you'll just come with me…'

Sarah tried to pull her arm away. 'Now, look! You may be evacuating this street but I don't live here. I'm staying in Tabernacle Street and that's where I'm going now. OK?'

'I'm sorry, miss, but you have to come with me,' the policeman insisted.

Sarah could not seem to pry his iron grip from her arm. 'You're just not listening to me, Constable. What's wrong with you?'

'We're evacuating everyone from the local area, due to the inclement weather…' the policeman began.

'You just said that…' Sarah felt a chill of terror as the hairs on the back of her neck stood up. She looked intently at the features of the constable. It was a placid, well-meaning face but the eyes were glazed over, lifeless. Something was very wrong. He began dragging her towards the gathering up ahead.

Sarah squinted through the gloom. She could see people being shoved roughly into the back of a Black Maria. Some were protesting, among them an elderly man waving a stick. He was clubbed to the ground by a truncheon-wielding policeman. Despite the savagery of the blows being inflicted, the policeman's face was completely blank and expressionless. An old woman in the back of the van began to scream.

'Leave my husband alone! He's done nothing wrong! Nothing!' She was silenced with a single blow to the head, knocking her unconscious.

Sarah looked away, horrified. She had to get away, otherwise she would be trapped like the people being herded into the vehicle. But Sarah also wanted to save them. Hodge was dragging her ever closer to the van. If she was going to act, it had to be now.

'Excuse me, Constable, but I think you've got something on your foot,' Sarah said benignly. Then she rammed the heel of her shoe downwards onto the policeman's ankle, which gave way beneath him. He let go of Sarah's arm and sank to the ground, his face still a blank.

Sarah ran off down a side street on the left, away from the stricken constable. She had to get back to Tabernacle Street. She had to warn Tommy and the others. She tried not to think about the people she had left behind.

The Doctor ventured out of the TARDIS, a cape, scarf and hat added to his usual attire. He held the tracker out in front of him, staring intently at its display. It indicated the source of the weather disruption was less than five minutes' walk away, beyond St Luke's Church. The Doctor pocketed the device and began striding towards the Xhinn vessel.

Tommy Ramsey sat down, having described what happened

147

outside St Luke's Church only twenty-four hours earlier. It seemed like a lifetime ago now. He looked around the dining room table. Fingers Blake and Stratford Simon were plainly puzzled, unable to take in what he had said. But there could be no doubting what Steve MacManus thought of it all.

'You know, I've heard some tall stories in my time,' he began. 'Wild excuses from men who knew they had earned my anger. Packs of lies from gamblers who can't cover their debts and just need one more chance to get themselves straight. But I've never heard anything to match what you've just described.'

Fingers and Stratford looked at each other, waiting for the coming storm. MacManus swiftly obliged them, pushing his chair back and standing up to pound on the table.

'What a load of tripe! People turning into floating creatures! Incinerating your men with blue lightning bolts! Do you call us here just to insult our intelligence, or was that just a happy coincidence?' he raged.

'I know it sounds impossible—' Tommy began.

'Sounds impossible? It is impossible! Where's your proof? Where's your evidence? Why should we believe a single word you've said, Ramsey?'

'Because it's the truth!' Tommy shouted. 'When the creature killed my men, the bodies disappeared – like God winked and took them away.'

'God winked? God winked!' MacManus sat back down and sighed. 'It'd be funnier if it wasn't so pathetic!'

Tommy looked desperately at the three visitors. They were his best hope of taking on this threat. Without them, he and his men stood no chance. If they fell, then all of the East End would follow.

'You won't think it's so funny when you're facing one of those monsters!'

'Do you see me laughing?' MacManus snarled.

Fingers and Stratford shook their heads. This was not going well.

The Doctor was close to the Xhinn vessel. According to his tracker, it should be within sight – but the smog was making seeing anything almost impossible. His quest was not helped by having little idea of what the spacecraft should look like. Did the Xhinn possess stealth technology? For all the Doctor knew, he could be standing on top of the vessel.

A croaking diesel engine spluttered into earshot and twin headlights appeared from the smog. It was a black police van. The Doctor ducked behind a tree as the vehicle rumbled past. Just before it disappeared from view, the tail lights dipped, and then were gone – almost as if the van was going down a slope. But this part of the East End was almost perfectly flat.

'Of course! The Xhinn must be underground – there's nowhere else to conceal a ship of the size necessary to travel vast distances through space.' The Doctor ran forwards, after the vehicle. But he was stopped by a blinding light which burst into radiance in front of him. It was a Xhinn. The creature raised its right arm and gestured at the Doctor.

A blue energy bolt surged forth, engulfing the Time Lord. He cried out in agony, then collapsed to the ground. Blue tendrils of light danced around his body. Then he winked out of existence…

In the back of the Black Maria, Rose Kelly's hopes for a happy break from London were rapidly diminishing. As they were driven through the smog-choked streets, the passengers began to grow apprehensive. The driver would not talk to them when they asked questions. Instead he accelerated, driving ever faster along the dim, dank streets. It was almost as if he could see in the smog when nobody else could. Rose was just thankful there were no other vehicles on the road, for they would certainly crash.

Suddenly the van was going down a steep slope, into pitch darkness. She could not help crying out and hugged her husband. Frank was trying to keep a brave face, but his hands were shaking with fear. As the vehicle descended, warm air flowed up to meet them. It was cleaner and clearer. For the first time that day, Rose's eyes stopped watering. She looked at their surroundings through the back window as the van drove on.

They were going down a steep tunnel, which moved from dark to light. But this was like no tunnel Rose had ever seen. Once she had walked all the way to the Isle of Dogs, then through the tunnel under the Thames for a family picnic in Greenwich. This tunnel was grey and bumpy, the walls glistening. It reminded her of a wet crocodile skin handbag.

After several minutes the tunnel levelled out and the Black Maria entered a vast white chamber. The back of the van was opened and Rose clambered out, followed by Frank and the other passengers. The walls were so high Rose could not see the ceiling. She looked around. There were half a dozen vans, all unloading passengers. She recognised neighbours from roads near Great Sutton Street. The police were obviously being very systematic, evacuating the East End one suburb at a time.

'I've never seen anything like this – where do you suppose we are?' she whispered to her husband.

'During the war the Government built dozens of secret tunnels and rooms under London. In case of emergency, Churchill could run the country from underground. Maybe this was part of that,' Frank replied, his words soothing. But his eyes betrayed an inner terror to his wife.

'What's wrong, Frank? What is it?' she asked.

'I don't know, Rose – but something ain't right here.'

Rose gave him a little hug. It was the first time he had called her by name since their honeymoon.

The Doctor came to and promptly began dry-retching. He hadn't eaten for days and his body had nothing to eject, but that didn't stop it trying. After a few moments of meditation he was able to restore the natural equilibrium and the spasms passed. He opened his eyes and looked around.

He was lying on a bench in an empty, oval-shaped room. All was white and the walls curved seamlessly down into the floor, and up into the ceiling. He could see no corners, no edges and no evidence of a doorway.

'An oubliette,' he muttered. 'Quite ingenious.' He laid a hand against his abdomen. The vomiting had no doubt been brought on by the use of such a crude, short-range matter transmitter. At least now he knew where all the corpses had been disappearing to.

The Doctor knew he was a captive of the Xhinn. But why had they taken him alive? Presumably for observation. So the oubliette was probably a test, to determine his intelligence levels. He decided to talk out loud. It would help mask his thoughts, in case the Xhinn were trying to probe him telepathically.

'Hmm, no doors, no corners – so no weaknesses. But perhaps this is simpler than it seems.' He began fishing around in his pockets. His fingers touched the sonic screwdriver but he pulled out a small rubber ball instead. The Doctor crouched down and rolled the ball along the floor at speed. It went up the curved walls and then began a series of spirals as it rose and fell. After a few elliptical circuits of the chamber it suddenly disappeared.

'Ah! The seamless walls are an illusion!' He rose from the bench and walked to the point where the ball had vanished, reaching out with his hands to touch the wall. The perfect whiteness of the oubliette made it almost impossible to know where the walls actually began.

The Doctor soon found the hole in the illusion. Viewed from the right angle, the narrow opening was blatantly obvious. But to have found it by touch alone could have taken hours. The Doctor peered into the hole. Inside was a white circle. He reached forward to press it.

Logically, this had to be the escape mechanism. It could be a death-trap, but his captors had already had ample opportunity to kill him. He pressed the circle. It turned black and the walls of the oubliette folded backwards, like the petals of a flower opening. Beyond was only darkness. The Doctor took a slimline torch from his pocket and stepped out of the room into the void. What would the next test be, he wondered.

Steve MacManus had heard enough. He walked out of the dining room in search of his bodyguards.

Tommy Ramsey called after him. 'Wait! You can't leave yet!'

'Try and stop me,' MacManus replied coldly. He found his men sipping cups of tea, served by Mrs Ramsey. 'You two – we're leaving. Now.' The bodyguards immediately put their cups down and fell into step behind their boss. He hurried down the stairs and began pulling on his coat, scarf and hat by the front door.

Jack Cooper hurried down the stairs after him. 'Mr MacManus! Stop!'

The gangster opened the front door. 'Why should I? Did Tommy send you? Have you heard that cock and bull story he's peddling?'

Jack put a hand out to stop MacManus. 'It's true – what Tommy told you, it's all true. I was there. I saw it with my own eyes!'

'Not you as well. I expected better from you, Jackie boy.' MacManus shook his head sadly. 'You can forget our agreement – I don't make deals with nutters. You're on your own. Now take your hand off me before I get one of my boys here to take it off – permanently.'

The two bodyguards stepped forward, eager to assist. Jack pulled his hand away hurriedly. MacManus walked out to his Rolls Royce. The driver opened the rear passenger door and MacManus got in. The two bodyguards followed him into the vehicle. MacManus gave Jack a final glance.

'You showed promise, lad. But I also reckoned you were a little too fond of lighting fires. It's a sickness. You should get it seen to.'

The Rolls Royce drove away, quickly being swallowed up by the smog. Jack shut the door and went back upstairs. Stratford Simon and Fingers Blake were also preparing to leave. Tommy was pressing them for an answer.

'I'll call you tomorrow morning – nine o'clock sharp,' Fingers offered. 'It's the best I can do.'

Stratford Simon made the same promise. Tommy accepted, grateful to get something out of the meeting.

'Thanks. I appreciate you sticking your neck out for me. It'll be well rewarded, if we get out of this alive, you mark my words.' Tommy slapped both of them on the back. The pair collected their minders and departed.

Jack reported MacManus's dismissive comments, but Tommy was not concerned. 'If either Fingers or Stratford join their firm to ours, we've got a real fighting force to be reckoned with. Things are looking up!' Tommy said.

*

The Doctor emerged from the darkness into a narrow corridor. Sarah was chained to a post at the other end of the corridor. She was dressed in a green velvet trouser suit with a white shirt. A Xhinn was hovering over her, its arm raised and pulsing with energy, ready to fire at her.

'Sarah! What are you doing here?' the Doctor asked. He began running towards her.

'They captured me! They – they're going to k-kill me!'

The Doctor stopped abruptly.

'Doctor! What are you doing? Help me!' Sarah pleaded.

'How do I know you're really Sarah, and not an illusion?' he asked thoughtfully. The Doctor closed his eyes and concentrated.

'Doctor, please! It's going to fire! Please!' The Xhinn blasted an energy beam through Sarah, who died screaming in agony. Once her cries had finished echoing in the corridor, the Doctor opened his eyes again.

Sarah and the chains were gone. Only the Xhinn remained, now aiming its arm at the Doctor. He smiled at it.

'That's very good. Plucking an image of someone dear to me from my memories and then giving it form and reality. I presume you scanned my mind while I was unconscious. But you made one mistake – her clothes. Sarah wears dresses in 1952.'

The Xhinn floated towards him, its arm pulsing with ever increasing energy. The Doctor refused to be frightened. 'Now, I think I have taken enough of your tests. I want to meet with the triumvirate!'

The real Sarah hammered on the door of 15 Tabernacle Street. She kept glancing over her shoulder, convinced she could still hear the police constable running after her. Mrs Ramsey opened the front door and Sarah fell inside, coughing and gasping for breath.

'Oh, my dear, you look parched. Would you—'

'Tommy – I need to see Tommy.'

'Thomas is upstairs in the dining room,' Mrs Ramsey said. Sarah took off her coat and scarf in the hallway before running up the stairs. She burst into the dining room, startling Tommy and Jack. They were just sitting down to lunch. Tommy threw his fork on the table in disgust.

'Where the hell have you been? I told Brick to make sure you stayed here today. The meeting's already over!'

Sarah collapsed into a chair, out of breath. Tommy poured her a glass of water from a pitcher on the table. She gulped the liquid down before relating what had happened to her. 'The police are evacuating people, but there's something wrong. It's as if somebody is controlling the police, like pulling the strings of a puppet!'

'The monster,' Tommy stated, matter-of-factly.

'You think so?' Jack asked.

'It's all too much of a coincidence – that thing yesterday, then the smog coming down, now this with the police. The creature is making a move for the East End – maybe for the whole of London!'

'What are we going to do?' Sarah asked.

'Any of the Old Bill come round here trying to evacuate us, they've got a shock in store. Nobody gets the better of Tommy Ramsey – nobody!'

'What about the people being evacuated?'

Tommy thought long and hard before replying. 'Right now, I ain't got the men or the firepower to take on all the Old Bill at once. By tomorrow morning I could have two or three times as many men, if the other firms come on board. For now, we just have to wait.'

Sarah was furious. 'I thought you were supposed to be the

East End's protector? I don't see you protecting anybody but yourself!'

Tommy grabbed her by the throat and threw her against a wall. 'Shut your mouth! Shut it!' He let go of Sarah, who slid down to the floor coughing. 'I've put up with a lot from you – but don't think you can take liberties! I decide when I'm ready to strike back, not some girl!'

He stormed out of the room, following by a grinning Jack. Sarah rubbed a hand around her neck ruefully. She wondered how the Doctor was doing in his efforts to persuade the Xhinn to leave. Right now, there didn't seem much hope of anybody else saving the day…

Rose and Frank Kelly were huddled in a corner. They had been herded into this empty room along with everyone else offloaded from the vans. That had been nearly a hundred people, leaving space and privacy at a premium. The police said they would soon be moved on to a safer place and apologised for the overcrowding. Not long after another flood of evacuees were being driven into the room, followed by a third wave. The room had no ventilation, no windows and nowhere to stand. If any more people were added, the crush would begin to suffocate those already trapped inside.

'I don't like this, Frank,' Rose said, biting back tears. 'There's too many people in here. Why are there so many people?'

'I don't know, love, I don't know.' He hugged her closer, but that just pushed them closer against the wall. Frank could feel his ribs bending under the pressure of the crowd pressing against him. 'Somebody open a door, for the love of God! My wife's suffocating over here!' he shouted.

But the only response was a hissing noise above them. A panel opened high in a wall and a walkway extended across the room. But it was far too high for any in the crush to reach.

One man clambered onto the shoulders of others and made a desperate leap upwards. He missed the edge of the walkway and fell back to the floor, toppling several people. The crowd collapsed inwards on the fallen, crushing them underfoot.

Frank put his hands over Rose's ears to block out the screams of pain. 'It'll all be over soon, love,' he said soothingly. 'You'll see.'

High above them the Xhinn floated forwards along the walkway, followed by the Doctor. He looked down with horror at the crush below. 'You're killing those poor people! What possible reason could you have?' he demanded.

'We are testing them,' the creature replied, projecting its words directly into the Doctor's mind. 'How else could we decide whether this species is worthy of being offered the salvation the Xhinn brings? They could also make a basic foodstuff, once the bodies have been sufficiently rendered down.'

Voices cried out in agony and anguish from below. The Doctor forced himself to look at the faces, trying to remember each and every one. Nobody deserved to die like that, but at least they could be remembered. 'That does not excuse such barbarity. Why, it's—'

'Inhuman? You forget – we are not human. Neither are you. What do you care for the fate of a few hundred savages from a backwards species?'

'Life is life. Just because a sentient being does not match your own, that does not permit you to torture and kill.'

'We would hardly call these creatures sentient.' The Xhinn moved onwards, already leaving the chamber behind. 'Besides, there are plenty more where they came from. This whole planet seems to be swarming with them.'

The Doctor closed his eyes. 'How many more must die?' he

whispered to himself before following the Xhinn. 'How many more?'

Rose died first, her breathing stopped but her eyes stared glassily up at Frank. He was glad she was out of pain now. He had caused her so much in their time together. He had been no sort of husband to her. Rose had deserved better than him. But at least she was out of pain now.

Frank threw back his head and gave a last, agonised scream as the crush snapped his ribs one by one. He felt the breath leaving his body and then a warmth flowed over him, gentle and giving like a lover's embrace. He surrendered himself, his arms still holding the only person he had ever loved…

Sarah found Brick up on the roof. He was wrapping little hoods of hessian around the heads of his pigeons. Before putting each hood on, he poured a drop of whisky over the fabric.

'What are you doing?' Sarah asked quietly.

'They're dying. They can't breathe,' Brick replied, tears streaming down his face. 'I thought if I gave them sort of gas masks, it might help. The fumes from the alcohol might keep out the worst of the smog.'

Around him the roof was littered with the bodies of his dead pigeons. A few still fluttered their wings feebly, but most were already gone.

'I tried to set them free earlier. Once I realised the weather was only going to get worse, I tried to set them free.' Brick couldn't bring himself to look at her. 'But they just kept coming back. They couldn't fly any more. Couldn't breathe, I suppose.'

Sarah hugged the mountain of a man, his huge body racked with sobbing. 'I'm sorry, Arthur. I'm so sorry.'

*

The white Rolls Royce was creeping along Old Street, only travelling at a few miles an hour. The driver had been forced to open his window to lean out to see. The windscreen wipers had seized up from the strain of trying to keep the front window clear. Steve MacManus shook his head angrily.

'I must have been mad to come out in this weather,' he fumed. A familiar face loomed out of the smog by the gangster's side window. He called to the driver to stop, then opened his door. Detective Bob Valentine got into the car.

'Hello, hello, hello – there's a policeman in my roller!' MacManus exclaimed, laughing at his own joke. The two bodyguards laughed along dutifully, but the crumpled detective did not smile. 'What's wrong – lost your sense of humour?'

Valentine just stared at him.

MacManus stopped grinning. 'I've been paying you plenty to feed Tommy Ramsey false information. Now it's time you gave me some true facts. What's he really up to? He gave me some story about killer creatures that shoot lightning out their arms. I don't believe a word of it. So why don't you tell me what's really going on?'

Valentine smiled. 'You want to know what's really going on?' The detective pulled a pistol from his pocket and shot both the bodyguards in the face. Blood sprayed across the shocked face of Steve MacManus. The driver struggled to pull a gun from inside his jacket. Valentine turned and shot the driver through the head. Then he trained the pistol at the gangster.

'Now who's lost their sense of humour?'

At St Luke's Church, Father Simmons had been praying for guidance. After more than an hour on his knees in front of the altar, inspiration struck. He painfully got to his feet and went to the telephone in the sacristy. He dialled the number for one of his parishioners.

'Mrs Potter? It's Father Simmons at St Luke's. I'm calling around all the most influential members of my congregation.' He really meant those with the biggest talents for gossiping, but all talents had their uses. 'I'm holding a special service tomorrow morning, to pray for relief from this terrible smog.'

He listened to several minutes of impassioned anecdotes about the effects of the weather, before politely interrupting. 'I know, it is shocking. I was wondering if you could help me spread the good word. The service will start here in the church tomorrow at ten o'clock.'

It took him another five minutes to end the conversation and start his next call. At this rate, Father Simmons was worried that he might still be calling people when the service was due to begin tomorrow!

'Now, what's this all about, Bob?' Steve MacManus was using his friendliest voice, smiling at the detective opposite. The gangster was painfully aware of the blood still dribbling from the corpses of the two bodyguards on either side of him. Unless he played this very carefully, MacManus knew he could be joining them in the hereafter.

'Do you believe in Heaven?' Valentine asked.

'You what?'

'Heaven. Pearly gates. Playing the harp. Sitting on clouds. All of that.'

MacManus was worried now. Having a conversation about the afterlife with a man pointing a loaded pistol at you was never a good sign. 'I hadn't really thought about it.'

'Tsk, tsk – in your line of business? You should have done. But then, let's face it, you're going to be spending eternity in the other place, ain't you? Hard nuts roasting on an open fire,

Lucifer prodding you with his pitchfork.'

'Like I said, hadn't really thought about it.'

'That's a shame.' Valentine started laughing. 'You know what I find the funniest thing of all? The real rib-tickler?'

'No…'

'You thought you were controlling events. Getting Jack the Lad to run your errands, using me to send Tommy Ramsey jumping to all the wrong conclusions. You honestly believed you were the man.' The detective leaned forwards, careful to keep his pistol just out of MacManus's reach. 'You were well wrong. And all those times you humiliated me, all those times you treated me like I was nothing, like I was less than nothing… Well, now they're all coming back to haunt you, ain't they? Goodbye, Steve.' Valentine shot his remaining bullets into the gangster. 'See you in hell.'

Soon after Frank Kelly died, small grates appeared high in the walls of the chamber. Yellow gas tumbled downwards on to the survivors, stealing the final breaths from their twisted bodies. Everyone was dead within moments.

The doorway reopened and expressionless policemen began to drag the corpses out, one by one. They put each body onto a conveyor belt outside the doorway. Once on the belt, the corpses rumbled away into darkness.

Elsewhere inside the Xhinn vessel, the Doctor was standing amidst the triumvirate. The three creatures floated around him in their random patterns, but each examined the visitor with remorseless intensity. The Doctor returned their gaze with interest, refusing to follow them with his eyes. Instead he stared at each member of the triumvirate as they passed him.

'Why have you come to this world?' he demanded.

'To analyse.'

'To investigate.'

'To decide.'

'Decide what?' the Doctor asked.

'If it is ripe.'

'Ready for colonisation.'

'Ready for the Xhinn.'

'But surely Earth can be of no strategic importance to the Xhinn?'

'It has resources.'

'A wealth of resources.'

'It will be a valuable asset.'

'Your experiments – how can you justify such horrors?'

'We need not justify.'

'We are the triumvirate.'

'We are the Xhinn.'

'You are avoiding my question,' the Doctor replied, exasperated. He found talking with this three-voiced entity hard work. Time to try another line of attack. 'You are a scouting force?'

'We are missionaries.'

'We are sent to educate these primitives.'

'If they will not learn, they will be swept aside.'

'So, if everyone on Earth embraced the ways of the Xhinn, they could all live happily ever after?'

'We do not care for their happiness.'

'We want their obedience.'

'We expect their worship.'

'Mankind should worship at the feet of the mighty Xhinn, is that it? And when's all this supposed to happen? You like to consider yourselves omniscient, but you didn't predict the need to accelerate your plans, did you?'

'Unfortunate.'

'But nothing more.'

'Soon more Xhinnships shall arrive.'

'How soon?' the Doctor asked.

'When this world has circled its star fifty times.'

'Then shall the Xhinn arrive.'

'Then shall the great work truly begin.'

'What if the people of Earth refuse to accept the ways of the Xhinn? Humans can be a delightfully stubborn species, as I'm sure you've already discovered. What then?'

'They are stubborn.'

'But they are fragile.'

'You saw the testing.'

The Doctor was furious. 'What you are doing is wrong!'

'We have studied the history of this species.'

'For centuries they have colonised this world.'

'They have subjugated and exterminated their own kind.'

'All in the name of civilisation.'

'All in the name of progress.'

'All in the name of their gods.'

'We do unto them as they do to themselves.'

'How can that be wrong?'

'But they have learned! They have changed! What's your excuse?' the Doctor demanded.

'We need no excuse.'

'We are the Xhinn.'

'We are the future of this world.'

Sarah and Tommy bumped into each other on the staircase, her coming down from the roof, him coming up from the kitchen. They stared at each other, neither refusing to give way. Finally, Tommy broke into a smile.

'Sums up our relationship. You're too stubborn to give way...' he said.

'And you're too stubborn to admit when you're wrong,'

Sarah replied.

'Speak for yourself!'

'I always do.' Sarah couldn't help but smile. For all his violence and fury, there was something infectious about Tommy. Just a shame he showed it so rarely. 'Look, I want to go over the road and visit Mary Mills. One of her daughters is sick from the smog.'

Tommy stepped aside to let Sarah past. 'Be careful.'

Across the road Mary was getting ever more concerned about Bette. Her youngest daughter's breathing was just a shallow wheeze now. Bette had always been a sickly child. She was born prematurely and never completely recovered. Every illness going around seemed to strike her down first and worst. The smog was going to be the death of her.

There was a knock at the door. Jean opened it, leaving her mother to care for Bette in front of the fireplace. 'There's a woman here to see you, Mum. Says her name's Sarah.'

'Let her in and close the bloody door, Jean!'

The eldest daughter came back into the front room, followed by Sarah. The visitor looked with concern around the room. The smog was seeping in through the gaps between the wooden frames of the sash windows. A film of grey moisture coated nearly every surface. The air was dank and sour, despite the blazing fire in the grate.

'How is she?'

'Dying. Can't hardly take a breath.' Mary looked up pleadingly. 'Can't somebody do something?'

Sarah just shook her head. 'The ambulances can't get through. The hospitals will be overflowing with cases like this. I wish there was something I could do…'

'You can,' Mary replied. 'Stay with us until… until it's over.'

Sarah nodded. She sat on the floor beside the distraught

woman and held her hand. It was the least she could do.

The Doctor decided that debating the nature of right and wrong was getting him nowhere. He had to use the only language the Xhinn understood – threats.

'I didn't want to have to resort to your methods. I thought we could resolve this peacefully. I see now that you are intent on destroying this world and all its species. So let me say this: I am sworn to protect this planet and its people. If you continue on this course of action, I will have no alternative but to destroy you all. You may consider this a first and final warning.'

There was a curious noise in his mind, like metal rasping against metal. The Doctor realised it was the Xhinn expressing mirth.

'You warn us?'

'You would destroy us?'

'How?'

'I am not of this world,' the Doctor said, 'but I have saved it before and, no doubt, I shall save it again.'

'We know you are alien.'

'We sensed your presence.'

'That is why we permitted this meeting.'

'That is why we tested you.'

'The room without a door.'

'The illusion.'

'The killing chamber.'

'You murdered those people – just to test me?' the Doctor asked. 'Why?'

'To see where your allegiances would be.'

'To test your attitude to these primitives.'

'Who are you?'

'I am the Doctor, a Time Lord from the planet Gallifrey. My

own people are a highly advanced and powerful force for good in the galaxy. The Xhinn would do well not to risk our wrath.'

'We know of the Time Lords.'

'It is true about your technological advancement.'

'But your species is weak, impotent, unwilling to intervene.'

'You present no threat to the Xhinn.'

'In time your world shall be as this one – a colony of the Xhinn.'

'Never! I will stop you, using any means necessary!' the Doctor pledged. 'I have a weapon that can destroy you all. Withdraw from this world or I shall unleash this nemesis.'

'You lie.'

'You cannot deceive the Xhinn.'

'You have no such weapon, or you would have used it already.'

The Doctor smiled bleakly. 'That's the difference between us. I give you a chance to leave. You simply destroy to get your way. The Xhinn like to think of themselves as missionaries, colonists, a noble species bringing civilisation to primitives. In fact you're just thieves and murderers, plundering and pillaging your way across the galaxy.' He looked down his nose haughtily at the circling triumvirate. 'You deserve no pity and you will have none from me.'

'Bravado.'

'Deception.'

'Self-delusion.'

The Xhinn all pointed at the Doctor simultaneously. His limbs became heavy as lead, unable to move. He strained just to stay standing but the pressure proved too much, forcing him downwards into a crouch. He pressed a hand to his chest, his face ashen.

'My hearts!'

*

Elsewhere in the Xhinn vessel, PC Hodge was stripping the clothes from bodies as they passed him on the conveyor belt. Further along the corpses fell into a vast vat, the contents a steaming red liquid from which a few limbs protruded. The area was rotten with the stench of death and cooking flesh.

Hodge looked down as the bodies of Rose and Frank Kelly reached him on the conveyor belt. In the jumble of corpses, they had been thrown back together. It was almost as if they were holding hands.

The young policeman's face remained impassive but a single tear rolled down his cheek. His eyes stared helplessly at the murdered couple.

The Xhinn were toying with the Doctor, firing low-intensity energy bolts into his writhing body. He twisted and rolled, trying to escape their torture. But the situation was hopeless. He was caught, at the mercy of the triumvirate.

'Tell us about this weapon.'

'Tell us all you know.'

'Tell us!'

'Never! I would rather die than help the likes of you,' he replied.

'A noble self-sacrifice.'

'We have encountered your kind before.'

'Martyrs in the making.'

'If you are a Time Lord, death can hold no terrors.'

'You will regenerate.'

'We could kill you again and again and again.'

'Perhaps you would prefer to go back to the killing chamber.'

'We have hundreds more captives to test.'

'You can witness their death throes.'

'Would that be more to your liking?'

The Xhinn halted the torture, giving the Doctor a brief

respite in which to answer. 'No. No more killing.'

'Your logic is flawed.'

'You ask for the killing to cease.'

'Yet you would kill the Xhinn.'

The Doctor got to his feet again. 'All right. You win. How can I help you?'

It was dusk by the time Bette Mills finally died, her gasps for breath slowly fading to nothing. Mary pulled the blanket up over her daughter's lifeless face. Jean and Rita were sobbing in a corner, the elder girl trying to comfort her inconsolable sister. Sarah got up and turned on the overhead light.

'Sun's gone down, though you'd hardly know it in this weather,' she said. 'This smog – it's killing thousands of people.'

'I don't care about thousands of people!' Mary spat angrily. 'I care about my daughter! Who's going to bring her back?' She threw herself over the body, hugging her youngest child.

Sarah felt hollow inside. When she had first read about the deaths of thousands of Londoners, it had seemed like a mystery to solve, an intriguing adventure to lure the Doctor from his inactivity. That idea seemed trivial and unworthy now. The people who died – they were just an abstract statistic, a number on a page. It was hard to care about someone dying if you had never known them, never shared their hopes and dreams and aspirations.

But the death of this child made it all too real for Sarah. She knew this grim reality was being repeated across London. She had read all the reports, her dispassionate journalistic attitude keeping her at arm's length from the horror and the tragedy of it. Not any more, she vowed. Something had to be done, somebody had to stop this killing mist and its murderous instigators.

Sarah approached Mary, pulling the distraught mother away from her dead child. 'Mary, you've got to listen to me. Mary!'

The grieving woman looked up. 'Yes, Sarah – what is it?'

'I've got to go now. I have a friend, he may be able to stop this smog. He says he can and I believe him. I've got to help him, however I can.'

Mary nodded.

'The police are evacuating residents from the East End,' Sarah continued. 'They say it's for your protection, to take you away from the smog. Whatever you do, don't go with them!'

'Why not?'

'The police – I think they are being controlled by some other force. I saw them beating an old man who wouldn't leave his home. There's something very wrong happening. So whatever you do, don't let them in.' Sarah shook Mary to get her attention. 'Do you understand me?'

'Yes, I understand.' Mary beckoned her two surviving daughters over and hugged them both. 'Bette's gone, but I've still got these two. Don't worry – the police won't get them.'

Sarah smiled. 'Goodbye, Mary.'

'Goodbye, Sarah. And good luck.'

'To us all.' Sarah walked out of the house, closing the door carefully behind her. Only after she was outside did the tears come.

The Doctor listened to the demands of the Xhinn triumvirate.

'You will tell us the truth.'

'Are you a Time Lord?'

'Yes,' he replied.

'You travel in space and time?'

'Yes.'

'How? The Xhinn would value such technology.'

169

'So you can plunder the past and future, as well as the present? Do you believe I would willingly give you such capability?'

'You said you would help us.'

'Give us this and we would spare this world.'

'The Xhinn will abandon all plans for its colonisation.'

'How do I know I can trust you?' the Doctor asked.

'You have no choice.'

'You must believe in the Xhinn.'

'You must believe.'

'All right, I agree to your terms,' the Doctor said. 'My time ship is not far from your own vessel. I will take one of the triumvirate with me to see it.'

The three Xhinn consulted silently before nodding their agreement. One of them broke from formation and floated down to hover by the Doctor. 'Prepare yourself for matter transmission. Many species find this unpleasant.'

'I've had quite enough of being scrambled by your transmat systems for one day.' The Doctor folded his arms stubbornly. 'I will walk out of here. You can show me the way. Lead on!'

The Xhinn hovered indecisively then moved off into the darkness, its pulsating blue energy illuminating a path for the Doctor. He followed the creature as it left the vast chamber.

Hodge was still stripping clothes from corpses when he noticed a familiar face standing beside him. It was Sergeant Diggle, who had inserted himself into the line of policemen working at the conveyor belt.

'Hodge! Can you hear me? If you can, don't look around. Just nod.'

The constable gave an almost imperceptible nod of his head.

'Good. I don't know what this horror show is, but I came

to my senses a few minutes ago. I think our minds were being controlled, but whatever is doing it has been distracted by something. God only knows what we've been doing. I can't seem to remember,' Diggle whispered.

'I can,' Hodge said. 'I just wish I couldn't.'

The sergeant leaned a little closer. 'Me and some of the lads are going to try and break out of here. Are you with us?'

'Yes!'

'We go in two minutes. Be ready. We don't know where we are or how to get out, but we're damn well going to try.'

'I'd rather die trying to escape than stay here, doing this,' Hodge said.

'Good lad. Watch for my signal.' The sergeant shuffled away, moving further along the conveyor belt.

All through their conversation Hodge had continued to work, tearing the clothes off the bodies passing in front of him. He closed his eyes, trying to block out the sickening scene passing before him.

The Doctor tried to make conversation while the Xhinn led him through its vessel. They were getting closer to the surface. The Doctor could feel the acrid stench of the smog growing stronger in the air. 'So, whatever happened to Callum? I imagine he caused you a few problems with that little display in front of the church.'

'That advance scout was neutralised. All energy and knowledge were reabsorbed into the triumvirate.'

'Yes, I noticed the energy spike. Hardly inconspicuous, was it? Must have put quite a kink in your master plan.'

'The missionary work continues. When the rest of the Xhinnships arrive, this world shall be joined with our quest.'

'Ah, yes, the divine journey of the mighty Xhinn. But where is it all going? Where does it lead? Or are you just doing what you've always done? What is the purpose of it all?' the Doctor asked. Ahead he could see the tunnel leading to the surface. Smog billowed down from above into the vessel.

The Xhinn gestured at a group of policemen approaching from one side. 'Already our subjugation of this species is well advanced. A simple chemical solution controls their actions. They do our bidding so easily.'

The Doctor looked at the policemen. He had seen other groups moving around the vessel, but those were like puppets, jerkily moving to the command of unseen controllers. This group seemed far more purposeful. 'Really? I do think you may be mistaken about that, old man.'

The policemen began running at the Xhinn. The group of twenty men were screaming and yelling, their faces riven with hatred. The leader had the insignia of a sergeant on his uniform.

'Damn you, monsters! Damn you for using us!' Sergeant Diggle threw himself at the Xhinn. The alien was so surprised it did not have time to power up its killing arm. The policeman knocked the creature to the ground and began flailing at it with his fists. 'They can fall! They can be beaten!'

The rest of the mob joined Diggle in attacking the Xhinn. The Doctor knew this was his chance. He joined the policemen, striking at the Xhinn with the deadliest blows known in Venusian Aiki-Do. But the element of surprise passed in seconds and the Xhinn recovered enough to start blasting at the men.

Diggle died first, projected up into the air by a bolt of blue energy. He twisted and screamed in its grasp before blinking out of existence. More and more of the policemen were forced back by the Xhinn weapon.

The Doctor yelled for the others to follow him and ran towards the exit. But they could not hear him over their own shouting and cries of anguish. As he reached the foot of the tunnel, the Doctor looked back. There was nothing more he could do for these unwilling slaves of the Xhinn.

He had to escape if Earth was to have any chance against this remorseless alien enemy.

The Xhinn floated back up into the air, out of its attackers' reach. The surviving policemen cowered before its presence, Hodge among them. He prayed for death but it had eluded him. Instead he felt the chill grip of the Xhinn taking hold of his mind again.

'You shall suffer for this attack. Suffer!'

Sarah walked into the kitchen at 15 Tabernacle Street. Mrs Ramsey was cooking a huge pot of stew for Tommy and all his men. Sarah sank down into a chair and put her head in her hands.

'You all right, love? You look like you've seen a ghost,' Mrs Ramsey said, humming away happily to herself.

'Mary Mills, one of her daughters just died.'

'Oh, that's terrible! Still, those that stray from the path of the righteous shall suffer more than most.'

Sarah looked at the little old woman with shock. 'How can you say that? A child has just died because of this smog and you're saying it's God's will?'

'Well, Mary was always a little trollop. None of those children have been baptised you know. That poor little mite will rot in Hell now.' Mrs Ramsey said this as if she were discussing everyday subjects like the price of potatoes.

'That's not a very Christian attitude,' Sarah commented.

'But it's the truth, my dear. None of us can escape that.'

Sarah got up from her chair. 'I think I'll go upstairs, if you don't mind. I seem to have lost my taste for home-spun philosophy.'

'Well, if you say so,' Mrs Ramsey replied, unconcerned. She called up the stairs after Sarah. 'Father Simmons is holding a special service tomorrow to say prayers for this fog to lift. Could you take me along?'

She got no reply but the sound of Sarah's feet stamping furiously up the stairs. Mrs Ramsey went back to her stew. 'Oh well, have it your own way.'

The Doctor emerged from the tunnel, still running. He dug in his pockets and pulled out the small torch. Night had fallen and the smog was now thicker than ever. The Doctor stood silently, getting his bearings. He could still remember the path which had led him to the tunnel. Now he just had to retrace his steps. That would take him past St Luke's Church.

'Time to pay a visit to Father Simmons.'

Down inside the Xhinn vessel, Hodge and the surviving rebels had been returned to their grim tasks. Their bodies moved at the command of the captors, even though the policemen were willing themselves to resist. The constable remembered a scrap of prayer from his childhood, long forgotten but now dredged up from the depths of his memory.

'Forgive me, Father, for I have sinned.' He repeated it over and over again in his mind, his lips moving in time with his thoughts. It was the only way he could block out the reality of what he was doing. 'Forgive me, Father, for I have sinned. Forgive me, Father, for I have sinned…'

The triumvirate was reformed now the third Xhinn had returned to their chamber. It reported the attack by the prisoners and the Doctor's escape.

'He is of no importance.'

'A man of empty threats.'

'His mind betrayed his fear.'

'He will return when he has no choice.'

'He will return, and his time machine shall be ours.'

'And the weapon?'

'Untested, untried.'

'No danger to the Xhinn.'

'The quest continues!'

Tommy phoned his last surviving lieutenant. Norman Page had been waiting at home all day for the call and said so. He was never a man to mince words.

'Where the hell have you been, Tommy? Do you know what's happening on the streets?'

'Yeah, the Old Bill is dragging people away in Black Marias. Any idea where they're being taken?'

'I had one of the lads follow them. Some underground tunnel north of Old Street. He said people went in but nobody came out.' Page was worried. It wasn't like Tommy to hold back from taking action. Usually the problem was quite the reverse. Tommy tended to jump in boots first and ask questions afterwards. 'Maybe they're being taken out of the city on the Tube. The underground was running this morning – it's about the only thing in London that still is!'

Tommy wasn't convinced. 'If they was using the Tube, they'd take them down the station. Stands to reason. No, this is something else – and I don't like it. Not one little bit.'

'So what are we going to do?'

'Sit tight for now.'

Norman could stand it no longer. 'You lost your bottle or something? That new bird of yours putting ideas into your head?'

'I'm gonna forget you said that. Tommy Ramsey takes orders from no one!' The gangster tried to keep calm. 'We can't do anything in darkness, it's bad enough trying to see in the daytime. We'll just end up hurting our own instead of striking back at whoever's responsible for all this.'

'So what's the plan?'

'Get everyone around here tomorrow morning, armed to the teeth. I'm expecting a call from Stratford Simon or Fingers Blake. If either of their firms joins us, we could have a hundred men.'

'And if they don't?'

'Then we go it alone. We're big enough and ugly enough to hand out some damage,' Tommy said.

'Go down fighting, you mean?'

'That's not my plan. But if I die tomorrow, I'm taking as many of these monsters with me as I can. They're going to rue the day they stepped on Tommy Ramsey's manor!'

The Doctor knocked on the door of St Luke's Church, glancing apprehensively around himself. He had expected the Xhinn to pursue him but there was no sign of that yet. His audience with the triumvirate had obviously distracted the Xhinn, weakening the grip of the aliens' mind control over its slaves. That gave the Doctor some hope. The Xhinn were a powerful enemy but this missionary force was limited in its capacity. It had not been designed to control a whole city, let alone an entire planet. There was still time to defeat the Xhinn, but the Doctor would need help if he were to succeed.

Father Simmons opened the door and let the Doctor in. 'What are you doing out there? You'll catch your death in that fog! Come inside, come inside!' The priest was holding a lit taper. 'You'll have to excuse me, I'm just lighting the gas lamps in the church. I want St Luke's to shine as a beacon of hope in these dark days.'

'Please, carry on,' the Doctor said. He watched as the priest moved around the church, touching the flame to the gas-fired lamps mounted on tall stone columns which reached upwards to the high ceiling. Around the outer walls were hung a dozen tapestries, depicting the journey of Jesus to his crucifixion. 'Don't you worry about having such valuable tapestries on the walls of the church?'

'St Luke's is lucky to have them. They were stolen during the war but were returned in 1946, I've been told. Tommy Ramsey apparently brought them back.'

'Hardly what I would expect from him. Mr Ramsey does not seem to be a very religious man.'

Father Simmons grinned at that. 'No, but his mother is a believer. I suspect she may have had something to do with their recovery and return. According to parish records, the tapestries have hung here since—'

'I'm sorry to interrupt you, but I didn't come here to talk about history. I came to ask for your help,' the Doctor said.

'I am just a simple parish priest. But I do all I can to aid this community. How can I help you?'

'Many people will die in the coming days. Many have died already.'

'The smog. It's a terrible tragedy but the Saviour moves in mysterious ways. I don't see how I can—'

'The smog is not a natural event. It is being caused by the Xhinn.'

'That creature we saw yesterday? The fallen angel?' Simmons blew out his taper and sat in a pew beside the Doctor. 'But how can one such sinner create such a foul cloud over all of London?'

'There is more than one Xhinn. They have come to bring their own gospel to this world. But it is a gospel of death and destruction, glorying in its own righteousness,' the Doctor said, explaining himself in terms that the priest might best be able to grasp.

'They worship a false god!'

'Something like that. Unless I intervene, millions of people will die. But if I act, I must be willing to sacrifice everything and everyone I hold dear. I must be willing to become like the Xhinn to stop them.'

The priest thought long and hard about the Doctor's words. 'I killed once. I murdered a man. Not for any cause, not to stop tyranny or prevent a war. Just for my own gain, just for my own benefit. I was like the Xhinn then – but I changed. I saw the error of my ways. I have devoted the rest of my life to seeking redemption for that moment, by doing the Saviour's work.' Father Simmons looked intently at the Doctor. 'Do you believe what you are doing is right?'

'Yes.'

'Do you believe this evil must be stopped?'

'Yes.'

'Then you must look to your own conscience to decide. All it requires for evil to triumph—'

'Is that good men do nothing,' the Doctor replied, completing the quotation. 'A simplistic notion but not without its own truth.' He was interrupted by a bleeping noise in his pocket. The Doctor took out his tracking device. The screen was pulsing to indicate the presence of the Xhinn.

'What does that mean?' the priest asked.

'The Xhinn are close. I have to get back to my laboratory.' The Doctor stood up to leave, putting the tracker back in his pocket.

'You look for the answer there, Doctor – I will pray to the Saviour for guidance.' He showed his visitor to the door. 'You know, Albert Einstein once said that science without religion was like a cripple.'

'He also said religion without science is blind. Goodbye,

Father.' The Doctor disappeared into the cloud of smog.

'Goodbye, Doctor,' the priest replied.

Sarah was listening to the BBC World Service in the parlour at 15 Tabernacle Street. The smog was mentioned during the weather report but its terrible effects hardly rated a mention otherwise. There were no official warnings for Londoners to stay off the streets or take any precautions. The evacuation of East End residents was not announced, even though Sarah had been listening for more than an hour. She switched off the radio as Brick came into the room.

'No mention of the evacuation on—' Sarah began, but stopped when she saw the look on his face. 'Arthur, what's wrong?'

'Dead. They're all dead,' he said quietly. 'I tried to save them, I did. But it was no use. No use at all…'

'There was nothing you could do.'

'I know. Doesn't make it any easier.' He wiped at his eyes and took a deep breath. 'Mrs Ramsey says dinner will be ready in five minutes.'

'Thank you, Arthur.' Sarah smiled at him, trying to raise his spirits.

'You know, you and Mrs Ramsey are the only two who call me by my proper name. The only two.'

'It's no more than you deserve. You've got a big heart.'

Brick almost managed a smile. 'You need it when you're my size.'

Father Simmons stood before the altar, thinking about what the Doctor had told him. Could it be true? Were thousands of people dying all around him? What was he doing to stop the tragedy? Faith could be a great comfort, but too great a faith could make you blind to reality. Had that happened to him?

179

The priest dropped to his knees and began to pray.

'Saviour, you came to me six years ago and showed me another way. Guide me now that I may know your will. Tell me what you would have me do!'

Simmons listened, reaching out with his senses, straining to feel again the incredible light and warmth of the Saviour's love. His god would never desert him in this hour of need – would it?

The Doctor opened the TARDIS door with his key and hurried inside. All the way from St Luke's Church he had been tensed, ready to run if the Xhinn appeared. It was vital that he have the time to prepare for a final confrontation.

In the control room he checked the atmospheric display. The needle was nearly through the amber and moving ever nearer the deadly red zone. One more day, maybe less, and London's air would be pure poison. The Doctor began sorting through the scattered circuits and wiring strewn across the central console. He would have to work through the night to have a chance of constructing his terrible weapon. He hoped against hope he would not have to use it…

Dinner in the Ramsey household was turning into a disaster. Vera had cooked up a storm but hardly anyone was touching their food. Brick stared listlessly at his plate, Sarah couldn't stop thinking about Mary Mills and her daughters, while Tommy's mind was obviously elsewhere. Only Billy and Charlie tucked into their food with gusto, oblivious to the mixture of emotions around the table. Mrs Ramsey tried unsuccessfully to tempt Sarah with a slice of buttered bread.

'Are you sure you wouldn't like a piece?'

'No, thank you Vera. I don't seem to have any appetite.' Sarah pushed her plate away. After Mrs Ramsey's diatribe earlier, Sarah was finding it very difficult to stomach the old woman's kindness. How could somebody be so nice yet cling to such outdated attitudes? Sarah tried to remind herself that Mrs Ramsey's attitude was still prevalent in this time and place.

Billy was first to spy the food going begging. 'I'll have your dinner!' He caught a vicious glare from Tommy at the other end of the dinner table. 'That's if nobody else minds.' After allowing a few seconds for others to speak up, Billy divided the spoils with his brother. Mrs Ramsey smiled contentedly.

'Does my heart good to see two growing lads enjoying their food.' She was less impressed with Tommy's fidgeting. 'I don't know what's got into the rest of you. That's good home cooking you're letting go to waste.'

Tommy got up from his chair and began pacing the room, like a caged tiger in a zoo. He lit a cigarette, decided he didn't want it and threw the unsmoked cigarette into the fireplace. His mother soon tired of the agitation.

'For goodness' sake, sit down, Thomas! Some people are still trying to eat, you know.'

Tommy almost shouted at his mother but thought better of it. 'I'm going to the front room, if that's all right with everyone.' He stormed out.

Mrs Ramsey turned her attention to Brick. 'What about you, Arthur. You've hardly touched your dinner.'

Brick looked bashful. 'I'm sorry, Mrs Ramsey. I'm just not very hungry.'

She patted him on the shoulder. 'That's all right, dear. Just finish what you can. Growing boy like you needs his strength.'

Sarah could stand it no more and followed Tommy into the front room. He was standing by the window, looking outside. A single lamp light was just visible but the street below was hidden by smog and darkness.

'You were right,' Tommy admitted. 'I should be out there, fighting for my people – not waiting for others to decide whether they will help me.'

'You were right too,' Sarah replied. 'You've got to pick the right battles to fight. Otherwise, everybody could lose.'

'I can't see us winning tomorrow. The creatures are holding all the cards – the smog, the Old Bill, those death rays. What have we got? Two dozen men at most and some shooters. Might as well be pea-shooters for all the good they did against that monster.' Tommy rubbed the stubble on his chin. 'But if we're going down, we're going down fighting. Better to die on your feet than live on your knees.'

Sarah felt she could almost have been attracted to Tommy – in another life, at another time and place. When he was vulnerable, he revealed a little of his inner self, the strength that drove him on and the genuine concern he held for this community. 'You could do with a shave,' Sarah said. 'How long is it since you slept?'

'Can't remember. Two nights, maybe three. Never been able to sleep well. My brain won't shut up. It keeps going over all the things I've got to do, like I've got to cram two lifetimes into every day.' Tommy closed the curtain and sat down in an armchair. He tapped a cigarette out of its packet and lit it. 'I always thought I'd die young, like my dad. He was younger than me when he copped it in the First World War.'

Sarah sat down opposite him. 'You thought of having a family yourself?'

Tommy smiled. 'The lads are my family, I suppose. It's hard to find the right woman in my line of work, know what I mean? Someone who understands—'

'But doesn't interfere?'

'Something like that. Most women are either terrified of me, or out for me money. You don't find many happily

182

married gangsters. Doesn't go with the territory. Guess I'm married to the firm.' Tommy looked at Sarah. 'You ask a lot of questions. Who are you really?'

'I told you – Sarah Jane Smith.'

'Oh I don't doubt that. But I'm no mug. I'm good at reading people, Sarah. That's what makes me the boss. I can tell when a man is lying or frightened or ready to die or ready to kill. I can inspire men, lead them to do things they'd never consider by themselves. I can get the best out of people – and the worst.' Tommy stubbed out his cigarette. 'But you're different. Your attitude, your confidence – it's like you know things a person shouldn't have a right to know. Who are you really?'

'If I told you, you wouldn't believe me.'

'Try me. After what I seen in the last two days, I'd believe anything.'

'All right.' Sarah got up and began pacing back and forth across the floor rug. 'I'm not a waitress or a barmaid. I'm a journalist, a reporter – I usually write for a magazine called *Metropolitan*.'

'Never heard of it.'

'I'm not surprised. It won't be launched until 1967.'

'Hang on, you've lost me.'

Sarah stopped pacing and forced herself to trust Tommy could cope with the whole truth. 'I'm from the future – more than twenty years in the future. I've come here because of a mystery and a tragedy.'

'Keep going. I don't know if I believe a word of it, but keep going.'

Father Simmons had been praying for hours. At long last he reached a decision. He would go beyond the walls of the church and try to help those in suffering. He would seek the truth outside as well as in. The priest fetched a long coat and scarf from the sacristy before venturing out into the night. He had only walked for a few moments when he heard the screaming.

'Help us! Somebody help us!'

Father Simmons began running towards the cries. He stumbled and fell, but picked himself up again and ran on. The screaming receded into the smog. Then it started once more, but now seemed to come from another direction. The priest ran towards the noise but it faded from hearing.

'I've got to stand still. The smog is playing tricks with the noise. I must concentrate with all my senses,' Simmons told himself. He began a breathing exercise he had learnt in the seminary, taught to help eager students focus on their inner thoughts and prayers. He reached out with all his senses. Now the screams seemed more pronounced. They were coming straight towards him!

Suddenly he was caught in the headlights of an oncoming van. The priest threw himself out of the way. As the vehicle rumbled past, he could hear screaming men, women and children trapped in the back of the police van. They cried out to him for help as they began disappearing into the smog.

Simmons ran after them, desperate to keep the tail lights in view. Just as they were fading away, the lights dipped downwards. The priest followed them and found himself in a tunnel. It descended below the city streets. The van was now far ahead of him, further down the tunnel. He ran after it, gasping for breath, his right side aching from muscle twinges.

Sarah explained to Tommy about the smog and how it coincided with thousands of deaths across London, especially in the East End. 'There was a cover-up, a conspiracy to disguise what really happened here – what is happening now.'

'Let's say I believe you,' Tommy began, 'and I'm not saying

I do, but let's say I believe you. What's all this got to do with me?'

'I'm not sure, in all honesty. Your conflict with Callum seemed to be the trigger for events, but we didn't know that when we came here.'

'We? Who's this we? You mean you're not alone in this?'

Sarah bit her lip apprehensively. 'No. I sometimes help a man who investigates and fights against menaces like this. He travels through time in a machine called the TARDIS.'

'The what?'

'TARDIS. Look, the name isn't important. What does matter is the machine could bring us here, to this time, to stop these creatures – to stop the Xhinn.'

'So who's this mystery man?' Tommy's eyes flashed with inspiration. 'The Doctor! You came here with the Doctor!'

'Yes. How did you know?'

'The eyes. You can tell a lot by looking into a person's eyes. His were, well, different. And not many old-age watchmenders dare to take on the Ramsey Mob, let alone beat two of me best men!'

'I'm not sure the Doctor would like being called old, but you're right – he is a remarkable man.'

Tommy was still puzzled. 'But what's it got to do with me? How did you know to seek me out?' Sarah pulled the fateful photograph from her pocket. Tommy examined it with wonder. 'That's St Luke's in the background! What's happened to it?' he asked, pointing at the subtle ripples in the building's structure.

'Nothing – yet.'

Tommy handed the photograph back to her. 'Do you know what's going to happen?'

'No. That's what is so frustrating. The events of what happened during the smog are never spoken about in the future. It's like the entire city decided to forget it ever happened. Will happen. Is happening! Ohhh!' Sarah sat down, frustrated by her inability to keep past, present and future separated.

Tommy had a final question. 'Do you know what happens to me?'

'You survive long enough to appear in this photograph.'

'No, I mean – afterwards.'

Sarah shook her head. 'I won't be your fortune teller. I wouldn't want anybody telling me what was going to happen in my life. I don't think you do either.'

Tommy pondered what she had said. 'No, you're probably right. I could live to a ripe old age, or get knocked down by a bus next Tuesday. Why spoil the surprise?' He smiled. 'What will you do – after all this?'

'Depends. If we succeed, I'll go back to my own time with the Doctor. If we fail… Well, let's not think about that.'

'You could always stay here in 1952.'

'I don't belong here, Tommy. Life is very different in the future,' she replied. 'And no – before you even ask – I will not tell you how it's different.' He began to speak but she cut him off again. 'And I will not tell you who wins the next twenty Grand Nationals either!' Sarah folded her arms to show her determination.

Tommy started laughing at her.

'What's so funny?' Sarah demanded.

'I was just going to say that's the first time you've called me Tommy!'

'Oh,' she replied, a little embarrassed.

'Still, if you could just tell me who wins next year's Grand National, that would be a start…' he suggested with a twinkle in his eye.

'Don't you dare!'

*

186

Father Simmons finally reached the end of the tunnel. The van had long since moved out of sight, but he could still hear the screaming of its unwilling passengers. He followed the terrible noise through a series of wide corridors and chambers, before emerging into a vast room. Several empty vehicles stood by a high doorway. A being of light and darkness floated by the door, facing away from the priest.

Simmons could hear the people screaming for mercy beyond the high doorway. He ran towards it, shouting. 'Let them out! Let those poor people out!'

The Xhinn slowly rotated to face him, glaring malevolently with its hundred eyes. 'Who dares?'

The high doorway slid sideways to reveal the death chamber. Dozens of bodies were strewn about the floor, some still twitching as the last clouds of gas dissipated around them. Father Simmons tried dragging them out of the room but it was too late. They were all dead. He staggered out of the death chamber, choking on the poisonous fumes.

'Why? Why did you kill them?' he gasped.

The creature tilted its head, as if listening to another conversation. Nodding several times, it gestured at the priest. Father Simmons felt a churning disorientation in his stomach. White light surrounded him and he blinked out of existence, followed by the Xhinn.

Once they were gone, a long line of policemen shuffled forward, PC Hodge at the front of the queue. One by one, the slaves dragged the corpses out of the death chamber and onto the waiting conveyor belt.

Sarah was drinking a mug of hot cocoa that Tommy had made for her. They sat in the kitchen, enjoying the quiet of the house. Everyone else had gone to bed. 'What will you do?' she asked. 'Tomorrow, I mean – what then?'

'The lads are coming in the morning, armed to the teeth. Once we're all assembled, we start taking back the streets.'

'How?'

'Brute force, some native cunning – the usual methods,' Tommy replied, smiling.

'Your mother wants me to take her to St Luke's for a special service. Father Simmons is trying to gather the community together.'

'You go if you want, but you be careful. Me mum can look after herself. She may not look it, but there's a core of steel inside that little old lady.'

'I don't doubt it. She gave birth to you, didn't she?'

'That's enough of your cheek!' Tommy asked to see the photo again. 'It's weird this, like seeing a glimpse of the future.'

Sarah finished the last of her cocoa. She rinsed the mug in the sink and dried her hands. 'Well, goodnight, Tommy. I'll see you in the morning.'

'Goodnight, Sarah. Sleep well.'

She walked out of the kitchen and up the stairs to her bed. Tommy almost called out after her but bit back the words. He could almost have been attracted to her – in another life, at another time and place…

He stared down at the photograph until long after midnight.

In the TARDIS, the Doctor was staring with frustration at the bulky array of circuits, wires and switches he had assembled. What he needed was a power source and a trigger mechanism.

He patted the pockets of his velvet smoking jacket. The long cylindrical shape of his sonic screwdriver was still inside. He pulled the life-saving gadget out. It had helped him escape many a fate worse than death. He activated its mechanism, sending a pulse of sonic energy towards the assemblage. Lights and circuits inside it began to flicker into life, then faded away.

The Doctor smiled with satisfaction. He could jump-start the device with the sonic screwdriver. That meant he could arm it from a safe distance. But he still needed a power source.

The Doctor looked around him. An assortment of batteries and energy cells littered the floor of the console room, but none would be big enough to give the power necessary for the device. There was only one thing for it.

He patted the central console gently. 'Sorry old girl, but my need is greater than yours.' The Doctor dropped to the floor and opened an inspection hatch below the many-sided console. 'Try not to take it personally...'

Outside the TARDIS, a church clock chimed twelve, its bells ringing out dully The smog choking London continued to thicken, becoming ever more toxic. The pea-souper was turning the city's air into nerve gas...

Sunday, December 7, 1952

Father Simmons woke with a thumping headache. He felt like his insides had been removed, spun around several times and pulled back into his body. His whole being seemed to be dislocated, at odds with itself.

He opened his eyes and wondered if he had gone blind. Darkness surrounded him, total and enveloping. He touched the floor beneath his feet but all around was nothingness, a void. What was this place? Why had he been brought here? Then he remembered the room full of corpses and began to cry.

'You were right, Doctor – there is a tragedy at work here. A murderous, foul tragedy being perpetrated against mankind.' The darkness felt almost appropriate to the priest, now he thought about it. 'I have been blind, just like the Doctor said. Blind to what's been happening around me. Blind to everything but my own beliefs.' Simmons looked up into the darkness. 'My Saviour, my Saviour – why have you forsaken me?'

'We have not forsaken you.'

'We have always been with you.'

'We are you.'

The priest smiled, his tears forgotten. 'I knew you could

never desert me. I knew you would guide me in this hour of need?'

'Why have you come to us?'

'What do you seek?'

'Why are you here?'

'I'm sorry, Saviour, I don't understand – where am I?' Father Simmons looked around him but the darkness remained.

'Let there be light.'

A dazzling brilliance engulfed the priest from above, blazing down on him. It was just as he remembered from that fateful night, six years earlier. He had been standing over the dying man when this same light found him. The Saviour had sought him out, chosen him at that moment.

The priest dropped to his knees in adoration, clasping his hands together to offer up a prayer of thanksgiving. 'I worship you, my Saviour, I praise you. I worship you, my Saviour, I praise you. I am Xavier Simmons, your most faithful servant.'

'We know who you are.'

'Do you know who we are?'

'Do you?'

Simmons was confused. 'You are the Saviour. You speak with the voices of the Holy Trinity – three voices of the one true Saviour, indivisible and whole.'

The air became alive with crackling energy. The priest felt the hairs on the back of his neck stand up. It was happening again – just as it had happened six years ago. He was going to be in the presence of the Saviour.

A glowing figure emerged from the light. It floated down through the air, coming to rest just out of the priest's reach. Father Simmons couldn't bring himself to look at the figure, such was the brilliance surrounding it. He threw a hand in front of his eyes to shield them.

'Look at us.'

'Look around you.'

'Look upon the face of your Saviour.'

The priest lowered his hand, forcing himself to look up at the glowing figure. As he watched, the blaze of light around it grew fainter, allowing him to see the figure properly, to see the Saviour for the first time.

The face of the Saviour had a hundred eyes. The face of the Saviour had no mouth. The face of the Saviour was the face of the creature that had presided over the murdered people in the death chamber.

The face of the Saviour was the face of the Xhinn.

The Doctor woke with a start. He had been dozing in an antique chair he had dragged into the control room. He went to the central console and examined the time readings. It was nearly dawn on Sunday morning. The atmospheric monitor showed the air quality outside at near toxic levels. Unless the build-up of smog could be stopped today, London would be a dead city.

The Doctor strode into the interior of the TARDIS and returned a few seconds later clutching an old leather satchel. He carefully picked up a delicate mess of wiring and circuitry from beside the antique chair. It had taken him nearly twelve hours to complete the device but he hadn't had a chance to test it yet. Dozing off had cost him that opportunity. 'This body of mine must be getting old,' he murmured.

The Doctor slid the device into the satchel, closed the flap and slung the bag's carrying strap over his shoulder. He looked around the control room, which was littered with discarded equipment and rejected prototypes. He must do some spring cleaning when he got back. He thought about what lay ahead. If he got back.

The Doctor operated the TARDIS's entry mechanism. The

heavy outer door swung inwards and smog curled inside, insidious and cold. The Doctor strode out of the TARDIS, humming quietly to himself as he left.

'No! No, this can't be right. It's some kind of trick!' The priest was shocked and confused. The creature spoke with the voices of the Saviour, the same voices he had heard in his prayers and in his dreams. But it had the visage of that creature which killed the men outside the church, the fallen angel. The creature that had been gloating over the dead bodies…

'You're not the Saviour! The Saviour is wise, all-knowing. The Saviour wants to rescue mankind from its mistakes, to guide men to the promised land! The Saviour is a kind and benevolent god!'

The Xhinn made a crackling, otherworldly noise. Father Simmons realised they were laughing at him. 'You're not the Saviour. You are an impostor, pretending to be the one true Saviour.' The noise only grew louder. 'Stop laughing at me! Stop laughing!'

'You have become blind to the truth.'

'You have believed what you wanted to believe.'

'You have worshipped us as your god.'

The priest looked around. Three Xhinn floated about him now, each keeping an equal distance from the others. Their voices echoed inside his mind, cold and guttural. Their words scratched at his thoughts like cockroaches scrabbling over exposed flesh.

'You stand before the Xhinn triumvirate.'

'Three voices, one mind.'

'Indivisible.'

Father Simmons clamped his hands over his ears, trying to block out their words. But it was no use.

'We are your trinity.'

'We are your true god.'

'We are your Saviour.'

Simmons shook his head but could not deny the reality of what they said. It was true, every word. All this time he had been worshipping at the feet of a false god. 'Then everything I have done…'

'Has been at our bidding.'

'Has been of our choosing.'

'Has been for our good.'

'The charitable words, all the things I have done for the community…'

'We let you have some independence.'

'We let you have your beliefs.'

'But you were our agent.'

'What do you mean?' The priest searched back through his memories, trying to recall the moments of divine inspiration that had directed his energies. One such moment stood out from all others. 'No – not that. Don't tell me that was your bidding. Anything but that…'

The Doctor emerged from the TARDIS and locked the door behind him. He was grateful for his alien respiratory system, which helped filter out the worst of the smog. This vile cloud was designed to weaken and debilitate humans. It made him feel ill but the effects were far less than for the natives of Earth.

He turned into Old Street and began striding towards the Ramsey household. To get close enough to use the weapon inside the satchel, he would need help from Tommy's men.

The Xhinn would not take kindly to another unannounced visit from the Doctor.

As he walked east past St Luke's Church, the Doctor heard voices crying out for help from a side street. He went to the corner and peered along the tiny road. Policemen were herding people out of their houses and into the backs of black vans. Those who protested were beaten and then thrown inside the vehicles, dead or alive. Despite the savagery of the tactics, the faces of the police remained calm and impassive. Each of them just kept repeating the same words, over and over again.

The Doctor recognised mind control at work, he had seen its evil effects often enough. It created an army of slaves, acting out the will of their controller. They were just as much victims as the people they were attacking. The Xhinn had turned the police into a private army, using mankind's own protectors against the citizens. Like Sarah before him, he agonised about whether to intervene. He turned away, no longer able to watch the brutal evacuation. The Doctor knew he had to fight the source of this disease of cruelty, not the symptoms. But how were the Xhinn controlling the police?

The Doctor remembered the words proudly spoken by Father Simmons outside the smouldering ruins of Fixing Time, boasting about negotiating a contract to supply bread to the local police stations. The Doctor started running towards Tabernacle Street...

'My bread factory – giving jobs to local people. Selling the bread cheaply to those in poverty. Giving something back to the community – that was all a lie?' Father Simmons asked, hoping against hope for a negative response. The Xhinn did not fulfil that hope.

'A ruse, to spread our influence.'

'The bread contains a drug, a chemical.'

'It makes human minds susceptible to suggestions.'

'Our suggestions.'

'Our will.'

'Our ways.'

'The bread sent to police stations is especially strong.'

'It makes them our drones, our slaves.'

'They serve us, dead or alive.'

'For ever and ever.'

'Amen.'

The priest shook his head helplessly. 'I thought I was doing good. I believed I was helping people.'

'You were just another pawn.'

'Another of our agents.'

'Like Callum.'

Father Simmons wasn't listening to the triumvirate. 'You tricked me! You clouded my mind! I would never have done your bidding if I had known!'

'Yes you would.'

'You were our most loyal servant.'

'Callum was a mistake.'

'An error.'

'He wanted power.'

'Anarchy'

'Chaos.'

'He broke with the ways of the Xhinn.'

'He had to be punished.'

'Extinguished.'

'Erased.'

The three consulted silently before speaking to Simmons again.

'Would you make the same mistake?'

'You can still do our bidding.'

'Share in the glory of the Xhinn.'

The priest shook his head. 'Never! You manipulated me, had me manipulate others just to suit your purposes. I could never go back to your ways. I could never betray my people.'

'So be it.'

'There can be only one consequence.'

'Are you ready for that?'

Sarah got out of bed. She had slept badly, her mind fixated on questions for which she had no answers. Had she been right to tell Tommy the truth about herself and the Doctor? Probably. She believed Tommy still had an important part to play in this crisis, whatever it might be. Had he believed what she said? Perhaps. It was a lot for anyone to take in.

As she got dressed, Sarah remembered her first experience of time travel with the Doctor. She had stowed away in the TARDIS and found herself in medieval England. Of course, she hadn't believed it was medieval England. Why should she? It looked like any forest anywhere, at any time. Even when she had been taken to a castle, she still thought it was some sort of pageant or contemporary recreation of the past.

By comparison to her experience, Tommy seemed to take her wild and unlikely story in good faith. Of course, he had already seen an alien killer manifest itself in murderous mood on the streets of 1952 London. After that, a woman claiming to be a time traveller from the future probably seemed a perfectly reasonable proposition.

Sarah went down to the kitchen where Mrs Ramsey had just finished serving breakfast. 'I'm sorry, dear, would you like me to cook you something? We haven't got long before the service starts and I don't want to miss it.'

'That's OK, Vera. I'll just have a slice of toast while you get ready. Then we can walk over to the church together.'

'Right you are, love.'

Father Simmons stood in the midst of the Xhinn, preparing himself for the worst. 'I'd rather die than go on serving you. I'd rather sacrifice my life, if it will save the lives of others.' He gazed up at the hovering figures of the triumvirate. 'You will never conquer this world. Mankind will stand against you to the last man. We would rather go down fighting than live as slaves to the likes of you!'

The Xhinn shared that strange, disturbing laughter again.

'Stop laughing at me! If you want to kill me, get it over with! I'm ready for death now. It would be a release after all this.'

'You are the most amusing being.'

'You speak so passionately about mankind.'

'You seem to believe you are one of them.'

'What do you mean?' the priest demanded.

'You are not human.'

'You never have been.'

'You are one of us.'

'No! No, that's not possible!'

'Look to your feelings.'

'You know it is true.'

'You know who you are.'

'No! You're lying! It's another trick! It can't be true!' Simmons shouted.

'Such faith.'

'Such belief.'

'So misplaced.'

The triumvirate all raised their arms and pointed at Father Simmons. He closed his eyes, waiting for the killing blast to strike him down. Instead he felt himself coming apart, as if his very soul was being disassembled and put back together again. White light engulfed him, spinning around in ever accelerating circles. Finally, the swirling maelstrom of light and darkness died away.

The priest was gone. In his place stood one of the Xhinn.

The Doctor heard another Black Maria approaching from the

west, heading towards Tabernacle Street. He darted into an alleyway before it reached him, avoiding the searching gaze of the policeman driving the van. The evacuation was moving ever closer to the Ramsey Mob's headquarters. If the Doctor didn't reach Tommy and Sarah soon, it would be too late.

He was about to step back onto Old Street when another vehicle stopped directly outside the alleyway. The Doctor pressed himself into the darkness, edging away from the main road. He would have to take a less direct route. There were just too many patrols to avoid on the key streets.

As he crept away from Old Street, the Doctor thought back to his conversation with Father Simmons in the church the previous night. If the bread factory was under Xhinn control, then the priest must also be working for the alien scouting mission. Simmons might even be Xhinn himself.

That explained the readout on the tracker, which had indicated a massive level of alien activity near the church. But the signal had been too strong for just a single Xhinn…

'Of course!' the Doctor exclaimed, careful to keep his voice quiet. 'The Xhinn vessel – its core must be beneath the church, buried underground. That's where the tunnel leads!'

The location of the Xhinnship had been troubling the Doctor since Callum's transfiguration. The clue had been in the photograph Sarah had shown him. St Luke's Church was visible in the background, a curious rippling effect visible in the fabric of the building. It was that which had made him come back to 1952. He recognised the effect as a warpshadow, created by the detonation of a terrifying weapon the Doctor knew could not be of human making.

He emerged from the other end of the alleyway and resumed his journey east. It was more urgent than ever that he reached Tommy and Sarah ahead of the Xhinn-controlled police.

*

Mrs Ramsey was finally ready to leave for St Luke's. She had spent many minutes fussing over Tommy and his men, who were gathered upstairs in the dining room cleaning and checking their shotguns and pistols. Norman had arrived just after breakfast, bringing more than a dozen men, all carrying armfuls of guns and ammunition.

Sarah popped her head round the door to say goodbye to Tommy and Brick. 'We're off – at last!' She rolled her eyes and smiled. 'We should be back by midday, all things being equal.'

Tommy wasn't happy about the two women leaving without an escort. 'You sure you won't take Brick with you, for protection?'

'Brick doesn't need our help – he can look after himself,' Sarah replied, getting a laugh from the men. 'See you later.'

'This can't be true. It can't!' The newly transformed Xhinn tried to speak but found itself projecting the words mentally instead. 'It's another trick!'

'This is the truth.'

'You are one of us.'

'You are Xhinn, like us.'

'No! I can't be! I remember growing up in Chicago. I went to ballgames and played truant from school. I got into trouble and ran away to join the army. I am Xavier Simmons!'

'Memories taken from the real Xavier Simmons.'

'Memories implanted into your mind.'

'You were the first of us to take human form.'

'You had to blend in with these primitives, become one of them.'

'You were our agent among the natives.'

'But you have been among them too long.'

'You have forgotten yourself.'

The Xhinn that had been Simmons kept shaking its head.

201

'No, you're wrong. I'm Father Xavier Simmons, of the parish of St Luke's.'

'You are Xhinn.'

'If you cannot accept that, you are no use to us.'

'Xavier Simmons died six years ago.'

'You replaced him.'

'You became him.'

'But you went too far.'

'Now, you must come back to us.'

'Or else…'

'Never! I could never be like you. I may be one of you, but I could never be like you! Never!'

'So be it.'

The triumvirate gestured at the Xhinn that had embraced its false humanity too well. White light engulfed the rebel Xhinn, tearing it apart. Energy surged outwards, released from the disintegrating being. It was soon absorbed by the triumvirate. They glowed brighter, enhanced by the fresh life force.

'More humans are gathering above us.'

'They expect the priest to see them.'

'A surprise awaits.'

Sarah had been surprised by how easily she and Mrs Ramsey had found the journey to St Luke's. Old Street was deserted. The evacuations had obviously moved on to other parts of the East End. Something was nagging at the back of Sarah's thoughts but she couldn't seem to focus on it.

Mrs Ramsey stopped on the steps of the church to gossip with another member of the congregation. A group of twenty parishioners were waiting for Father Simmons to open the church. 'This smog is terrible, isn't it?' said one of the elderly ladies. 'Never seen anything like it all my days. Don't seem natural.'

Mrs Ramsey shook her head vigorously. 'You do talk a lot of nonsense, Edith Cartwright! Next you'll be telling us the tea leaves warned you not to come out this morning.'

'Well, now that you mention it…'

'Superstitious nonsense! I'm sure Father Simmons wouldn't approve of such notions. We should be looking to him for guidance from our Saviour.'

The doors of the church swung inwards. A warm glow emanated from inside the building, friendly and welcoming. 'Shall we go inside?' Sarah asked. 'I don't want to be out in this smog any longer than I have to. Who knows what it's doing to our lungs, being out in this…'

'You're probably right, dear. In we go!' Mrs Ramsey led the congregation inside, leading from the front as always. The doors swung closed behind them, seemingly of their own volition…

Tommy looked at his watch. It was ten o'clock. They had waited long enough. The calls from Fingers Blake and Stratford Simon never came, but that was no surprise. Tommy planned to make their lives very difficult if he got through the next twenty-four hours in one piece.

'All right, let's go,' he announced, rousing the men. 'Now we don't know what we're going to be up against. It could be more of these monsters, could be the Old Bill – could be anything. So I want you to stay sharp and keep in touch with one another. Make sure you can always see the man next to you and you won't get lost in the smog. Everybody got that?'

There was a nodding of heads.

'Jack, I want you to stay here.' The second-in-command began to protest but Tommy was having none of it. 'I don't care what you think. I need you here to keep watch on the house and keep everything running smoothly.'

Jack reluctantly agreed to Tommy's ruling.

'All right. Norman, I want you to take ten men and head south towards the City Road. Brick and me will be going the other way with the rest.' He looked around the room. 'So what are you all waiting for? Move it!'

The remains of the Ramsey Mob filed out the door and downstairs to the street, Page leading the way. Brick and Tommy brought up the rear. The gang boss locked the front door after himself. 'I remember a time when you could leave your door on the latch. Not any more.'

Page had already taken his men and disappeared off into the smog. Brick called the others to him and then led them away from number 15. Tommy was the last to leave, clutching his sword in his hand. It might not have stopped Callum but it would certainly make any copper with a brain think twice. Tommy smiled to himself. Probably not very effective, then!

Across the road Jean Mills watched the men disappearing into the smog. 'Mum, Tommy Ramsey and his men are out on the street with guns!'

'About time somebody did something,' Mary replied. She was sitting in front of the fireplace. Rita had now taken Bette's place on the sick bed. The child was wheezing and coughing, her face pale and grey. Mary didn't think she could stand to lose another daughter to this smog.

Jean closed the curtains, trying to keep the mist out. But the front room was slowly filling with the insidious mist, despite the roaring fire in the grate. The elder daughter took the family photo down from the mantelpiece. Nobody wanted to be reminded of the dead girl lying next door on the kitchen table, a crisp white bed sheet laid over the body.

'Mum, is Rita going to be all right?' she asked.

'I hope so, love,' Mary replied. She had run out of tears

to cry. Her face was now drawn and tired from exhaustion. If only the girls had been older, they might have been strong enough to survive this silent killer.

Tommy's group encountered no resistance until they reached the northern end of Tabernacle Street. There a Black Maria was unloading a dozen policemen on to the road, all armed with truncheons. They stared at Tommy and his men with glassy eyes, as if in a trance.

One of the policemen stepped forward and pointed at Tommy with his truncheon. 'We're evacuating everyone from the local area, due to the inclement weather…'

'Don't shoot them unless you have to!' Tommy yelled over the policeman's mantra. 'Put your man down, but don't kill them.'

'Why not?' asked Billy, who was standing near Tommy.

'Look at them! They ain't in control of themselves,' he replied. 'It's like they've been brainwashed. Somebody else is pulling the strings – the coppers are just their puppets.'

The policemen began marching towards the mobsters, all repeating the same meaningless mantra, over and over.

Tommy ran forward and punched the leading policeman in the face. He staggered before the blow but then came forward again. Tommy smashed the policeman over the head with the hilt of his sword, then drove his knee into the crumpled constable's stomach. Still the policeman tried to stagger onwards.

All around the same scene was being played out as Tommy's men attacked the policemen. Brick smashed the heads of two constables together, knocking them unconscious. He went to Tommy's aid, clouting the constable with the butt of a shotgun. The policeman finally fell to the ground.

'Thanks, Brick, I appreciate it.'

205

A shot rang out as Billy blew a hole through the head of a sergeant who ignored all attempts to subdue him. The headless corpse lunged at Billy and locked its hands around his throat in a deadly grip. Charlie came to his brother's rescue, tearing the fingers away from Billy's neck. Charlie smashed his rifle down on the back of the headless corpse's legs, breaking its knee joints. The dead sergeant collapsed onto the road, his hands still clutching at the air. The effect would have been comical were it not so macabre.

Tommy realised the stricken policemen were getting up again too soon. The two Brick had knocked out were clambering back to their feet. His own attacker was trying to get up once more. 'What's happening? These plods should be out for the count!'

'I killed one and it kept on coming!' Billy shouted.

It was Brick who first realised what was happening. 'They're already dead. These policemen – they're already dead!'

Tommy knew Brick was right. The policemen didn't have glassy eyes – they had lifeless eyes. They were already dead, somehow brought back to a sort of life and sent in to quell any resistance from local residents.

'Fire at will!' Tommy shouted. 'These things aren't the Old Bill – they're walking corpses! Take them out any way you can!'

He lashed out with his sword, slicing the head from his own attacker. Two more flashes of the blade severed the zombie's arms. They lay twitching on the road, grasping and grabbing at anything within reach.

Tommy's men turned their guns on the advancing policemen, blowing holes through the walking corpses. But several of the mobsters were too slow to react. They fell beneath the feet of the zombies. The screams of the dying men chilled the hearts of their friends. Tommy's men were holding their own but the oncoming policemen were slowly driving them back. A second van filled with reinforcements pulled up behind the first.

Tommy recognised that his men were slowly losing the battle. He yelled for everyone to retreat to the house and stood guard while the others ran back down Tabernacle Street. When the last of his men had passed him, Tommy ran after his men, back towards number 15. He wondered how the others were doing.

Norman Page soon realised the horrific nature of the foe his men were facing. 'Give 'em both barrels, boys! It's the only way to put them down!' He unloaded his shotgun into the chest of a sergeant but the lifeless body kept lumbering towards him. Norman tried to slot new cartridges into the shotgun but the sergeant was on him before he could snap it shut again. Norman lashed out with the heavy butt, knocking the zombie sideways.

The others were faring just as badly. Two men had been overrun by the policemen, others were blasting away with their guns but making no impression on the slow advance. Norman realised they had to get away from this relentless enemy.

'Fall back! Everybody, fall back to the house!' he shouted. He turned and began running back towards number 15. But someone was coming out of the smog towards him. 'Tommy, thank god it's you—' Norman began. Then he realised the figure emerging from the mist was another policeman. Norman and his men had been outflanked.

'They must have come along Epworth Street, got in behind us,' he said. But no one was listening. The mobsters were caught between two advancing lines of lifeless policemen, with no side street to escape into. Norman tried banging on the front doors of several houses but nobody would open up.

He snapped shut the shotgun and took aim at the nearest policeman. 'Come on, then! Come and get me! Come on!'

Tommy got back to his front door to find the Doctor waiting for him with the rest of the men. 'What are you doing here? How did you get here?'

'I came up a side street. This place is crawling with police patrols,' the Doctor replied. 'It took me more than an hour to get here from St Luke's. I've been banging on the front door but nobody answers it.'

Tommy unlocked the front door and let everyone inside. Once in, he bolted the front door and stationed two men in the hallway to stand guard. 'Jack, you still here?' he yelled up the stairs.

The young man appeared at the top of the flight. 'You're back quickly! What was all that shooting about?'

Tommy ran up the stairs, pursued by Brick and the Doctor. 'Change of plan. Those monsters are using dead coppers against us. They keep getting up again, no matter how many times we shoot them!'

'But that's impossible!'

'So's nearly everything that's been going on! I want you downstairs guarding the front door. Nobody gets in without my say-so – got that? Good. Jump to it!'

Jack went downstairs to join the rest of the men on guard duty. The Doctor and Brick followed Tommy into the dining room. Mrs Ramsey was sitting in her favourite chair, knitting happily.

'Mum! Am I glad you got back home safe – it's madness out there!' Tommy said. He glanced around the room. 'Where's Sarah?'

The Doctor looked alarmed at this. 'She's not here with

you?'

'She went with Mum to a special service at St Luke's this morning,' Tommy explained. 'Where's Sarah, Mum?'

'I don't know, dear,' the little old lady replied. 'We must have been separated in the fog on our way back.'

'What happened at the service?' the Doctor asked, concern in his voice.

'Father Simmons never turned up. We waited a few minutes and then decided to come back home,' Mrs Ramsey said with a smile. 'Silly me, I forgot to take my knitting along.'

Tommy rolled the rug away from the floor at one corner, revealing the floorboards underneath. He pushed one of them and it pivoted upwards, revealing a secret compartment beneath the floor. 'I imagine you've got something to tell me, Doctor,' Tommy said as he reached under the floor.

'You don't seem very surprised to see me here.'

'No. Sarah and me had a little chat last night. She explained a few things, about you two being travellers – if you know what I mean.' Tommy pulled out a sawn-off shotgun and threw it to Brick. 'Fixing watches ain't the only kind of time problems you repair.'

The Doctor stroked his chin thoughtfully. 'An interesting way of putting it. Yes, what she told you is true. We came here to stop a tragedy. I need your help.'

Tommy fished another shotgun out from under the floorboards and threw it to Brick. 'You've got it. But right now, I'm not sure how much use I can be. Looks like those coppers have taken out half my men already. So whatever you're planning, you better make it snappy.'

'I have a weapon that may stop these creatures, the Xhinn. But I need to get close enough to them to use it,' the Doctor explained.

Tommy got two boxes of ammunition from the hidden

compartment before putting the floorboard back into place. 'This weapon, it better be more use than our shotguns.'

'Bullets are no use against these beings.' The Doctor patted the satchel slung over his shoulder. 'But what's in this bag should do the trick.'

'Should do the trick? You mean you don't know?' Tommy asked, his voice incredulous.

'It's not something you can easily test, I'm afraid,' the Doctor replied.

Someone was banging against the front door. Tommy peered out through a gap in the curtains. 'No time like the present, then. The police are outside our front door.'

Mary Mills jumped at the sound of banging on her front door. She got up to open it then remembered Sarah's warning from the previous night. Mary went to the front window and peered out through a gap in the curtains.

A young constable was knocking on the door. He seemed perfectly normal to Mary. She was about to tell Jean to let him in when the constable looked directly at her. Mary could not stop herself from screaming. He was missing half his face, the half which had been turned away from the window. Gunpowder burns were visible on the edges of the massive wound. The head had been blasted at point-blank range. Yet the young constable was still standing. He walked to the window and began banging against it.

'We're evacuating everyone from the local area...' the policeman slurred through what remained of its mouth.

Mary closed the curtains so Jean could not see the horror outside. 'Who is it, Mummy?' the girl asked.

'It's a policeman. He wants to take me away for a few hours,' Mary replied, a plan already forming in her thoughts.

'Can we come too?'

'No, you have to stay here and look after Rita. She's too sick to go anywhere right now.'

'Oh, Mummy…'

'No, Jean – it has to be this way. You'll be safe here.'

The banging continued on the window, joined by a second person banging on the front door. Mary knew the flimsy wood would not keep the lifeless policemen out for long. They knew someone was inside. It was only a matter of time before they broke in. But there was still some hope…

Jack was starting to worry. He had four men jammed up to the front door, keeping it shut. The other eight men stood ready for action on the staircase. The police were hammering against the front door but without success – so far. Then Jack heard glass smashing. He opened the door into the ground-floor parlour to see two policemen climbing through the shattered windows.

'Hell's teeth!' Jack pulled the door shut and shouted for two men to keep hold of the handle. He ran back through the house to the kitchen and opened the back door, almost expecting to see a lifeless constable waiting outside. The back alleyway was empty. Jack summoned another two men and told them to stand guard in the alleyway.

'This is our escape route. It's our only way out of here. You see any sign of the police, yell your bloody heads off – got that?'

Mary picked Rita up, mattress and all. She carried her stricken daughter into the hallway. 'Jean! Open the door to the understairs cupboard, quick!'

Mary's eldest daughter pulled back the door to reveal the cramped, cluttered space beneath the stairs. There was just room for Mary to lay Rita down on the floor. 'Jean, you get in there with her.'

'But I don't want to, Mummy. I want to be with you,' the ten-year-old girl protested. 'Why can't I be with you?'

'Because I have to go with the policemen. You can see how sick your sister is. If she goes outside now she'll die, just like Bette. You don't want that, do you, love?' Mary stroked Jean's hair, trying to persuade the child.

'No, Mummy.'

'Good. Now do as I tell you, there's a good girl.'

'But why do we have to be inside the cupboard? It's warmer in front of the fire,' Jean said.

'It's like a game of hide and seek,' Mary replied, trying to keep the terror from her voice. The hammering on the front door was becoming ever more impatient. The policemen could be through it at any moment. 'You hide in here and later on, when it's safe, you can come out.'

'But how will I know when it's safe?'

'When it's all been very quiet for a long, long time.' Mary gently pushed Jean into the cupboard. As a child Mary had spent many unhappy hours underneath the stairs. Her father would beat her, then lock the sobbing child inside the cupboard. She had sworn never to be so cruel to her own children. Now it was probably their only hope of survival. 'Remember, you have to be as quiet as mice in there.'

'But no squeaking,' Jean volunteered.

'But no squeaking,' Mary agreed, forcing herself to smile. She gently closed the cupboard door. 'Goodbye, my loves.'

The front door began to splinter from the constant hammering. Mary slid home the bolt locking the cupboard door and walked into the kitchen. She pulled back the sheet from her dead daughter's face.

In the hallway, the front door buckled and then collapsed inwards. Three policemen shuffled into the house, searching each room with their lifeless eyes. They found Mary standing in the kitchen, holding Bette s cold body in her arms. 'I'm ready for you now. It's just me and my daughter. Please be careful – she's asleep and I don't want to wake her.'

'This smog, it's not natural,' the Doctor said. 'The weather is being controlled by the Xhinn. They are using it as a weapon against the people of London. Unless the Xhinn are stopped, it will poison everyone in the city by Tuesday.'

'That thing Callum turned into – there's more than one?' Tommy asked.

'At least three, maybe more. They have three leaders. Stop them and all this will cease.'

Tommy watched through the windows as his neighbours were being dragged out into the street by the zombie policemen. 'What about the Old Bill? Why are they helping these monsters?'

The Doctor pointed at a plate of bread and butter on the dining room table. 'The Bread of Life. I believe it contains a powerful psychotropic drug.'

'Psycho what?'

'Mind control, brainwashing – call it what you like. It makes humans susceptible to telepathic prompting. The drug builds up in the human body, until it reaches a critical density. Put enough of the drug into a person and they will carry on following orders, even after their brain is clinically dead.'

Brick had been listening intently to all this. 'That means the priest—'

'Father Simmons is working for them. He may even be one of them. He told me that Bread of Life was supplying its product to the local police canteens,' the Doctor said.

'That damned priest! Jack said he was trouble.' Tommy cursed himself for not taking Simmons more seriously as a threat. Now so many were suffering for that mistake.

Jack burst into the dining room. 'Tommy, we've got trouble.'

'You don't say.'

'The police are coming in through the windows. The street's swarming with them now. We can still get out the back alley, but we have to go now!'

'Send four men up here. Keep two on the front door, the rest of you are going out the back,' Tommy commanded, checking his shotgun was fully loaded. He shoved boxes of spare ammunition into his jacket pockets.

'Where are you going?' Jack asked.

'We're taking the scenic route. Now get going!'

Jack made for the stairs, shouting for the four nearest men to come up. Tommy adjusted his tie in the mirror over the fireplace. 'It's time to take the fight to these creatures. The only way the bug-eyed monsters are taking these streets is over my dead body!'

'That can be arranged, dear,' Mrs Ramsey said. She was slowly advancing on Tommy, her knitting needles stabbing forward in short, choppy motions. It would have been comical but for the savage malevolence in her eyes...

Mary let herself be dragged out into the hallway and towards the street. One of the policemen was banging at the door of the understairs cupboard. Mary collapsed to the floor, as if overcome by the smog billowing in from outside.

The three policemen pulled her upright and dragged her out into the street. Mary climbed up into the back of a waiting van, where several of her neighbours were waiting. They looked at her with hollow, terrified eyes. 'Are you all right, love?' one woman asked.

'I'll be fine,' Mary replied, her eyes fixed on the entrance to her home. The last of the policemen emerged from the house and crossed the road to join those attacking number 15. The vehicle drove away towards Old Street. Mary slowly rocked back and forth, hugging her dead daughter's body. 'I'll be fine.'

'Mum, what are you doing?' Tommy asked. His mother was making short stabbing motions with the knitting needles as she walked towards him.

'Be a good boy and die, Thomas,' she replied, getting ever closer.

'Shoot her!' Brick shouted.

'I can't!' Tommy said. 'She's me mum!' He raised the shotgun barrel to fire but couldn't bring himself to pull the trigger. Mrs Ramsey pushed the gun aside and lunged at her son.

The Doctor lashed out with one arm, the edge of his hand chopping against the side of Mrs Ramsey's neck. The little old woman crumpled to the floor, her arms still twitching for several seconds afterwards.

'You killed her!' Tommy cried out.

'Nonsense,' the Doctor said. 'I simply rendered her unconscious and incapable of harming you. She was drugged like the policemen, probably from a communion wafer. But she seems to have resisted the drug's influence for much longer than the police.'

'She's a very strong-willed lady,' Brick observed.

'That's what saved you,' the Doctor told Tommy. 'She didn't want to hurt her own son, just as you didn't want to hurt her. She'll recover soon enough.'

Billy and Charlie rushed into the room to see what all the commotion was about, followed by two more Ramsey men. Tommy told them to tie up his mother. The two brothers looked bemused but followed the orders without question. They carried Mrs Ramsey out and laid the old lady down on her bed.

Tommy shouted down the stairs to Jack. 'How's it going down there?'

'They'll be through the door any second. If we're going, we've got to go now Tommy!'

'You go. Take the lads out the back. I'll see you outside St Luke's Church in an hour.'

'What about you?'

Tommy smiled. 'I'll be all right. You worry about yourself. Now go!' Tommy went back into the living room. 'Doctor, will me mum be safe if we leave her here? We can't risk taking her with us.'

'I believe so,' the Doctor said. 'To the policemen she will be just another drone, like themselves. They should ignore her. It's us they want.'

'That's what I'm counting on,' Tommy replied. 'Brick, get upstairs and open that skylight. You four, go help him with the ladder. Doctor, you said you needed my help – you ready?'

The Doctor slung the leather satchel over his shoulder. 'Ready.'

'Then let's go!'

Downstairs Jack sent the first four men out the back door. They ran to the end of the long, narrow yard to a gate at the far end. Once beyond that, they signalled the all clear. Jack ran back through the kitchen into the hallway. He grabbed up his double-barrel shotgun before yelling to the two men still holding the front door shut.

'You two! Get out through the back door – now!'

'But the—'

'Now!' Jack shouted. The two men ran back through the house, passing Jack and then out through the kitchen into the back yard. They were followed by the two men that had

216

been clinging on to the door of the ground-floor parlour. As they passed Jack, both doors opened. More than a dozen policemen surged through the two doorways.

'I hope you've got a search warrant,' Jack said, 'otherwise I shall consider this as breaking and entering.'

'We're evacuating everyone from the local area,' the leading policeman began to say. His head was blown off by a shotgun blast from Jack.

'And that's what I call a legitimate act of self-defence.' Jack blasted a hole through the chest of the first policeman, who toppled backwards. His body partially blocked the hallway, slowing the progress of those behind. Jack had time to reload both barrels.

'See, I don't like burglars – horrible, furtive little men who haven't got the bottle to rob you face to face.' Jack shot twice, further blocking the hallway with another twitching corpse. He calmly reloaded as the zombie policemen got ever closer. 'Give me a dangerous villain with an iron bar any day'

Jack got off one more shot before he was forced to start retreating back through the ground floor of the house. He glanced up the stairwell to see Tommy give him a parting wave. 'They're all yours!' Jack shouted. He turned and ran, pulling the doors shut behind him. Jack emerged from the back door at speed into the yard, yelling at the men ahead of him. 'Move it!'

Brick was first up onto the roof, followed by Billy and Charlie. The brothers were shocked by the array of dead pigeons littering the roof.

'What happened here?' Billy asked. 'Some sap lost all their little birdies to the smog?' Brick advanced on the teenager, his fists clenching and unclenching. Charlie remonstrated with his brother by ramming an elbow into Billy's ribs. 'Sorry,

Brick – I mean, Mr Brick. I didn't mean anything by it…'

The Doctor was next up through the skylight, followed by the other two Ramsey henchmen. Last came Tommy himself, pulling the ladder up behind him. He was out of breath but smiling. 'That was a close thing. Jack's leading most of the Old Bill out the back as a diversion, but a few came up the stairs after us.'

Tommy leaned over the skylight and shot down onto the landing below. A dull thud announced that one of the pursuing police was now out of action. Tommy closed the skylight and told Billy and Charlie to carry the ladder.

'Why?' asked Billy before his brother could get another elbow jab in.

'Because we might need it to get down from another roof,' Tommy said, rolling his eyes in despair. 'Honestly, I worry about the next generation.'

The Doctor looked over the side of the roof, down into Tabernacle Street. More than twenty police were crowding through the front door into number 15. 'The decoy is working. If we go now, we should make it.'

Tommy nodded to Brick. 'You know these rooftops better than anybody – lead on.' The big man vaulted the adjoining wall with number 17 and jumped down to the roof of the neighbouring terraced house. The Doctor went after him, followed by the four Ramsey henchmen. Tommy brought up the rear. He looked over the back sides of the houses but could not see any further because of the smog. 'I wonder how Jack and the rest of the lads are doing…'

The back gate of number 15 led out into a narrow alleyway. This ran parallel to Tabernacle Street and provided rear access to all the adjoining houses. Jack led his eight men south, towards the cross-junction with Epworth Street. Motioning for the others to keep quiet, he pulled open the gate at the end of the alleyway and peered outside. A policeman was standing directly in front of the gate, about to open it.

'Hell's teeth!' Jack exclaimed. Before he could pull his shotgun up and fire, the zombie constable had pulled a whistle to its lips and begun to blow a shrill note. It was cut short by the shotgun blast, swiping the face away. But the damage had been done.

Jack yelled for everyone to retreat. 'Run! Out the north end of the alley!'

The group pelted up the thin path, gasping for breath in the acrid mist. Before they reached the other end, the north gate was pulled open by another policeman. The drones began pouring into both ends of the narrow channel, cutting off the exits. The escape route had become a death trap. Jack and his men were outflanked and outnumbered.

'It's not over yet!' Jack vowed. He kicked open a back gate and ran up the path to a kitchen door. 'Open up! Now!' There was no response from inside. Jack stepped aside and called for the two largest men among the eight. 'Get this door down – now! All our lives depend on it.'

The two men began hurling themselves at the kitchen door. Jack organised the others into three rows of two. The front pair lay on the ground, the next two kneeled and the final pair stood at the back. All six checked their guns, waiting for the lifeless foe to force its way into the tiny back yard.

One of the men started praying. 'The Lord is my shepherd, I shall not want. He leadeth me—'

'Shut up!' Jack snarled. 'I don't see the good lord getting us out of this. If we want to survive, we've got to stay together, stick up for each other. Everybody got that?'

The eight men murmured their assent.

'All right, then – no more bloody praying. How's that door

coming?' Jack demanded. The two men throwing themselves against it shook their heads.

'It's too heavy, Jack,' one replied. 'We can't budge it.'

The zombie policemen flooded into the narrow back yard. The six men fired, reloaded and fired again. The corpses began to pile up but still the policemen kept coming, clambering over the bodies of their fallen brothers. They were relentless and they were getting closer.

'Do I have to think of everything myself?' Jack aimed his shotgun at the door lock. He turned his head away before pulling the trigger. 'Don't want any shrapnel ruining my good looks, do I?'

The door splintered inwards around the lock. Two more hefty shoves pushed it open and the trio fell inside. Several pairs of shiny black boots were lined up on the floor. Jack looked up to see three policemen already waiting for them in the kitchen. They reached down towards him…

The van carrying Mary and her neighbours rolled past the Bread of Life factory and down into the tunnel beneath it. Warm air rushed past the passengers as they descended. Mary could remember going to Bank tube station once with her father, before the war. They had gone down several escalators and spiral staircases to reach the correct platform. The journey downwards had seemed to take forever, Mary remembered. The further beneath the city they went, the warmer the air around them became. She had worried that they would end up in the centre of the Earth if they kept going, or maybe even Hell.

The priests who visited Mary's school always told the pupils to be good, lest they be sent down to burn for all eternity in the fires of Hell. The young Mary had deduced that Hell must be a very hot place, deep underground. Now it seemed she had been right all along. How she wished it were otherwise.

After an interminable journey into stifling heat, the tunnel finally levelled out and the van emerged into a vast chamber. One by one the passengers meekly got out and allowed themselves to be herded into lines by policemen with dead eyes and blood-splattered faces.

How very English, Mary thought. Forming an orderly queue for your own death. She was sure they were all going to die. But she felt no tears, no regrets. She just couldn't bring herself to care any more. As long as Jean and Rita survived, it didn't matter what happened to her now. Mary still cradled the lifeless body of her youngest child in her arms. Bette would always be the youngest now, never grow up, never grow any older. Frozen forever as a coughing, wheezing six-year-old, eyes uncomprehending and confused as life left her frail body.

No, Mary didn't care what happened to herself any more. Like all the others, she shuffled meekly towards the tall doorway of the death chamber.

Tommy looked back along the rooftops. He saw one of the skylights open outwards and a policeman emerge onto the roof, followed by another. The trap was closing around the fugitives faster than they could escape it.

Ahead of Tommy the group was approaching the last house in Tabernacle Street. Brick was in front. He peered over the edge of the roof. The street below was clear. Brick gave a happy thumbs up sign to those following him. Billy and Charlie were labouring along beside the Doctor, who was starting to feel the weight of his satchel bearing down. The two other Ramsey men were close to Brick when the skylight just ahead of them popped up into the air. A constable pulled himself up onto the roof and lurched towards the two henchmen. They ran at him, shoving him towards the edge of the roof. But as the policeman toppled over he grabbed them by the arms. All three went over the edge together. A sickening crunch followed from the ground below.

Brick shoved the skylight back in place and sat on it until the others reached him. 'We ain't got long. Unless we get off this roof soon…'

'I know,' Tommy said. 'Let's go – over the side.'

Billy and Charlie lowered the ladder over the wall. It just reached a balcony below. Charlie climbed down first while his brother held the ladder in place. The Doctor was next, followed by Tommy. Charlie grabbed a drainpipe by the balcony's edge and began sliding down it to the ground. The others followed his example, the Doctor protesting as he descended.

'You know, this is hardly dignified for a man of my age.'

'Shut your mouth and keep moving,' Tommy growled. 'Unless you fancy your chances against what's behind us.'

Brick was last off the roof, following Billy down the ladder. As soon as the big man got off the skylight the policemen were clambering up onto the roof. Brick just pulled the ladder away from the roof in time to stop the pursuers using it for their descent.

Less than a minute later all five men were on the street. They avoided looking at the broken bodies of the fallen men, except Tommy. He crouched down to close their eyelids. 'Somebody's going to pay for this,' he vowed to himself before standing again.

'Where to now?' Charlie asked.

'St Luke's – whatever's going to happen, it'll be around the church,' the Doctor replied.

The five men began running west along Old Street.

Jack rolled aside, avoiding the grasping hands of the zombie policemen. Instead they grabbed the two Ramsey men who had broken down the back door into the kitchen. Jack realised the house must be filled with the enemy. The only escape was the back door. He scrambled out into the yard where the other six were fighting hand to hand with the remorseless flood of policemen coming into the narrow space.

But the yard was too confined for effective combat. Sheer weight of numbers was overwhelming the six men. Jack hoisted himself up on to the roof of the outhouse. From there he could jump over the fence into the neighbouring property.

'Don't leave us behind!' one of the men cried out.

But Jack did not look back. He threw himself over the fence, falling awkwardly to the ground on the other side. A stabbing pain shot up through his right leg, making him gasp in shock. Jack tried to stand but could not put any weight on his injured leg. Bones pushed against the cloth of his trousers in strange places. He had dislocated his knee. Already he could feel the joint beginning to throb warmly. Jack leaned against the high wooden fence, trying to catch his breath.

This was not how he planned to die, caught in some grubby back alley like a rat in a trap. His death was meant to be glorious, not long after the moment of his greatest triumph. Perhaps a million-pound robbery, or taking control of all the East End. A few days to savour the moment then a quick, painless death in his sleep. Then his body would be cast out to sea on a burning pyre, like some Viking hero. That was the way to go. Not like this…

The screams of the men in the next yard jolted Jack back to reality. He glanced around the yard for a weapon. The zombie policemen would soon find him and Jack didn't want to think about what would happen next. His eyes lit on a petrol can in a corner. He hopped over to it and picked the can up. It was half full. Jack was planning his next move when the policemen began swarming into the narrow yard.

*

Mary stood in a corner, hugging her dead daughter. Her neighbours stood around the chamber, bewildered and shivering with fear. Mary smiled bleakly. It hadn't been much of a life. A few moments of pleasure set against so many years of work and struggle. She hoped her children would live to see a better day, a better world. She hoped she was going to a better place.

Clouds of gas began to billow from the grills high up the walls of the chamber. Mary breathed deeply, welcoming the toxic fumes into her body. She slid down the wall into a sitting position, still clutching Bette's lifeless form. Some long-forgotten words crept into Mary's mind as she was dying. The twenty-nine-year-old woman began mouthing them slowly.

'Hail Mary, Mother of God, pray for us sinners, now and at the hour of our death.' Mary closed her eyes for the last time. 'Amen.'

Jack poured out most of the petrol in a semicircle around himself, keeping his back against the rear of the house. He kept a last reserve of the accelerant in the can, which he put on the ground between his legs. He pulled his precious Zippo lighter from the inside pocket of the suit jacket and ignited the flame. As the policemen drew nearer, Jack bent over and lit the semicircle of petrol.

It burst into flame, hungrily consuming the gasoline on the ground. One of the policemen tried to step across the line of fire but his trousers caught light. He stumbled away, flames racing up his uniform and engulfing his head.

'Don't like that, do you?' Jack sneered. 'I love it. Fire is alive, it's powerful. It doesn't need friends, it doesn't need family, it doesn't need a mum or a dad. It just needs fuel and oxygen. Then it can burn for ever.'

Another policeman tried to cross the flames and was

driven back by the intense heat. But the ring of petrol was burning away too quickly. Soon it would be gone and Jack would be vulnerable. He was trapped, surrounded and unable to escape. He stared at his warped reflection in the polished metal casing of the lighter.

'I wanted to burn for ever too. But I guess it's better to burn out young than get old, all your fire gone, no spark left.' Jack made a decision. He glared at the policemen gathering around him. 'Who wants to come with me?'

Jack picked up the can and poured the last of the petrol over himself. It stung his eyes but he didn't care any more. He ignited the lighter one last time. Around him the flames on the ground were spluttering out. Jack touched the lighter to his sleeve. He screamed as the flames shot up his arm and around his head.

Jack threw himself at the nearest policeman.

Brick, Billy and Charlie were leading the way to St Luke's, while the Doctor and Tommy followed just behind them. The smog got denser the closer the group came to the church, cutting visibility to an arm's length. The leading trio disappeared into the mist, leaving the Doctor and Tommy behind.

'Brick! Slow down, or we'll lose each other!' Tommy shouted.

'All right Tommy!' a voice replied from up ahead.

'All right Tommy?' another voice hissed quietly. The gangster turned to see Detective Valentine emerge from the smog, a shotgun aimed at Tommy's chest. 'Who's your friend?' Valentine asked, jerking his head at the Doctor.

'My name's Smith, Doctor John Smith – but everyone just calls me the Doctor.' He offered a handshake to Valentine, who ignored it.

'I'm not everyone, am I, Tommy?' the detective replied.

'I'm your stooge, your little flunky, fetching and fixing at the sound of his master's voice.' He nudged the gangster in the chest with the end of the shotgun. 'You don't mind if I call you Tommy, do you? I know you prefer to be Mr Ramsey, but since our circumstances have changed…'

'Now then Bob, there's no need to go overboard,' Tommy said.

'Oh, it's Bob now is it? I don't recall inviting you to use my first name.' Valentine swung the butt of the shotgun around, striking Tommy in the side of the face. The gangster staggered but stood his ground.

'You treated me like dirt,' Valentine said. 'You took my weakness and exploited it, turned me into a bent cop, a standing joke on the force. I was just a washed-up drunk waiting for a pittance of a pension. But things are different now – the shoe's on the other foot.'

'What are you on about?' Tommy asked.

'I saw your friend Steve MacManus earlier.'

'He's no friend of mine!'

'He's no friend of anybody's any more – I spread his brains over the back window of that precious car of his. Of course, he was never anybody's friend to start with so I doubt many will mourn his demise.' Valentine paused for effect. 'You've probably been wondering where all your best men have got to – Dave Butcher, the others. I took care of them as well.'

'Why you—' Tommy was cut short by another vicious blow to the head.

'Compensation, you see, for all those times you humiliated me. Now it's your turn, Mr Tommy Ramsey.' Valentine smiled. 'You thought I was your little lapdog, but I've got a new master now. They speak to me in my head, telling me what to do. They sent me to kill you and anyone else I thought might offer some resistance.'

226

'Look, old chap, we really don't have time for—' the Doctor began.

'Shut up, or I'll shoot both of you!' the detective shouted.

The Doctor took a step towards him. 'It's just that we're in quite a rush—'

'I said shut up!' Valentine swung the shotgun towards the Doctor, his finger beginning to squeeze the trigger. 'I don't know who you are, big nose, but you can keep your hooter out of my business. Permanently!'

Tommy grabbed for the shotgun but the detective was ready for him. He neatly side-stepped the crude lunge, sticking out a leg for Tommy to trip over. The gangster went sprawling on the road. Valentine turned back to the Doctor. 'Now, where was I?'

The Doctor silenced him with a chop of the hand, the finely directed blow catching Valentine's windpipe. The detective was choked for breath, dropping the shotgun. The Doctor followed up with another strike, this time punching two fingers into a nerve cluster on the side of the neck. Valentine went down, the left side of his body numb and useless.

'As I was saying before I was so rudely interrupted,' the Doctor announced, 'we really don't have time for settling old scores.'

'That's where you're wrong,' Tommy replied. He picked up the shotgun and held the end of the barrels beneath the chin of the stricken detective. 'There's always time for settling old scores. Goodbye – Bob.'

'Tommy, don't—' the Doctor protested but it was too late. Tommy pulled the trigger, a smile playing around his lips.

Brick, Billy and Charlie ran back to find the two men arguing over the headless corpse of Detective Valentine. 'What the hell happened?' Brick asked.

'This murderer just executed another man!' the Doctor said furiously.

Tommy was unrepentant. 'It was self-defence.'

'He was lying on the ground, unable to move!'

'But he tried to kill me. He tried to kill both of us,' Tommy replied. 'You should be grateful I stopped him.'

The Doctor shook his head sadly. 'Murder can never be justified.'

Tommy leaned close to the Doctor's face, their noses almost touching. 'Yeah? Well how are you planning to stop the Xhinn? Ask them nicely to leave?'

'I already tried that.'

'Then I guess you still need me and my methods.' Tommy smiled triumphantly. 'Face it, Doc – you and me, we're quite similar.'

The Doctor glared at the gangster. 'You couldn't be more wrong.'

'We'll see.' Tommy reloaded the shotgun and motioned for everyone to get moving again. 'Let's go!'

At Mary Mills's house, Jean and Rita were still hiding in the understairs cupboard. Jean was desperate to go to the toilet but did not dare leave the cramped space for fear of discovery. She had promised Mummy not to go out and she would keep the promise as long as possible.

Rita started coughing and wheezing again as the air in the cupboard became increasingly stale. Jean wondered how long her sister would survive. Bette had faded away over several hours and now Rita was showing the first signs of the same slow, painful process.

Something creaked in the house. Jean had jumped at the first few noises they heard while hiding in the cupboard, but that was just the house shifting. At night she sometimes thought the house was like an old man breathing, the way floorboards creaked and groaned. But this noise was different. Somebody was at the front door.

Jean put a finger over her sister's lips, willing her not to cough. Then the elder girl crept to the door of the cupboard and pressed her face against the wood. She peered through the gap between door and wall, trying to catch a glimpse of what was happening.

The footfalls grew nearer, as someone stepped into the hallway from outside. Wood splintered and broke apart as the visitor stood on the broken front door. The steps got louder as the intruder shuffled along the hallway, getting ever closer to the cupboard.

Jean saw movement as a dark shadow passed the cupboard, but she could not make out the shape of it. She craned her head round, trying to follow the figure. A smell like rotting fruit began to fill the hallway and filter into the cupboard, putrid and disgusting. Then Jean heard the sniffing.

The intruder was breathing in heavily through its nose, then hissing the breath out through its teeth. Jean could see the intruder twisting its head, as if trying to locate the source of an elusive scent. Then the figure turned around beneath the naked light bulb in the hallway and Jean forced her fingers into her mouth to stop herself screaming.

'Can you hear that?' Brick asked. 'Sounds like screaming, people screaming.'

The quintet had reached St Luke's and was making final preparations before entering the church. The Doctor opened his satchel and flicked a switch on the device. Lights began blinking into life as the power supply began to spread its energy through the assemblage of wiring and circuitry. The others were reloading their weapons and filling their pockets with spare ammunition. In the heat of battle there would be no time to stop and open boxes of bullets before reloading. All five men were stopped by the sound of screams.

'Where's it coming from?' Tommy asked. The smog deadened sound, making it difficult to determine from which direction it was emanating. A light flashed briefly from a building in the distance, accompanied by more screams.

'The bread factory, over there!' Brick said.

There was another flash of light, accompanied by a single, female scream. This time the source was inside St Luke's Church. The stained-glass windows were illuminated from within by a powerful beam.

'And that was the church,' Tommy said. 'Where's Jack and the rest of the lads? There's only five of us here. We can't split our numbers up even further!'

The Doctor gazed at the church before making his decision. 'I recognised that last scream. It was Sarah. She's still inside St Luke's.'

Tommy took a step towards the church but the Doctor stopped him. 'No, I'll save Sarah. I brought her to this place, it's up to me to see she gets out alive. You have to go to the bread factory and try to close it down. More and more police stations are falling under the control of the Xhinn. London is dying from this smog, but you've seen how the Xhinn use even the dead to do their dirty work.'

'That's where the Old Bill is getting all the reinforcements!' Tommy realised. 'So no more bread, no more coppers to fight?'

'Exactly. You have to shut down that factory. Stopping the bread supply will take away their army, make them weaker and more vulnerable.'

'What about you?'

'I've got to face the Xhinn myself – that's why I came here.

Unless I can stop them, this world will be ripe for colonisation. This is just a scouting mission. Stop it and the main Xhinn force might think twice.'

'Might?'

The Doctor smiled weakly. 'It's the best we can hope for.'

'What about Miss Smith?' Brick asked.

'If they haven't already killed her, then she's a hostage. It was Sarah who persuaded me to come here, to stop this tragedy. I won't let her become another victim of the Xhinn.'

'I'm coming with you, Doctor,' Brick said.

'But Brick—' Tommy began to protest.

A single glance from the big man silenced his boss. Tommy turned to Billy and Charlie. 'You boys ready for some action?'

The brothers grinned at each other. 'Too right!' they agreed.

'Then let's get going,' Tommy replied. 'Good luck, Doctor.' He shook hands with Brick. 'Thanks for all your help, Arthur. It's appreciated.'

Brick didn't trust himself to speak.

Tommy and the brothers ran off into the smog, towards the bread factory. They were quickly swallowed up by the yellow and grey mist. The Doctor and Brick walked to St Luke's. They paused in front of the church.

'Brick, I want you to stand guard outside these doors. Let nobody else in,' the Doctor said. He held up a hand to silence the big man's protests. 'I know you want to save Sarah – we both do. But what I have to do will be very dangerous. I need you here, guarding my back. Fair enough?'

'Fair enough.'

'Good man.' The Doctor checked the contents of his satchel, straightened the frilled cuffs of his shirt and opened the door to St Luke's Church. Light blazed from within, almost blinding him. Squinting to see his way forward, the Doctor stepped inside and the door closed slowly behind him.

Brick took up sentry duty outside, listening intently for noises from within.

Jean could not help staring at the dead policeman. She knew he was dead because his lower jawbone was missing, along with the flesh and skin that should have surrounded it. His clothes were soaked with dried blood, as if someone had spilled beetroot juice down his front.

Jean noticed the dead man still had his tonsils, even though his tongue was missing. Her own tonsils had been removed when she was five. Her mummy had promised she could have all the jelly and ice cream she wanted afterwards but Jean's throat had been so sore she didn't feel like having any. She wondered if the dead man liked jelly and ice cream.

He seemed to be staring right at her, but his eyes had no life. They were more like a doll's eyes, empty and cold. Instead he was trying to sniff them out. Jean closed her eyes and started praying silently to herself, lips mouthing the words. Please don't let the bad man find us, she thought, and please look after Mummy and Bette. Jean knew Mummy had gone away to die but she hadn't cried in front of Rita. Better to be brave. Better not to let her little sister know the truth, that they would never see Mummy again.

When Jean opened her eyes, the bad man had turned away again. He shuffled into the kitchen. We're safe, Jean thought – then Rita began coughing again. Jean crouched by her sister and clamped a hand over Rita's mouth.

'Sssh! Please don't cough, Rita – please!'

The footsteps returned to the hall and Jean almost screamed when the door to the cupboard rattled. He was trying to get in! The door shook and shook but it did not budge. Finally, after what seemed like forever, the footsteps shuffled away again. Jean listened as they went down the hall, out the front door and onto the street.

They were safe – but for how long?

Tommy, Billy and Charlie peered through the windows of the bread factory. Inside was a scene to match any horror Tommy had seen in his violent, murderous life.

More than two dozen men and women were working inside the factory. Each looked utterly exhausted, as if they had not rested for hours, even days. Their faces were sallow and drawn, black rings under their eyes. Clothes stained with sweat and blood hung from their sagging bodies. Their arms strained to move the long bread shovels and heavy wooden blades used to stir the dough.

A dozen policemen stood around inside the factory, watching the workers. If any of them slowed the pace of work, a policeman would stride forward and beat the culprit repeatedly with his truncheon. As the trio watched, one such broken body was pushed to one side and an invisible signal passed between the police.

In one corner of the factory floor a crude cage had been constructed. Dozens more people were wedged inside, some already dead, others dying. When a worker fell, the police opened the cage and selected three people from inside. One was made to replace the missing worker. The other two were forced to pick up the body of the fallen man and place it on a conveyor belt. This propelled the body slowly towards a giant metal wheel, studded with cruel spikes. As the body was fed into the maw of the machine, the spikes began to vibrate – tearing the body apart. The unfortunate victims were still alive as they entered the machinery. None survived more than a few moments.

'Christ almighty!' Charlie whispered. His brother was too busy vomiting to speak.

Tommy's face was like stone, a muscle rippling in the jawline the only clue to his thoughts. 'This stops today,' he told the brothers. 'We can't take all those police guards on our own, but maybe some of the workers will help us.'

'They can hardly stand,' Billy said, wiping the vomit from his chin.

'Nobody wants to die like that,' Tommy replied. 'Given the chance, I reckon they'll fight to get out of there.'

'What do we do?' Charlie asked.

Tommy glanced through the window again, assessing points of entry and the enemy's position. 'You stay here. Vomit boy will come with me. When you get my signal, come in through this window shooting. Put your man down, because you'll only get one chance. Reckon you're up to it?'

Charlie gulped hard and nodded. 'What's the signal?'

Tommy smiled. 'You'll know when you hear it. Good luck.' He ran off along the perimeter of the building, shotgun at his side.

Billy embraced his brother before following Tommy. 'See you inside.'

Charlie watched him go then checked his shotgun one last time. Better safe than sorry. Seconds later he heard glass smashing and two shotguns firing. Charlie smiled as he backed up, ready to launch himself inside. Tommy had been right – he knew the signal. Charlie threw himself through the window, rolled on the ground and came up shooting.

The Doctor closed the church door and leaned against it, one hand shielding his eyes from the brilliant glare. Once they had adjusted, he was able to focus on the gathering in the centre of the church.

Sarah was floating in the air, her arms held out sideways as if being crucified by invisible forces. Her face was riven with pain, each breath gasped in as if her rib cage was slowly collapsing. Tears ran down her cheeks.

Around her floated the Xhinn triumvirate. The creatures of light and darkness were flicking shards of energy at the suspended Sarah, each jagging into her body, making her writhe in the air. The Doctor could hear the metal upon metal rasp of Xhinn laughter in his mind.

'Where's Father Simmons?' he asked.

The Xhinn whirled to face him, the torturing of Sarah forgotten for now.

'Doctor!'

'So kind of you to come back.'

'We knew you would.'

'Now we shall take your time machine and learn its secrets.'

'I asked you a question – where's Father Simmons?'

'Aren't you more interested in this human?'

'She is your travelling companion, isn't she?'

'You care about her, don't you?'

The Doctor did not deny it. 'You already know this. You stole the knowledge from my mind to create one of your tests.'

'You wouldn't want to see her hurt, would you?'

'She seems such a fragile creature.'

'Yet she has survived for several hours here.'

'Why did you abandon her?'

'I didn't, as you well know,' the Doctor replied tersely. 'Release her.'

'You are in no position to give orders, Time Lord.'

'She came here of her own free will.'

'She agreed to be our captive to save you.'

'She shall be our mouthpiece on this world.' The Xhinn Triumvirate turned inwards towards Sarah. 'Won't you?'

'Never!' she replied between gasps for air.

'How tiresome.'

'How stubborn.'

'How regrettable.'

All three Xhinn gestured. Energy lanced at Sarah, stabbing her with bolts of blue light. She twisted and buckled in the air, then hung limply.

'What have you done to her?' the Doctor demanded.

'Fear not.'

'She has only lost consciousness.'

'For now.'

'When she awakes, we shall resume.'

'We can keep her alive for days, even years in this state.'

'Would you like to watch?'

'No.' The Doctor walked towards the Xhinn. 'You really are the most petty, vindictive creatures, aren't you?'

'You dare to question us?'

'To criticise us?'

'To mock us?'

'Why not?' the Doctor replied. He sat down in a pew, placing the satchel carefully beside him. 'I mean, if this is the best you can do – torturing a member of a species you have already decided is primitive and no match for the mighty Xhinn. Hardly the work of a great and important civilisation, is it?'

The Xhinn moved away from Sarah to surround the Doctor. He continued to taunt the triumvirate.

'I mean, you can't even control your own kind – let alone an entire planet of hostile aliens. Look at what happened with Callum, he nearly ruined your entire invasion schedule with his actions.'

'An error.'

'An oversight.'

'Quickly corrected.'

'Then there's Father Simmons – I notice you haven't

answered my question about what happened to him? He was one of the Xhinn, I presume?'

'He has been punished.'

'He went too far.'

'He is no longer.'

'Dear, dear – went native, did he? Too long mixing with this primitive species you seem to despise so much?' The Doctor smiled. 'Got in with a good crowd, you might say.'

'You would do well not to mock us.'

'The Xhinn are a noble civilisation.'

'But we are not above vengeance.'

The Xhinn triumvirate pointed at the Doctor, surrounding him with the same crippling energy shackles that bound Sarah in the air. He rose slowly up from the pew, his arms and legs straining against the invisible bondage.

'Feel the grip of the Xhinn.'

'Feel it tighten around your body.'

'Feel it crush the life from you.'

Tommy burst through the doors into the bread factory, his shotgun ready to fire. A policeman lurched towards him. Tommy fired twice, taking both legs off the approaching guard. No point wasting bullets blowing holes in them, Tommy thought. Better to disable them from causing any more trouble – sort out the living from the dead later.

Billy appeared, flying through a side window. He quickly got up off the floor and began firing, his shots concentrated on the bread-making machinery – just as Tommy had suggested. A few rounds carefully aimed brought the factory to a grinding halt. That meant the workers were now free to help them.

'We're getting everybody out of here! But we need your help,' Tommy shouted as he reloaded. Two more policemen were advancing on him. 'Pick up your tools and use them on the guards!'

Charlie was last into the factory. He blew the head off the nearest policeman, then ran on to fire point-blank into the chest of another. The ventilated zombie fell backwards into the bread mixing vat, disappearing into the viscous dough. Charlie was still reloading when the next policeman was upon him. The teenager was picked up off the ground and thrown across the factory. He slid into a wall and lay there, the breath knocked out of him. Already another of the remorseless, relentless enemy was moving toward him.

The two nearest workers made weapons from their tools, attacking the oncoming policemen with their long-handled bread shovels. But both were swatted aside by the much stronger guards, propelled by the will of the Xhinn. Their necks snapped like dry kindling and the bodies were thrown aside. The policemen returned to their original quarry, Charlie. He was still lying on the ground, his shotgun just out of reach.

Tommy ran to the cage. He smashed at the padlock with his gun butt, breaking it open. Tommy threw the padlock aside and pulled the cage apart. 'Come on! Now's your chance to escape – come on!'

A few of the men and women inside got to their feet and began dragging the others out. But most inside the cage were already dead. The rescuers had arrived too late to save them. Better to die in here than go through that mincing machine, Tommy thought.

One of the captives was pointing over Tommy's shoulder. 'Look out…' he gasped.

Tommy ducked to one side as a policeman lurched at him. Tommy clubbed it to the ground and tucked the end of his shotgun barrel into the zombie's mouth. 'Eat this,' the gangster sneered, pulling the trigger.

Billy was leading the remaining workers out of the factory when he heard his brother cry out for help. Two policemen were holding his brother down on the conveyor belt as it pushed him towards the rending machine.

Billy pushed the last of the escaping workers out the door and took aim with his shotgun. But he didn't dare shoot the policemen, for fear of hitting Charlie. His brother was only moments away from being torn limb from limb. Instead he fired at the machine, blowing a hole through its pneumatic hose pipes. The grinding wheel slowed and stopped, with Charlie's legs only inches away from the spikes. Billy ran to help his brother fight off the assailants.

Beyond the rending machine a metal cage was appearing, sliding up out of the floor. It was an elevator laden with more zombie policemen. Now Tommy and the two brothers were outnumbered six to one.

'Billy! Charlie! We've got to get out of here!' Tommy shouted. The brothers ignored him, too busy fighting to stay alive in the far corner. Tommy ran towards the main exit only to find it blocked by another half dozen policemen. Now there was no escape – they were trapped inside the factory.

The Doctor writhed in the air but could not escape the Xhinn triumvirate's deadly grip. 'If you kill me, you are only sentencing yourselves to death.'

'More threats?'

'How tiresome.'

'You have no weapon that can stop us.'

The Doctor managed a smile amidst the crushing pain. 'You're wrong. If you don't believe me, see the certainty in my mind. You cannot read my thoughts, but I will let you know my emotions.'

The Xhinn delved into his feelings.

'It is true.'

'You believe you can destroy us.'

'But belief and reality are not the same.'

'Let the girl go,' the Doctor winced, 'as a sign of good faith. Show me how magnanimous the mighty Xhinn can be. Then I will reveal the device that will destroy you.'

The Xhinn consulted silently amongst themselves. One of them waved an arm at Sarah. She fell to the floor with a sickening thud and lay still.

'Sarah! Sarah! Are you all right?' the Doctor shouted.

On the ground Sarah stirred slightly. She lifted her head and smiled at the Doctor, before slumping back to the floor unconscious.

'We did as you asked.'

'We released the girl.'

'What is this weapon?'

The Doctor nodded with his head at the satchel. 'It's inside that bag.'

The Xhinn nearest the satchel moved towards it, raising an arm. Energy pulsated around the end of the limb.

'I wouldn't attempt to destroy it if I were you,' the Doctor said. 'Any attempt to tamper with the device will prematurely activate it.'

'What is it?'

'Open it – very carefully! – and see,' the Doctor replied.

The nearest Xhinn pointed at the satchel, which levitated just above the seat of the pew. The assemblage of wiring, circuitry and power cells emerged slowly from inside and then rested atop the satchel, which sank back down onto the pew. The Xhinn studied the device intently.

'A primitive construction.'

'Modest power source.'

'How can this threaten the Xhinn?'

The Doctor grimaced, still straining against his bonds. 'It is a Time Bomb. When fired it vastly accelerates the passage of time within its blast radius. Millennia pass in moments. The Xhinn are a long-lived species, but I doubt even you could survive such a chronometric extrapolation.'

The Xhinn were appalled. 'But such devices are barbaric!'

'All civilised cultures have outlawed its use!'

'This contravenes all known weapons treaties!'

The Doctor did not look proud of himself. 'You talk of barbarism, yet you have tortured and killed thousands of people on this planet without flinching. You call yourself a civilised culture, yet you are poisoning the people of this city hour by hour. You talk of weapons treaties, yet you revive those you have killed and use them as undead weapons against those who resist tyranny!'

The Xhinn regarded him coldly.

'Self-justification.'

'Self-righteousness.'

'Self-deception.'

'Yes, you're guilty of all those too,' the Doctor replied. 'I came to you before. I asked you to leave, to forget this world. There are millions of others which are better suited to your needs, where no sentient species like mankind would be sacrificed at the altar of your own self-aggrandisement. But you wouldn't listen! I said I didn't want to have to resort to your methods to stop you – but you didn't listen! I said I was sworn to protect this planet and its people – but you haven't listened! Well listen to me now.

'You have given me no alternative but to destroy you. I gave you a first and final warning before. Now I give you a last chance. Leave this world while you still can. Leave now and I will deactivate this device. Only I know how and you cannot take that knowledge from my mind. Leave now, or die here with me. It's your choice. But you should hurry. The Time Bomb will detonate soon.'

The Xhinn looked at each other and nodded. Before they could act, the Doctor added one final note of caution. 'By the way – I wouldn't try using your short-range matter transmission technology to escape either. The warpshadow it causes would trigger the device instantly.'

The Doctor smiled at them. 'Of course, I could be lying about some or all of what I've just said. It's up to you to decide what's true and what isn't.'

Tommy blew the head off another of the oncoming zombies, but no sooner did he disable one than two more stepped forward to take its place. He had managed to cross the floor of the factory and regroup with the two teenage brothers. But Charlie and Billy were both out of ammunition and had been using their shotguns as clubs to strike out at the enemy. All three men were caught in a corner of the factory by a stack of forty-four gallon drums.

Tommy dug into his pocket and pulled out the last of the ammunition. He loaded it into the shotgun and prepared to shoot. 'Last of the shells, boys. You got any bright ideas, now's the time for 'em!'

'Don't shoot!' Charlie replied.

'You what?' Billy was just as amazed by his brother's words as Tommy. 'Bruv, it's the last of our ammo. After that it's hand-to-hand combat, and they outnumber us five to one!'

'Exactly!' Charlie said. 'Save the bullets – I've got a better idea.' He rapped his knuckles on the sides of the drums. 'Help me tip it over!'

Billy and Charlie got one of the drums over on to its side. Tommy caught on quick. 'Now – roll it in among them!' he commanded. The two brothers shoved the drum into the zombie policemen, knocking several over.

Tommy took careful aim and fired at the drum. It exploded into a ball of flame, dousing the surrounding guards. 'Hell! I don't know what chemicals are in these drums but they burn good,' Tommy said with delight. 'That must be what the Xhinn are putting in the bread!'

The brothers sent another drum spinning out among the policemen. Tommy fired and was rewarded with another explosion.

In less than a minute the factory was ablaze as the burning liquid inside the two punctured drums spilled out across the floor. The burning drones staggered around the factory like human torches.

Tommy laughed at the spectacle. 'Burn, coppers, burn!'

Charlie tapped him on the shoulder. 'I wouldn't gloat just yet, Tommy.' He pointed down at the pool of approaching liquid. It was gushing across the floor towards their corner. 'We're standing in front of one almighty bomb.'

'Christ, you're right!' Tommy grabbed one of the drums and stacked it on top of another. 'Come on! If we build this high enough we'll be able to get out that window!'

High above them was a small window, just below the eaves of the factory roof. It was at least two storeys high.

All three men quickly began stacking drums to create a crude pyramid in the corner, clambering up its sides as they constructed it.

By now the flaming liquid was lapping around the bottom of the drums standing on the floor. Tommy urged the brothers to work faster. 'When the bottom drums get hot enough, they'll go too – blowing us all to kingdom come!'

He looked up at the window. They were still more than the height of a man short of their goal. Then the burning policemen began climbing up the stack of drums after them…

The Xhinn triumvirate had paused to consider what the Doctor said. While they were communicating telepathically, he whispered to Sarah. She was still lying on the church floor, but had begun moving again.

'Sarah! Sarah! Are you all right?' the Doctor hissed.

'Oh, I'll never drink cocktails again,' she moaned. 'Where am I?'

'In St Luke's Church,' the Doctor said. 'It's Sunday afternoon.'

'Sunday afternoon? But the last thing I remember was biting into a slice of toast for breakfast! What happened?'

'Mind control drugs in the bread.'

'I've always said there's too many additives in food these days, but that's going a little over the top isn't it?' She glanced around and was shocked by the hovering aliens overhead. 'Are they…?'

'The Xhinn? Yes.'

'Who's winning – us or them?'

'It's stalemate for the moment.'

Sarah could not help but smile. 'That's an improvement on our normal situation, Doctor. Whenever I regain consciousness I'm usually facing certain death or life imprisonment.'

'Well, don't count your blessings just yet!' The Xhinn had finished their silent discussion and were resuming their usual triangular floating formation. 'Here comes the verdict,' the Doctor said.

Before the Xhinn triumvirate could announce its decision, the church was rocked by a massive explosion nearby.

'What the hell was that?' Sarah asked.

'Tommy Ramsey's contribution to events, I imagine,' the

Doctor replied. 'When in doubt, shoot first or blow it up – ask questions later.'

'Just like the Brigadier!'

The Doctor knew better. 'Tommy Ramsey is nothing like the Brigadier.'

The Xhinn released the Doctor from his bonds. He fell to the floor beside Sarah. The floating aliens passed judgement on the Doctor's claims.

'We have listened to your words, Time Lord – but we do not believe them. Your presence here has been a deception, a decoy to delay us while your associates attacked our other base of operations. You shall pay for that deception with your lives.'

'You couldn't be more wrong,' the Doctor said.

'Silence!'

'You have said enough.'

'We have listened too long.'

'We have looked into your feelings.'

'You are willing to sacrifice yourself to save this woman.'

'But you are not willing to sacrifice her to save yourself.'

'That will cost both your lives.'

A new voice interrupted the Xhinn. 'You know what, Brick? I think these aliens are all mouth and no trousers.' Tommy Ramsey was standing in the doorway of St Luke's Church, aiming Brick's shotgun at the Xhinn triumvirate. The big man stood behind Tommy, closing the heavy wooden doors. 'No flaming bottle, if you know what I mean.'

'Miss Smith, are you all right?' Brick asked.

'Just about, Arthur.'

The Doctor got up and brushed himself down. 'Brick, I thought I told you to stop anyone else from coming in. I was most specific.'

'Don't blame him, Doc,' Tommy replied. 'I overruled you. No point being boss if I can't get me own way, is there? And I didn't want to miss the send-off for our unfriendly neighbourhood scum.'

'What happened in the bread factory?'

'Let's just say the Bread of Life is toast.' Tommy smiled. 'Burnt toast. Billy and Charlie are getting the survivors to safety. Now, where's Father Simmons? He's got a lot to answer for.'

'Gone. The Xhinn missionary force floats before you, in all its glory,' the Doctor said sarcastically.

'Well, I think they've overstayed their welcome. Time they went back where they came from.'

'Silence!'

'We lose patience with you, humans!'

'The Xhinn triumvirate shall tolerate you no more!'

The three aliens unleashed an energy blast that nearly took Tommy's head off. He dived to the right behind a pew, while Brick went the other way. The Doctor pulled his companion behind a tall wooden pulpit, shielding them from the aliens' line of sight.

'Sarah, I've got to get to the Time Bomb. Will you be all right here?'

She nodded, biting her bottom lip. 'Be careful Doctor!'

He smiled benignly at her. 'Always.' Crouching low, he ran to one of the tall stone columns supporting the roof of the church. Peering around its edge, he could see Tommy and Brick were pinned down at the back of the church. The Xhinn Triumvirate were floating towards them, arms raised, ready to strike them down. The Doctor stepped out into the open.

'I thought it was me you wanted?' the Doctor shouted. 'That's why you had Mrs Ramsey bring Sarah here, as bait to trap me, wasn't it?'

A bolt of light sent him scurrying for cover. He looked for Tommy, caught the gangster's eye and nodded. 'Of course, I doubt the mighty Xhinn are ready for time travel. No flaming bottle, as Mr Ramsey so eloquently put it.'

Tommy fired at the Xhinn, getting their attention. They swivelled back towards him, ready to strike. Tommy reloaded and fired again, but still didn't hit any of the alien trio. The Xhinn were methodically vaporising Tommy's cover.

Behind the pulpit Sarah began to despair. Tommy might be top dog among the East End gangland, but he couldn't hit three glowing targets floating in the air. Her eyes followed the line of fire and she realised what was happening. Tommy wasn't shooting at the Xhinn. He was shooting past them.

The first gas lamp exploded with ear-splitting ferocity, sending a fireball pluming outwards from its wall mounting. It was quickly followed by a second explosion, as Tommy got his aim in. The next fireball skewed sideways, setting fire to the tapestry hanging nearby. The ancient fabric was ablaze in seconds, flames dancing up the wall.

'Now!' Tommy screamed. He ran around the side of the church, shooting and reloading. The Xhinn rotated slowly to follow his progress, blasting repeatedly at Tommy as he ducked and weaved his way around the church. It was only a matter of time before the triumvirate scythed him down.

The Doctor dropped to the floor and scuttled over to the pew where he had left the Time Bomb. It was still lying on the wooden bench, untouched and unnoticed for the moment. The Doctor stretched out a hand towards it but had to duck back down into shadow as one of the Xhinn floated overhead.

Brick emerged from behind his cover and ran down the main aisle, beneath the Xhinn. He joined Sarah behind the pulpit, a random energy blast searing past his head.

'Arthur, are you OK?' Sarah grabbed his hand.

'Yes, but I've got to get you out of here.'

'Doctor's orders, Arthur?'

'Something like that. Ready?'

She gave his fearsome fingers a squeeze of confirmation. Still holding hands, they ran out into the centre aisle. A Xhinn was waiting for them.

Tommy stopped behind a column, keeping the thick stone pillar between himself and the Xhinn. The aliens were getting closer with each attempt and his own shots were only creating minor chaos. He needed to strike a major blow to give the Doctor a chance to use his weapon against the Xhinn. Tommy glanced around and saw a copper tube running along the opposite wall of the church. It was the main pipe feeding gas to the many lamps.

'Get that and I'll cause some serious damage,' he said with satisfaction. Tommy took careful aim and fired. Moments later, the lamps began exploding along both sides of the church, one after another. As each lamp exploded, it sent a massive fireball scorching out into the centre of the church. The Xhinn looming over Brick and Sarah was caught in a fireball, its flesh screaming as the flames incinerated the alien in seconds. The pair were thrown to the ground by the scorching heat of the flash fire.

The death of one of the triumvirate drove the other Xhinn into a frenzy. They began spinning like tops, firing randomly as they turned. Energy beams seemed to fill the air, like sparks from a Catherine wheel.

In the Xhinn vessel underground, the surviving policemen regained control of themselves. They looked around in wonder at the interior of the spaceship and in horror at the litter of corpses and colleagues. The zombie policemen collapsed to the ground, released at last from their reanimation.

PC Hodge stared at his blood-stained hands. For hours he had been working in the gassing chamber, herding the Xhinn's victims inside and then dragging the dead bodies back out again. He had been willing himself to stop, to step aside from this butchery – but his will was not strong enough to resist that of the Xhinn.

The worst thing had been witnessing what the monsters forced him to do, unable to resist. The stench of death had assaulted his senses, filling his nostrils, sending his body into retching convulsions. Hodge decided to kill himself when this was over. It was the only way he could ever hope to block out the memories. But perhaps there was still some good he could do first.

One of Hodge's colleagues shouted to the others. 'Come on! Something's happened – we're free! We've got to get out of here!'

'No,' Hodge said, his voice strained and brittle. 'Remember what we've done here, the people who have died. Let's try and save those who are left!'

The Doctor got hold of the Time Bomb and hastily examined its two display units. The device was now fully charged and ready for use. It just needed to have a detonation countdown. The Doctor hunched over the device, punching numbers into a keypad. Beside him half the pew was destroyed by a random blast of alien energy, but he tried to ignore the mêlée around him. Get this wrong and he would live out all his remaining regenerations before he could get clear of the building.

Two numbers appeared on the digital display unit, with a blinking light beside them. The Doctor activated his sonic screwdriver, providing the final trigger for the Time Bomb. The countdown began.

25, 24, 23…

'Everybody – get out!' the Doctor shouted. 'We've got less than half a minute.'

'Now he tells me,' Tommy said wryly. He was near the altar, at the furthest part of the church from the doors. The gangster starting running, shooting wildly into the air. Brick got to his feet and pulled Sarah upright. Pushing her ahead of him, the big man started lumbering towards the exit. The Doctor watched them go past and then pushed the Time Bomb towards the two remaining Xhinn.

20, 19, 18…

The device slid to a halt beneath the aliens, who were still recovering from the demise of one-third of the triumvirate. They looked down at the Time Bomb with dismay. The Doctor began running after Brick and Sarah. Tommy vaulted the altar and ran down the steps to the main aisle. The Xhinn turned away from each other. One faced the retreating trio running for the doors, while the other focused on Tommy, who was running towards the two aliens.

15, 14, 13…

Both Xhinn raised their arms and let loose deadly bolts of energy. Tommy dived to the floor, the beam just passing over his body as it slid across the cold stone surface.

The Doctor ducked to one side and felt an energy beam pass his head. Sarah fell to the ground screaming, her legs suddenly useless.

10, 9, 8…

Tommy was trapped beneath a row of pews, the Xhinn hovering above.

Sarah looked back. Brick was lying on her legs, pinning her to the floor. His eyes stared into hers, sad and pleading. 'I'm sorry,' he whispered. The Doctor grabbed Sarah and tried to pull her out from under Brick.

The Xhinn fired down at the pews protecting Tommy, vaporising them.

5, 4, 3…

The Doctor managed to free Sarah and began pulling her towards the exit. 'No! We're not leaving him!' she screamed.

Tommy rolled out into the side aisle, just avoiding another deadly energy beam. He pointed his shotgun at the stained-glass window overhead.

Sarah and the Doctor dragged Brick towards the doors. Behind them both Xhinn turned towards the Time Bomb, their arms raised. Tommy fired his shotgun, blowing a hole in the massive window.

2, 1…

The Doctor and Sarah fell through the doorway, onto the stone steps outside, still dragging Brick behind them. Tommy flung himself at the church window as the shattered glass rained down around him. The two Xhinn fired at the Time Bomb, just as the device triggered its own detonation.

The Time Bomb exploded in a ball of black light which rapidly began expanding outwards from the device, swallowing everything around it. The Xhinn were enveloped by the darkness, their arms still pointing down at the device. The dark globe of energy surged outwards, folding itself around the interior of the church. Black light blazed from the windows of the church, throwing menacing shadows into the smog cloud outside. It sank down through the stone floor, into the soil below and caught the edge of the Xhinn vessel buried beneath Old Street. The darkness spread out through the vessel, consuming the living circuitry and structure.

Hodge was running up the tunnel when he heard the roar of the Xhinnship dying around him. Ahead the young constable could see the rescued people running for their lives, urged on by the rest of the policemen. The tunnel began collapsing around them.

Inside St Luke's Church the black light explosion turned to black fire, silent and searing. The counter on the face of the device began racing through a series of numbers. Zero became ten, ten became a thousand, a thousand became a million. The numbers passed ever faster until the counter melted, no longer able to keep pace with the rate of change.

Sarah stared up in terror at the glowering shadows bursting through the doors of the church. 'Doctor, what's happening?'

He watched the dark light show with quiet fascination. 'The passage of time is being vastly sped up within the boundaries of the explosion. Millennia are taking mere moments. No living creature can survive such a catastrophic chronometric acceleration.'

'Like seeing your life passing before your eyes.'

'Yes, but the Xhinn are seeing their own future pass before their eyes – while they are still living it.'

Two terrible cries assaulted the minds of the Doctor and Sarah, as the Xhinn cried out in telepathic anguish.

'It is believed the Xhinn can live for thousands of years, by absorbing the energy released when one of their kind dies. The two caught in the blast are trying to feed off each other's energy as they die.'

'Cannibalism?' Sarah said with a shudder. The death-cry of the Xhinn was fading away as the black fire inside the church subsided. She crawled over to Brick, who was lying face down on the steps. Sarah rolled him over with difficulty and listened to his chest. There was no heartbeat. He was dead.

'He died saving me,' she said, too numb to cry.

'Another victim of the Xhinn.' The Doctor rubbed his hand

against his forehead. 'I may never forgive myself for this, Sarah.'

'You did what you had to do.'

'That doesn't make it right. Murder can never be justified.'

'It wasn't murder,' Tommy said, as he walked around the corner of the church. 'You saved us all. That can't be murder.'

'I'll thank you not to tell me what's right and what's wrong, Mr Ramsey.' The Doctor got wearily to his feet and went inside the church.

'Who rattled his cage?' Tommy asked. He crouched besides Brick's body. 'I'll be hard pressed to replace you, Brick. Best enforcer I ever had.'

'His name was Arthur!' Sarah shouted, flailing at Tommy with her fists. Tears of anger ran down her face. 'His name was Arthur and he saved my life! He was worth ten of you!'

Tommy pushed her away and stood up, shoving his hands into his pockets. 'Have it your own way.'

Inside St Luke's the Doctor sat in a pew, pulling apart the Time Bomb. The device had served its terrible purpose. Now it must be destroyed, so it could never be used again.

Sarah joined the Doctor inside the church. The device had blown out all the fires, leaving the smouldering remnants of the tapestries hanging limply on the blackened walls. There was no sign of Xhinn, except for two silhouettes burnt into the ceiling.

Sarah pointed them out to the Doctor. 'When the atomic bombs were dropped on Nagasaki and Hiroshima in 1945, those nearest the explosions were vaporised almost instantly,' she said. 'All that was left of some were silhouettes of their shadows on the walls.'

The Doctor pulled the last circuits apart and pushed the components into his satchel. 'I hope I never have to resort to such a weapon again.'

Sarah looped her arm through one of the Doctor's arms. They sat in silence for a while, contemplating the empty church.

'I hate to agree with him Doctor, but Tommy's right – you did save us all.'

'Not the thousands killed by the smog and its effects. Not all those who were sacrificed on the altar of the Xhinn's grand quest for new worlds to colonise. Not Father Simmons, who believed he was doing the work of God, but found his noble efforts had been warped and twisted by the Xhinn.'

'You said it yourself – we can't save everyone. We had to prevent a greater tragedy,' Sarah insisted. 'We did.'

The Doctor was still not convinced. 'In the year 279 BC, King Pyrrho of Epirus won a victory over the Romans that proved so costly in consequence, it was as if the Romans had won anyway.'

'A Pyrrhic victory' Sarah said. 'Hardly an apt comparison, Doctor.'

He got up and slung the satchel over his shoulder. 'Did I ever tell you about meeting Pyrrho?'

'No, I don't think you have.' Sarah followed the Doctor outside.

'A great military tactician – but he just didn't think things through…'

Monday, December 8, 1952

The killer smog over London began to disperse as the new day dawned. It would be several days before the city's public transport system could return to normal, but the first trains were running again between stations. Traffic on the roads was still minimal as buses remained in garages for another day and car drivers stayed home. But weather reports talked of a gradual freshening of the air over London.

The East End had been hardest hit by the events of recent days, yet it seemed to be bouncing back quickest from the tragic loss of life. Neighbours rallied around families who had lost loved ones or had relatives in hospital. In the streets around Old Street regular police patrols were conspicuous by their absence. Few policemen had reported back to duty and those that did seemed too ashamed to go far from the station. None of the men who escaped from the Xhinn vessel before it was destroyed were able to meet each other's eyes.

Rumours about what had happened were rife and tales about life and death during the smog would serve as gossip fodder for years to come. By mid-morning an army detail had appeared and began a strictly regimented clean-up of the streets. The sergeant in charge of the men knew only that there had been some sort of riot between the locals and the police, but nobody was talking. It was as if nobody dared speak about what had taken place…

PC Hodge couldn't face going back in to the station. It would only remind him of what had happened and his head was already full enough. He had spent the night scrubbing at his hands until his fingers were rubbed raw, but he couldn't seem to get the blood out from under the fingernails. He burnt his uniform but he couldn't get the smell away from his body.

Finally, it became too much. Hodge got his father's service revolver from the war out of its hiding place in the front room. It was still loaded, in case trouble ever came calling. Hodge's father had died two winters before, but he had shown the gun to his son before the end.

Hodge's father had been so proud of his son's plans to join the police force. Now the uniform, the job – it would all just be a reminder of how that pride had been twisted and perverted by the aliens. Hodge climbed up on the roof of the terraced house and walked out to the edge of the building. He pressed the end of the barrel to the side of his head and started praying.

'Our Father, who art in Heaven, hallowed be thy name. Thy kingdom come, thy will be done on Earth, as it is in Heaven.' Tears streamed down Hodge's sobbing face as he pulled the trigger.

The Doctor and Sarah emerged from the TARDIS at midday. Sarah had spent a restless night in her bedroom, tossing and turning as her mind tried to resolve all that had happened. She could hear the Doctor pacing back and forth along the time machine's corridors. He never needed much sleep but the encounter with the Xhinn had disturbed him too.

The smog was growing thinner and there was even a hint

of weak sunshine in the sky. The Doctor examined a small gadget he held up in his hands. 'Yes, the worst of the smog is over. London should be free and clear of it by Wednesday.'

'That's good news!' Sarah replied, trying to cheer him up.

'But the damage has already been done, my dear. Ambulance men and undertakers will still be removing bodies from homes for weeks yet. The terrible cost of this tragedy in human lives is only just beginning.'

'But we won! We defeated the Xhinn! Surely that counts for something,' she said, her eyes full of pleading.

'Yes, you're right.' He pocketed the gadget and strode towards St Luke's. 'Come on, let's go see how the clear-up is doing.'

Tommy Ramsey had appointed himself as taskmaster for the restoration of the church building. A dozen men were inside repainting the walls and scrubbing away all the scorch marks from the columns. A pile of broken and partially disintegrated pews had been made outside the front doors. Billy and Charlie carried another shattered bench outside and dumped it on the pile.

Tommy was still barking orders at the men when a sheepish figure shuffled into view. It was Billy Valance. 'Hello, Tommy. You OK?'

'Where the bloody hell have you been?'

'Sore throat. Think it must have been the fog. Knocked me for a right wallop. I only got my strength back this morning,' Valance explained weakly.

'Get out of my sight,' Tommy hissed.

'But I was sick, really. I was—'

'I said get out of my sight!'

Valance slunk away towards Whitecross Street. He was dismayed to see the Doctor approaching him and quickly changed direction. Valance had already suffered twice at the hands of the watchmender. He didn't want a third helping.

'Still making friends and influencing people?' Sarah said to Tommy. The Doctor continued past them, heading for the bread factory.

'Where'd you get to?' Tommy replied. 'I've been looking all over for you.'

'Why? I thought I made my feelings pretty clear yesterday.'

'We all say things we regret in the heat of the moment.'

Sarah shook her head. 'I meant every word of it. I do believe Arthur was worth ten of you. He was kind and gentle. He only did your dirty work out of a misplaced sense of loyalty. He didn't enjoy hurting people.'

'Me neither,' Tommy protested.

'The Doctor told me what you did to Detective Valentine.'

'Well, that was personal.'

'You can't just make arbitrary decisions like that, Tommy! What's wrong is wrong! Don't you understand?'

The mob boss shrugged and smiled. 'Sorry, Sarah, but I live in a different world from you. Your morals don't work for me.' Tommy noticed Billy and Charlie loitering by the pile of broken pews. 'You two, stop earwigging my private conversation and look lively! Go inside and make yourselves useful!'

Sarah decided to change the subject. 'How's Vera?'

'Mum? Back to her usual self, dispensing tea and scolding bad manners. I ain't told her about the incident with the knitting needles. She'd be mortified and it's not like it was really her trying to kill me. Anyway, she's got her hands full at the moment.'

'How come?'

'The woman across the street disappeared yesterday. We think she must have been one of the unlucky ones the Old Bill "evacuated". God only knows whether she's dead or alive. So Mum's decided to look after the two girls.'

'Mary's dead?' Sarah asked, her face suddenly ashen.

'Probably. I didn't see her in the bread factory, so, chances are…'

Sarah sank down on to the steps, her legs suddenly giving way beneath her. 'So much death and destruction. So many good people dead – and for what?'

Tommy sat beside her and slid an arm around her shoulders. 'Saved the world, didn't we? Ain't that enough?'

Sarah shook her head. 'Not for Mary. Not for her girls, who have to grow up without a mother. Not for all the other people killed, or lost, or hurt…'

Tommy offered her a handkerchief but she refused it. Sarah would always remember Mary, the courage she showed as her daughter was dying. Sarah determined to find out what happened to the girls, when she got back to her own time. It was the least she could do.

Tommy stood up and looked at the mess around him. 'Will the true story ever be known, Sarah?'

'Who'd believe it? The Government will use D-Notices to suppress anything that could compromise national security. And then there's the Coronation next summer…'

'Don't want to spoil the Queen's big day,' he agreed.

'It'll rain, you know.'

'What – on the day of the Coronation? Never.'

'Oh yes. A right downpour,' Sarah said, standing up again.

Tommy scratched the stubble on his unshaved chin. 'Hmm, might be worth a flutter on that. I wonder what the odds are?'

Sarah jabbed an elbow into his ribs. 'Don't you dare!'

The Doctor returned from the ruins of the bread factory. 'Well, no sign of the Xhinn vessel. It must have been consumed by the Time Bomb's fallout.'

'So it's all over? We can go home?' Sarah asked.

'We can go home,' he agreed. 'But this was just a Xhinn missionary force. The main colonisation fleet may still be on its way to Earth, homing in on the final signals from its scout ship.'

Tommy was aghast. 'So the Xhinn could still attack Earth? When?'

'Not for another fifty years, if what the triumvirate told me was true,' the Doctor replied. He was looking up at the steeple of St Luke's. The structure seemed out of proportion to the church below it. 'I wonder…'

Tommy was still doing his sums. 'That means they could turn up in…'

'2002 or 2003.' Sarah supplied the answer.

'Well, I won't be around to see them,' Tommy said happily. He pulled a battered packet of cigarettes from his jacket pocket and lit one.

'You won't be if you keep smoking those,' Sarah noted quietly.

'You what?'

'Nothing.'

'Excuse me, but do you know what's happened here?' Two men had joined the trio outside the church. The man speaking was clutching a pencil and notebook, while his colleague held a camera. 'My name's Terry Sharp, I'm a reporter for the *Bethnal Green News*. This is our photographer, Bob Cohen.'

The Doctor, Sarah and Tommy looked at each other.

'A gas leak.'

'An explosion.'

'A fire.'

The words had come out as a simultaneous gabble from the threesome. Terry just looked confused. 'Sorry, just one at a time if you don't mind. My shorthand isn't bad but I can't cope with three people all speaking at once.'

'There was a gas leak,' the Doctor said, 'inside the church.'

'It caused an explosion,' Sarah added.

'Which led to a fire,' Tommy said, finishing the explanation.

'Right. Could you tell me a little bit more?'

Sarah excused herself from the conversation. The last thing she wanted was to return to her own time and find herself quoted in a local newspaper article from 1952. Life with the Doctor was complicated enough.

She looked up at the church. The Doctor had told her about the warpshadow. She could just make out the ripples in the church's structure.

A pigeon flew down and sat on the church's wrought-iron fence. The smog had wiped out so many of London's animals. But now the deadly shroud was lifting, and life was returning to the city. Sarah remembered Arthur and his dying pigeons on the roof. He had been so sad. He was dead himself just a day later.

What was it the Doctor had said to her in the TARDIS? 'We want to save everyone – but we can't.' So Mary and Bette and Arthur had died, and a murderer like Tommy Ramsey lived to fight another day. It didn't seem fair.

The photographer was taking pictures of the scenes outside the church. He caught Tommy and the Doctor on film just as they were saying goodbye to each other. Sarah smiled – the photographic prophecy had been fulfilled.

The Doctor was saying goodbye to Tommy. 'I have to thank you, Mr Ramsey. With your help a much greater tragedy has been averted here.'

Tommy grinned. 'I know how much it must hurt to give me any praise. But you deserve all the credit, Doc. I was just the brawn – you were the brains behind this operation. If you ever want a job…'

Sarah could see the Doctor's nostrils flaring. 'Time to go!' she announced and grabbed him by the arm. 'Goodbye, Tommy!'

'Maybe I'll see you again some day!' Tommy called after them. He noticed the reporter lurking, still looking for a better angle.

'So if a gas leak started the fire in the church, what happened to the watchmender's shop?' Terry pointed at the burnt-out remains of Fixing Time across the road.

Tommy's good mood swiftly evaporated. 'Mind your own bloody business – before I mind it for you! Don't you know who I am?'

EPILOGUE

London – August, 2000

The old man stamped his boots on the footpath outside St Luke's Church, trying to keep his feet warm. The temperature was unseasonably cold and it seemed to chill him to the bone.

He could still remember the events of 1952 as if they were yesterday. The Doctor, the Xhinn and that terrible smog. Sometimes he thought he could still taste its acrid stench at the back of his throat. It had been a terrible time.

The churchyard was overgrown now, the windows of St Luke's long since gone – smashed in by kids with stones, probably. There were chains and padlocks on the wrought-iron gates. The church itself had stood empty since the late 1950s. The building had been declared unsafe due to subsidence.

The old man chuckled at that. Subsidence! Hardly a surprise if you knew what had been hidden underneath the church. It was amazing the whole street hadn't toppled into the ground. A large sign by the gates suggested the church was going to be converted into an arts and musical centre for the local community. Well, perhaps some good might come of the place after all.

The fifty years were nearly gone. He had been waiting patiently all this time, watching his face grow tired and haggard in the mirror, watching the world change around him. Would the Xhinn return? Would the triumvirate be proved right after all? Only time would tell.

The old man craned his neck back to glance at the steeple. It was dwarfed by the modern buildings around it. Trees in the churchyard which had been mere saplings five decades ago now obscured the view further. Was the Xhinn antenna still hidden inside the steeple? Was it still sending a signal to the waiting fleet of Xhinnships, inviting them to take this planet as their own?

So many questions, but no answers.

The old man shook his head, putting such debates to one side. Why dwell on things you can't change, he told himself. He could remember when he was able to change his own form. He could remember when he had power and abilities beyond the imagination of ordinary humans. He could remember the moment when that all changed, when he was cursed to walk forever in this form, alone in a world where he didn't belong.

'Never! I could never be like you. I may be one of you, but I could never be like you! Never!'

'So be it.'

They had stripped away his true self and cast him out, a wandering nomad in the form he had adopted. Now he was trapped in this body, a cage of flesh and bone. Trapped on this world, waiting to see if the Xhinn would return.

Xavier Simmons shuffled away, pulling his coat closer around him.

'So be it.'

HISTORICAL NOTE

Amorality Tale is a work of fiction. However, elements of the story are based on historical fact. London was beset by a killer smog in December, 1952. Thousands of people died as a result of the smog, which was brought about by a combination of air pollution and adverse weather conditions.

A disproportionately high number of those deaths happened in the East End, where pollution levels were worse than in the rest of London. Official estimates for the death toll range between 4,000 and 12,000 people. Recent investigations have shown the full extent of the tragedy was suppressed by the British Government of the time, to prevent a greater outcry.

Even more shockingly, London suffered from more killer smogs after the tragedy of 1952. The Government distributed gas masks to affected areas knowing the masks were ineffective in combating the effects of the smog.

It took years before the Clean Air Acts of 1956 and 1968 finally put paid to the burning of coal in domestic fires, a major contributor to the pollution problem. Clearances of slum dwellings in the East End and the movement of industrial factories out of the city helped resolve the trouble.

St Luke's Church and its surrounding streets are all real,

all part of London's Old Street in the East End. St Luke's was closed in the late 1950s due to subsidence. By the time this book is published, work to refurbish and reopen the church may have been completed. If you get the chance, pay a visit to this long-forgotten building.

Tommy Ramsey is a fictional character based on several real-life gangsters who operated in London during the 1950s. Sharp-eyed readers may also spot two infamous characters from the East End gangland making appearances within these pages…

ACKNOWLEDGEMENTS

The Read-Through Crew: Robert, Alison, Jon, Paul, Peter, John and Co.
   Soundtrack: Terror Version by Dominic Glynn
   Special Effects by Loonatik & Drinks
   Videotapes: Amanda

Also available in the Doctor Who *History Collection:*

BBC

DOCTOR WHO

The Stone Rose

Jacqueline Rayner

ISBN 978 1 849 90906 8

A 2,000 year old statue of Rose Tyler is a mystery that the Doctor and Rose can only solve by travelling back to the time when it was made. But when they do, they find the mystery is deeper and more complicated than they ever imagined.

While the Doctor searches for a missing boy, Rose befriends a girl who it seems can accurately predict the future. But when the Doctor stumbles on the terrible truth behind the statue, Rose herself learns that you have to be very careful what you wish for.

An adventure set in Roman times, featuring the Tenth Doctor, as played by David Tennant, and his companion Rose Tyler.

Also available in the Doctor Who History Collection:

THE ROUNDHEADS
MARK GATISS
ISBN 978 1 849 90903 7

With the Civil War won, the Parliamentarians are struggling
to hang on to power. But plans are being made to rescue the
defeated King Charles from his prison…

With Ben press-ganged and put on board a mysterious ship
bound for Amsterdam, Polly becomes an unwitting accomplice
in the plot to rescue the King. The Doctor can't help because he
and Jamie have been arrested and sent to the Tower of London,
charged with conspiracy.

Can the Doctor and Jamie escape, find Ben and rescue Polly –
while making sure that history remains on its proper course?

*An adventure set in the aftermath of the English Civil War, featuring the
Second Doctor, as played by Patrick Troughton, and his companions Ben,
Polly and Jamie.*

Also available in the Doctor Who *History Collection:*

THE WITCH HUNTERS
STEVE LYONS
ISBN 978 1 849 90902 0

With the Doctor wanting to repair the TARDIS in peace and
quiet, Barbara, Ian and Susan decide to get some experience
of living in the nearby village of Salem. But the Doctor knows
about the horrors destined to engulf the village and determines
that they should leave.

His friends are not impressed. His granddaughter Susan has
her own ideas, and is desperate to return, whatever the cost.
But perhaps the Doctor was right. Perhaps Susan's actions will
lead them all into terrible danger and cause the tragedy that is
already unfolding to escalate out of control.

*An adventure set during the seventeenth-century Salem Witch Trials,
featuring the First Doctor, as played by William Hartnell, and his
companions Susan, Ian and Barbara.*

Also available in the Doctor Who *History Collection:*

DEAD OF WINTER
JAMES GOSS
ISBN 978 1 849 90907 5

In a remote clinic in eighteenth-century Italy, a lonely girl
writes to her mother. She tells of pale English aristocrats and
mysterious Russian nobles. She tells of intrigues and secrets,
and strange faceless figures that rise up from the sea. And
she tells about the enigmatic Mrs Pond, who arrives with her
husband and her trusted physician.

What the girl doesn't tell her mother is the truth that everyone
at the clinic knows and no one says – that the only people who
come here do so to die.

*An adventure set in eighteenth-century Italy, featuring the Eleventh
Doctor, as played by Matt Smith, and his companions Amy and Rory.*

Also available in the Doctor Who *History Collection:*

HUMAN NATURE
PAUL CORNELL
ISBN 978 1 849 90909 9

Hulton College in Norfolk is a school dedicated to producing
military officers. With the First World War about to start, the
boys of the school will soon be on the front line. But no one
expects a war – not even Dr John Smith, the college's new
house master…

The Doctor's friend Benny is enjoying her holiday in the same
town. But then she meets a future version of the Doctor, and
things start to get dangerous very quickly. With the Doctor
she knows gone, and only a suffragette and an elderly rake for
company, can Benny fight off a vicious alien attack? And will
Dr Smith be able to save the day?

An adventure set in Britain on the eve of the First World War, featuring
the Seventh Doctor, as played by Sylvester McCoy, and his companion
Bernice Summerfield. This book was the basis for the Tenth Doctor
television story Human Nature / The Family of Blood *starring*
David Tennant.

Also available in the Doctor Who *History Collection:*

THE ENGLISH WAY OF DEATH
GARETH ROBERTS
ISBN 978 1 849 90908 2

The Doctor, Romana and K-9 are hoping for a holiday in
London in the sweltering summer of 1930. But the TARDIS is
warning of time pollution. And that's not the only problem.

What connects the isolated Sussex resort of Nutchurch with
the secret society run by the eccentric Percy Closed? Why
has millionaire Hepworth Stackhouse dismissed his staff and
hired assassin Julia Orlostro? And what is the truth behind the
infernal vapour known only as Zodaal?

With the heat building, the Doctor and his friends set out to
solve the mysteries.

*An adventure set in 1930s London, featuring the Fourth Doctor, as
played by Tom Baker, and his companions Romana and K-9.*

Also available in the Doctor Who *History Collection:*

THE SHADOW IN THE GLASS
JUSTIN RICHARDS AND STEPHEN COLE
ISBN 978 1 849 90905 1

When a squadron of RAF Hurricanes shoots down an
unidentified aircraft over Turelhampton, the village is
immediately evacuated. But why is the village still guarded by
troops in 2001? When a television documentary crew break
through the cordon looking for a story, they find they've
recorded more than they'd bargained for.

Caught up in both a deadly conspiracy and a historical mystery,
retired Brigadier Lethbridge-Stewart calls upon his old friend
the Doctor. Half-glimpsed demons watch from the shadows as
the Doctor and the Brigadier travel back in time to discover the
last, and deadliest, secret of the Second World War.

*An adventure set partly in the Second Wold War, featuring the Sixth
Doctor, as played by Colin Baker, and Brigadier Lethbridge-Stewart.*